CHAPTER ONE

"The fairy has lost her wings."

Sophie Downing held up the Christmas decoration so her grandmother could see.

"Oh my," Janet Downing said. "So, she has. What will we do now?"

Sophie thought for a moment. Then she stood on the stool in front of the Christmas tree and fixed the wingless fairy to the top of the tree.

"Maybe they'll grow back before Christmas."

"That's a very good point," Janet said. "It is the season for magic, after all. What next?"

It was two days before Christmas and Janet had left it late to put up the decorations this year. It was the first Christmas without her husband, and she knew that if it wasn't for Sophie she probably wouldn't have bothered. Sophie was six now and Janet adored her.

"There are too many silver balls," the young girl said.

"Baubles," Janet corrected.

"There are too many. We need to put some more red ones on the tree to balance it."

"You're the boss."

"I can do it," Sophie said.

"Then I shall make us something to eat. Sandwich? Ham and cheese?"

"No tomatoes," Sophie reminded her.

"No tomatoes," Janet repeated. "Got it."

She'd spread some butter on four slices of bread when the doorbell rang. She replaced the knife on the breadboard and went to see who it was. She wasn't expecting anybody, but it was the time of year when people tended to pop round without warning.

It was a courier. The logo on the badge on the man's uniform was a company Janet was unfamiliar with. He was holding a small brown box.

"Mrs Downing?"

"That's me," Janet said. "I wasn't expecting anything."

"I'm just the delivery guy, Ma'am."

Janet thought he had a friendly face. He didn't look very old – perhaps early to mid-twenties and his manners were refreshing. He had an accent – Janet thought it could be Australian.

She waited for him to hand over the parcel, but he didn't.

"Do I need to sign for it?" she asked.

"That won't be necessary, Ma'am."

He held out the package and Janet took it.

"What's going on?" she said when she looked back at him.

He'd taken out a green balaclava and he was sliding it over his head.

"Let's go inside."

He was holding a hunting knife in his hand.

"Don't scream. It won't change a thing if you scream. Step back inside and close the door please."

Janet felt like she was asleep and dreaming. Surely this couldn't be real – this was the sort of thing that happened to other people. She found herself doing as he'd instructed, and she suddenly remembered Sophie. The six-year-old was busy decorating the tree in the living room.

"Please don't hurt my granddaughter."

"I'm not going to hurt her."

Janet walked down the hallway towards the kitchen. She cast a glance inside the living room as she went. Sophie was oblivious to what was happening. The little girl was singing quietly to herself as she concentrated on making the tree look as pretty as possible.

"Sit down please."

The masked man closed the kitchen door and took in the room. He moved the knife closer when Janet remained standing.

"Please sit down."

She sat on one of the stools around the breakfast bar.

"I've got money," she said. "You can take what you like."

"I don't need money."

He removed a mobile phone from his pocket and swiped the screen. Then he frowned.

"No signal. Do you have Wi-Fi?"

Janet thought this couldn't get any more surreal.

"Could you give me the Wi-Fi password please."

Janet gave it to him and soon afterwards some familiar music started to play. It was a song she hadn't heard for quite some time, but it brought back a flood of memories.

"My son will be home any minute," she said.

"No, he won't."

After checking his watch, the courier ordered Janet to stand up.

"Please don't hurt me," she said.

The song was reaching the chorus. Even though Janet hadn't heard it for years, she could recall every word.

"Turn around please."

Janet did as she was asked. The song was reaching its climax now. The music faded and then it started again from the beginning. The kitchen door opened, and Janet froze.

"I'm hungry," Sophie said.

"Hello," the courier said.

"Hello," Sophie said. "Why are you wearing a mask in the house?"

"I don't like people looking at my face."

Two seconds later Janet Downing experienced an intense burn in her upper back, and she screamed out.

"The pain won't last long."

Janet wasn't aware of the man's hands gripping her below her shoulders. She knew that he was helping her to the floor, but she couldn't feel a thing.

"What have you done to her?" Sophie screamed out.

"Her spinal column has been severed."

Blood was gushing from the deep wound, but Sophie couldn't see it. Janet had been placed on her back.

"I'm calling the police," Sophie said.

"Not yet."

The courier glanced at his watch again. "We still have thirty-two minutes. Make your sandwich."

"I'm not hungry anymore."

Janet's mouth was moving but her vocal cords weren't functioning properly. She had no idea what was happening to her. She couldn't feel anything, and the sensation was terrifying. Her brain was sending signals to her limbs – she knew she had to do something to protect her granddaughter, but the signals were getting lost somewhere along the way. The music was still playing. It was the same song on repeat, and it seemed to get louder with every repetition.

"Four minutes."

Janet wasn't sure if she'd lost consciousness at some point. Her thoughts were disjointed, and the music wasn't helping. She didn't even know if Sophie was OK and she wasn't able to communicate with her. She couldn't even turn her head to check.

"Thirty-six minutes for thirty-six years is charitable, I think."

"Who are you?" Sophie said.

"I'm not going to hurt you. Call the police as soon as I leave, OK."

"OK," Sophie said. "And an ambulance?"

The courier shook his head and smiled at her. Sophie would later explain to the detectives who spoke to her that she knew he was smiling, even though he was wearing a balaclava. She could tell from his eyes.

"I want you to stand facing the door. When the music stops you can find a phone to call the police. Do you know the number?"

"Three nines," Sophie said.

"Clever girl."

"Everybody knows that."

"Please stand facing the door. It won't take long. I'm not going to hurt you."

Sophie let out a huge sigh and did as she was told.

"Thirty-six minutes. One for every year – you got to feel exactly how he felt for thirty-six years. Almost nothing. And now you will feel absolutely nothing at all."

Janet was aware of the blade of the hunting knife in front of her face. "I'm not here to judge you. It's important that you know that. I'm here to pass judgment – there's a big difference."

Janet Downing's existence was obliterated in no more than three seconds. The serrated edge of the knife sliced through both carotids quickly and the blood ceased to pump soon afterwards.

CHAPTER TWO

"You could have made more of an effort."

DI Oliver Smyth was looking Detective Sergeant Jason Smith up and down. He'd expressed his disapproval as soon as Smith had set foot inside the office and taken off his jacket. He was dressed in a pair of jeans and a faded T-Shirt that once had a print of a Led Zeppelin concert poster on it.

"They're not here to assess my fashion sense, boss," Smith said. "What do you think is going to happen today?"

"This is just the initial disciplinary hearing," DI Smyth said. "There will be no hard decisions made today. They'll listen to your side of things and decide whether they have grounds for disciplinary measures only once they've taken everything into account. That can take time."

"Will I be suspended in the meantime?"

"You're asking the wrong person."

"Could you point me in the direction of the right person then."

"Relax," DI Smyth said. "As far as I'm aware, nothing new has come up. What it boils down to is basically a case of your word against the professor's, and that's not going to wash."

Smith was facing charges of tampering with evidence and gross misconduct. The man who had made the accusations against him had been charged with his involvement in five murders and Smith hoped that that would work in his favour. He would argue that this was simply the result of sour grapes, and there was no proof to substantiate the charges he was facing.

"Do you think the professor might have something up his sleeve?" he said.

"Such as?" DI Smyth said. "He has nothing to support his claim that you tampered with evidence. You made sure of that, and gross misconduct is extremely difficult to make stick. The men and women on the disciplinary board are on your side."

"I thought they were supposed to be impartial," Smith said.

"Don't be so naïve. Look back through the disciplinary cases from the past few years and you'll see a common pattern. The police force does not go out of its way to muddy its own reputation. You'll be fine. Just be yourself in there and you'll be fine."

* * *

Smith had experienced disciplinary hearings before, but this one had to be the shortest he'd ever been a part of. It took the disciplinary panel less than twenty minutes to hear Smith present his side of the story and respond to the allegations that had been put forward. Smith couldn't gauge the mood of the men and women in the hearing, but he didn't expect them to give much away at this stage in the proceedings. He was thanked for his time and informed that a decision would be made in due course.

"You've dodged another bullet," DI Smyth said to him afterwards.

"We don't know that yet," Smith said. "They didn't give much away in there."

"There's no case to answer. The professor is going to be sorely disappointed. If they thought there was even a slight possibility that you were involved in something that might later bring the police into disrepute they wouldn't have hesitated to suspend you, pending the final decision. Consider it a wake-up call. You got away with it this time, but you might not be so lucky next time."

"I'd do it all again if I had to, boss," Smith said.

"I'll pretend I didn't hear that. It's been a stressful time for you, so I suggest you take the rest of the day off."

"I don't want to take the rest of the day off. I want to work. God knows how much longer I'm going to be allowed to do my job."

"You do realise that it's Christmas on Saturday?"

"What's your point?" Smith said.

"You're booked off until the twenty-seventh."

"Since when?" Smith said.

"Since Whitton reminded me that you haven't had Christmas off for years. You have a family – enjoy the festive season with them."

"I'm not a big fan of Christmas, boss."

"Tough. You're not due back at work until Monday."

Smith didn't think it was worth arguing. He left DI Smyth's office and headed upstairs to the canteen. The place was much busier than usual, and it was quite clear that not much work was getting done. Someone had tried to make an effort to get into the festive spirit by pinning some tinsel onto the walls. A tiny Christmas tree stood in the corner of the room.

Smith got himself a coffee from the machine and joined Whitton and Bridge at their usual table.

"Well?" Whitton said.

"The boss reckons it'll blow over," Smith told her.

"You can't have many of your nine lives left," Bridge said. "What did they say?"

"Not much," Smith said. "It was just the prelim hearing, and they'll only make a decision when they've looked through the evidence."

"As far as I can see," Whitton said. "There isn't any evidence. It's a simple case of *he said, she said*, and I think it will be thrown out."

"I hope so," Smith said. "Since when did you book leave on my behalf?"

"Ah that."

"Ah that," Smith repeated. "You could have asked me first."

"What would your answer have been?"

"I would have preferred to work."

"There you have it then."

"You know how I feel about Christmas," Smith said.

"Of course, I know, but you can't let what happened more than twenty years ago spoil things for the rest of the family. The girls are really looking forward to having us all together. My parents will be coming round, as well as Darren's family."

"Where the hell are we going to put them all?" Smith said.

"We'll make a plan."

"Why don't we just go to the Hog's Head?" Smith suggested.

"You are not having a steak and ale pie for Christmas dinner."

"Why not?"

"Because this year, Christmas is going to be special."

"I can't think of anything more special than one of Marge's steak and ale pies," Smith argued.

"We're having Christmas Day at our house," Whitton said. "And that's all there is to say about it."

CHAPTER THREE

Duncan Jordan eased his foot off the accelerator when the cheery voice on the GPS announced that his destination was coming up on the right. It had to be some kind of mistake. There was nothing but fields for miles. He stopped the car by the side of the road and tapped the screen of the phone to reset the GPS. He found the location pin he'd been sent and started the process from the very beginning. He cursed quietly to himself when he realised that there had been no mistake – the location he'd been directed to was right in front of him, and all Duncan could see was a narrow lane that appeared to lead nowhere.

He got out of the car and locked it. He walked up to the gravel path, held the phone in front of him and the GPS told him once more that he had arrived at his destination.

"Fuck it."

He wondered if he'd been scammed. It was very common these days. He'd forked out a lot of money for this, and the very nature of the transaction meant that discretion was imperative. Not only that, but Duncan also knew there would be no possible way to recuperate what he'd lost if this was a con. He swore again and he was ready to return to his car when the phone beeped. A glance at the screen told him he'd received another pin location.

The voice from the phone told him to turn right onto the gravel path, and according to the map on the screen his destination was just under a mile away. Duncan looked across the fields. He could make out a small structure in the distance. After a brief internal debate, he decided that he had nothing to lose, and he set off along the track.

When he got closer, he saw that the structure was an old farm outbuilding. Next to it was a field that looked like it had been recently ploughed, and this struck Duncan as odd. Why would a field in the middle of nowhere have been ploughed in winter? And where was the tractor? There were no vehicles to be seen.

Duncan approached the building cautiously. A glance at the phone told him that this was definitely his final destination, but there wasn't a soul in sight. He didn't think he was about to be robbed. He'd been instructed to come alone, and he'd also been told to bring nothing with him apart from the mobile phone he'd been sent shortly after he made the payment. Surely someone wouldn't lure him all the way out here to steal a phone that wasn't even his.

As he got closer, Duncan saw a figure emerging from the building. It was a man, and he'd spotted Duncan too. He remained where he was and waited for Duncan to come closer.

The man didn't introduce himself. He gestured for Duncan to follow him inside the old barn and Duncan saw no reason not to. There were no other people inside and Duncan wondered what was going to happen. The man reached behind a desk of sorts and pulled out a small wooden box. He placed it on the desk and tore a sheet of paper from an A4 notepad. Duncan saw that it was some kind of questionnaire. He was handed a pen.

"Welcome."

The man had a warm, soothing voice.

"Answer all the questions carefully. We can only do what you wish if you tell us concisely and clearly what it is you want out of this."

"How exactly is this going to work?" Duncan asked.

The man put a finger to his lips. "No questions. Take your time with your answers. When you're finished, place the paper in the box and make sure it's locked. Take the box to the field next to the barn and place it in the hole that has been prepared. Only one hole has been dug at the far side of the graveyard."

"How will I know when the transaction is complete?" Duncan said.

"No questions."

"I paid a lot of money for this," Duncan said. "I want a guarantee that I'm going to get what I paid for."

"Answer the questions and place the box in the hole. Do not pay any attention to the gravestones in the graveyard. Please leave the phone on the desk."

The man left him to it. Duncan realised that he was sweating even though it was four degrees outside. He looked at the questionnaire in front of him, read the first question and gasped.

CHAPTER FOUR

Whitton told Smith that she needed to check to see if any emails needed her attention before she left the station for four days. Smith decided to go and smoke a cigarette while he waited for her. The DCs King and Moore were standing by the front desk. PC Baldwin was talking to someone on the phone behind it.

"I'm off," he said.

"What are your plans for Christmas, Sarge?" DC King said.

"Doing whatever I'm told to do apparently," Smith said. "What about you?"

"Me and Harry will be working. The joys of being single."

"Do you want to swap?"

"Are you kidding me?" DC King said. "DS Whitton would kill me."

"I'll see you in a few days then," Smith said.

He was prevented from leaving when Baldwin held up her hand. Her other hand was covering the handset of the phone.

"Hold on, Sarge," she said.

Smith waited. Baldwin resumed her conversation. Smith listened as she got an address from the person on the other end and told them to leave the house and go somewhere safe. She finished up by assuring them that help was on the way.

"What was that all about?" Smith asked her after she'd sent a car out to the address.

"A dead woman. A man came back from last-minute Christmas shopping and found his mother dead in the kitchen."

"Did he sound legit?" DC Moore said.

"He sounded absolutely distraught, Harry," Baldwin said. "He said his six-year-old daughter was in the kitchen with his dead mother."

"Shit," Smith said. "Is the girl dead too?"

Baldwin shook her head. "She's not injured but according to her father, she's in a bad way. The patrol car and ambulance should be with them within ten minutes."

"Give me the address," Smith said.

* * *

He arrived at the house in Heslington just as a man and a young girl emerged from the front door. A police car was parked outside the property but there was no sign of the ambulance. Smith called Baldwin and he was told that it was two minutes away. He got out of his car and walked over to the man and little girl. He wondered where the police officers were.

"An ambulance is on the way," he told the man.

He wasn't sure if he'd understood. The man looked to be in his thirties, and his face was blank. There was no life in his eyes, and he seemed to be looking at Smith without registering him.

"I'm a police detective," Smith said. "There's an ambulance on the way. Where are the police officers who were here?"

The man simply shook his head. His arm appeared to be glued to the little girl's shoulder.

The expression on her face was even more disturbing. She stared, unblinking at something across the road. With her eyes fixed in their sockets she resembled a statue, frozen in time. Smith crouched down in front of her. "What's your name?"

Nothing.

"You're safe now," Smith said. "You and your dad are going to ride in an ambulance. Have you ever been in an ambulance before?"

He wasn't going to get anything from the girl, that was quite clear.

The ambulance pulled up five minutes later. Smith intercepted the paramedics before they reached the house.

"We've got a man and his daughter, and both of them appear to be suffering from severe shock. It's possible that the little girl is a witness to a murder."

"What are their names?" the taller of the two paramedics asked.

"They're not talking," Smith said. "What took you so long?"

"It's the silly season," the shorter woman said. "We were called out to a pub in the city centre. Waste of time – the two drunks who'd beat the crap out of each other were hugging like bloody lovers. I hate this time of year."

PC Miller and PC Griffin emerged from the house and Smith wondered what they'd been doing inside for so long. He walked over to them to get some answers. PC Miller was pale, and he was sweating. PC Griffin looked even worse. His shifty eyes were facing downwards and the skin on his face looked almost grey in the mid-afternoon half-light.

"What were you doing inside the house for so long?" Smith said.

"Sorry, Sarge," PC Miller said. "I needed a moment to get my composure back. It's a mess in there."

"Is she definitely dead?"

PC Miller nodded. "She's been butchered."

"Did the little girl say anything?"

"No, Sarge."

"What about the son?" Smith said.

"We couldn't get a word out of either of them."

"Is it that bad in there?"

"Worse. PC Griffin puked in the sink in the kitchen."

"Great," Smith said. "I'll make sure Webber is aware of it. You have notified Forensics, haven't you?"

"Of course, Sarge," PC Miller said. "I'm sorry – I just wasn't expecting this."

"Don't beat yourself up about it," Smith said. "It might be an idea to get yourself checked out by the paramedics."

He walked away and took out his phone. He wanted to make sure that Grant Webber was definitely on his way. He didn't have to. The black Suzuki belonging to the Head of Forensics pulled up and Grant Webber and Billie Jones got out. Webber spotted Smith and came over.

"What's going on?"

"Looks like a dead woman," Smith said. "I haven't been inside."

"That wasn't what I meant," Webber said. "What are you doing here?"

"I was standing next to Baldwin when the call came in, and I thought I'd come and take a look."

"Of course you did. Is there anything I need to know before we get to work?"

"Like I said," Smith said. "I haven't been inside the house, but I believe PC Griffin lost his lunch in the sink in the kitchen."

CHAPTER FIVE

"We're still waiting for a lot of the details," DI Smyth said. "But I can confirm that we have a murder. We didn't get anything out of the man or the little girl, but a neighbour identified them as Peter Downing, and his daughter, Sophie. The dead woman is Peter's mother, Janet. Early indications suggest she died due to a deep laceration to her neck. The son found her in the kitchen when he came home from doing some shopping."

"It's possible that Sophie witnessed the murder," Smith said. "But she appears to be in a state of deep shock, and I couldn't get anything out of her at the scene."

"I apologise for cutting short any leave you may have been looking forward to," DI Smyth said. "But we need everyone on board. This is a nasty one. We have a witness who saw a man standing outside Mrs Downing's house earlier this afternoon. The witness thinks he was a courier. He was holding a parcel in his hand."

"Did we get a description?" Bridge said.

"Not a great one. The witness thinks he was tall and slim, and he was wearing a courier uniform."

"It'll be easy to check if any deliveries were made to Mrs Downing's house this afternoon," Smith said. "We need to speak to the little girl."

"She's six years old, Sarge," DC Moore said.

"I'm experiencing a weird sense of déjà vu here, Harry. What's your point?"

"Do you really think we're going to get anything out of a girl that age?"

"She has a pair of eyes, and a pair of ears," Smith said. "Sophie Downing is our main priority."

"Hold your horses," DI Smyth said. "We'll work through things systematically. A door-to-door is underway. This happened in the middle of the afternoon, so we might get lucky. Most of the residents will have been home and we'll see what comes of that. As of now we know very little about Janet Downing apart from what the neighbour told us. Who was she and why did someone go to great lengths to kill her? This was a brazen attack and whoever carried it out left little doubt about their intentions. They went inside that house with the sole intention of killing her."

"They were taking a chance with the granddaughter there," DC Moore said.

"What part of *brazen* do you need translating, Harry?" Smith said. "And with respect, boss, I think you're wrong. We need to talk to Sophie before we focus on anything else."

"That little girl has just experienced something nobody her age should ever have to go through," DI Smyth said. "No doubt she's extremely traumatised and she needs time to process what happened before she has to face a police interrogation."

"I disagree."

"Of course you do."

"We need to speak to her while the events are fresh in her head."

"She's six years old, Sarge," DC Moore said.

"Haven't we already had this conversation? Where is she now?"

"Sophie and her father were both taken to City Hospital," DI Smyth said.

"I'm heading over there," Smith said. "You can argue this until the cows come home, but we need to see what that little girl has to tell us."

He got up and left the small conference room, ignoring DI Smyth's protests as he went.

"He's acting manic again," Bridge said.

"He's stressed about the outcome of the disciplinary," Whitton said. "He doesn't know if he'll have a job and he's making the most of it."

"Is Christmas cancelled?" Bridge asked.

"It looks that way," DI Smyth said. "Any thoughts about this one?"

"Why would someone kill a fifty-two-year-old woman?" DC King wondered.

"We'll focus on the motivation at a later stage," DI Smyth said. "Let's look at the details of how the murder was carried out first. We know that the son left in his car at around noon."

"How do we know that," DC Moore said. "If the son and granddaughter aren't talking?"

"An observant neighbour. The woman who lives across the road happened to see Mr Downing leave. Apparently, she likes to keep an eye on the goings on in the street."

"You've got to love nosy neighbours," Bridge said.

"There was no sign of forced entry to the property," DI Smyth said. "So, it's safe to assume that our killer gained entry by posing as a courier."

"Did the nosy neighbour see the courier?" DC King said.

"No, she did not. But the other witness definitely remembers someone in a courier uniform. Let's consider a possible scenario. Mrs Downing answers the door to a courier, he gains entry to the house and subsequently kills her."

"Why would she let him in?" DC King said.

"Why indeed? Perhaps she was threatened with something. We know that she was killed in the kitchen. We'll know more after the post-mortem, but Webber believes a knife with a sharp, serrated blade was used to kill her. Forensics didn't find anything like that in the kitchen, so it looks like the killer took it with him."

"Do any of the houses in the vicinity have CCTV?" Bridge said.

"A couple," DI Smyth said. "And we'll be looking at the footage in due course."

"If the killer arrived by car," DC Moore said. "We might get lucky."

"It's early days," DI Smyth said. "But everything about this murder makes me think we're going to get to the bottom of it quickly. This wasn't particularly well-thought out. The killer stood outside the house in plain view of the whole street. Far too many things could have gone wrong, and I believe he only managed to carry out the killing because he got lucky. We'll catch this man – it's only a matter of time."

CHAPTER SIX

Smith sensed that the murder of Janet Downing wasn't as simple as it appeared to be. There was more to the brutal killing than they could see on the surface, and he didn't think this was an investigation that was going to be resolved quickly. He was hoping to get some answers from the little girl who'd been present when the murder was carried out. He knew instinctively that Sophie Downing was going to be instrumental in helping them move forwards.

He found a parking space in the car park at City Hospital and got out of the car. He lit a cigarette and inhaled deeply. His phone started to ring and the sound of Ozzy Osbourne singing *See you on the other side*, told him it was Dr Bean. Smith answered it immediately – the Head of Pathology had something important to tell him.

"Kenny," he said. "What have you got for me?"

"I could be phoning to wish you all the best for the festive season," Dr Bean said.

"I doubt that. You've found something important."

"We found something," Dr Bean said.

"That was quick."

"It wasn't difficult to spot. Your victim had her spinal column severed."

"I thought she died due to the wound to her neck."

"That's what killed her," Dr Bean said. "But she also suffered a deep laceration to her upper back. I'm guessing at the moment, but the location of the wound looks to be on the upper thoracic vertebrae – possible T-1 or T-2. It will have resulted in instant paralysis."

"Wouldn't that have killed her?" Smith said.

"Not immediately. She would probably have died eventually, especially without urgent medical attention, but it's quite possible she could have lasted a couple of hours."

"Do we know which wound was inflicted first?" Smith said.

"The injury to her back will have resulted in massive blood loss," Dr Bean said. "You'll have to speak to Webber about that."

"The patterns of blood at the scene will be able to tell us that story. When will you be doing the postmortem?"

"In precisely twenty minutes."

"Can I join you?"

"Why would you want to do that?"

"It's been a while," Smith said. "I'm here at the hospital anyway – I need to see if I can get a little girl to talk, but that can wait until after the PM."

"It's a date then," Dr Bean said. "You know where to find me."

After a quick conversation with Grant Webber, Smith's suspicions were confirmed. The pooling of the blood on the kitchen floor suggested that the wound to Janet Downing's spinal column was inflicted first. When her carotid arteries were severed there was very little arterial spurt. She was still alive when she had her spine severed.

Smith couldn't remember the last time he'd attended a post-mortem. It had been a good few years and he wondered if much had changed in that time. He was given protective clothing and Sarah Monk asked him if he really wanted to be there.

"Why not?" Smith said.

Dr Bean's assistant didn't comment on this.

"She's still fresh," Sarah said. "So, there might be a few surprises."

"Who doesn't like surprises?" Smith said. "Where's Kenny?"

"He's just grabbing a quick bite to eat from the canteen. He prefers to have a full stomach when he cuts up dead bodies."

The post-mortem room felt warmer than Smith remembered and he wondered if it was because of the icy temperatures outside. Janet Downing had been placed face-down on the metal table at the back of the room. Smith wondered why she hadn't been laid out on her back. Next to the table were trays containing various surgical instruments. All of them had been sterilised and they would be sterilised again afterwards.

Dr Bean adjusted his face mask and coughed.

"You're probably wondering why she's on her front."

"It had crossed my mind," Smith said.

"The spinal cord injury is intriguing me," Dr Bean said.

"And you want to see if you were right," Smith said. "T1 or T2, you said."

"I think I'm right. But there's only one way to find out."

The wound to her upper back was still raw. The skin around the laceration was ragged and uneven. Smith had seen the result of knife attacks before and this one looked different to any of them. When a blade enters the flesh, parts of the skin are forced inside the body, and when the knife is pulled out that skin returns to the position it was in before. The wound on Janet Downing's back was much wider than it should be.

"He twisted the knife," Smith said.

"Correct."

With a scalpel, Dr Bean made two incisions over the wound, top and bottom. He selected a clamp and peeled the skin away.

"The tissue is badly damaged. There isn't much muscle to speak of here on the upper back and there's virtually no fat, but you can see that the trauma is extensive. The blade went in deep; it found its target and the knife was twisted hard to ensure that the spine was severed."

"How easy is it to do that?" Smith asked.

"It's not particularly difficult. If you know what you're aiming for."

"Are you saying that it was intentional?"

"Definitely. This was no accident – he wanted her spinal column severed. Hmm. Sarah, please explain to DS Smith where the blade of the knife went in."

Sarah Monk bent down and examined the part of the spinal column that had been severed. fragments of cartilage and bone were sticking out at random angles.

"It's not pretty," she said. "But that's smack bang in the middle of T1 and T2."

"You were right," Smith said before Dr Bean got there first.

"I was right," Dr Bean said anyway.

"I've seen enough."

"We're not finished."

"I've got what I wanted," Smith said. "Thanks, Kenny."

CHAPTER SEVEN

"I believe she's suffered what's known as a post-traumatic semi-catatonic episode."

Smith had tracked down the doctor who had been treating Sophie Downing since she was brought in. Dr Donna Frome was a short woman with pink hair. Smith didn't think she looked old enough to have qualified as a doctor.

"When will I be able to talk to her?" he asked.

"She's not responding to any outside stimuli at the moment," Dr Frome said.

"When will she snap out of it?"

This earned him a smile from the pink-haired doctor. "I'm afraid it's not quite as simple as that. Sophie has suffered a terrible shock, and her brain has reacted by shutting down the doors to the outside world. It's a defence mechanism that sometimes kicks in after extreme trauma."

"Do you know the details of what happened?" Smith said.

"I was told that it's possible that she witnessed her grandmother's murder."

"I think she did," Smith said. "And that's why it's imperative that I speak to her. Do you have any idea when she'll be up to that?"

"I'm sorry," Dr Frome said. "It really is impossible to say. And even when she does start to show signs of recovery, I would be reluctant to let you question her. It's possible she could regress if you push her too hard."

"I'm not planning on pushing her," Smith said. "I'm trying to catch the man who killed her grandmother. I'm trying to do my job."

"As am I," Dr Frome said. "And I cannot put my patients at risk. That little girl has a long road ahead of her, and I will not allow anything to hinder her recovery. I'm sorry."

"Me too," Smith said. "Is there any chance at all that she'll come back to the land of the living anytime soon?"

"I'm afraid I can't answer that. The human brain is a complex machine, and no two brains are the same. I'll let you know as soon as there's any change in her condition, but it's not going to be anytime soon."

Smith nodded. "Thank you. Could you let me know as soon as Sophie's condition improves?"

"Of course."

Smith gave her one of his cards and thanked her again.

He left the hospital and headed for his car. The news about Sophie Downing had come as a bit of a blow and Smith needed to think about another plan of action. He lit a cigarette and leaned against his car. Sophie had seen the person who killed her grandmother – Smith was certain of that, but she'd shut herself off from the world because of it. It was going to be impossible to talk to her about what happened.

Something occurred to him as he threw his cigarette butt into the distance.

"Did you tell your dad what happened?"

He made his way back to the entrance of the hospital. He'd just reached the front doors when the blare of a siren filled the air and when he turned his head, he saw an ambulance exiting the grounds at high speed.

Dr Frome didn't hide her frustration when she spotted Smith walking towards her. The pink-haired doctor even went as far as to turn around and pretend that she hadn't seen him.

"Sorry to bother you again," Smith said to her back. "I need to speak to Sophie Downing's father. Do you know where he is?"

Dr Frome sighed. "I'll find out for you."

Five minutes later Smith walked inside one of the private rooms. Peter Downing was sitting on the bed. A tube was feeding a saline solution into a vein in his left wrist. He looked up at Smith and offered him a weak smile.

"How are you doing?" Smith said.

"Not great," Peter said.

"Can I ask you a few questions?"

"I've already spoken to someone."

Smith was unaware of this. "Who did you speak to?"

"A bloke in uniform came by about an hour ago."

"Did you get his name?" Smith said.

Peter shook his head. "My mind isn't working properly at the moment."

"What did he look like?"

"Shortish. Mid to late twenties. Pretty ugly bloke with eyes that are too close together."

"PC Griffin?" Smith guessed.

"That sounds familiar. I think he was one of the officers who came to the house."

"What did he want?"

"He was asking how Sophie was mostly. I don't know – it was like he was really concerned."

Smith was surprised – this didn't sound like the PC Griffin he knew.

"I know this is hard," he said. "But can you talk me through the time you arrived home."

"I suppose so."

"Was the door locked or unlocked?" Smith said.

"It was unlocked."

"Was it open?"

"No."

"OK," Smith said. "I want you to think back to before you went into the house. Can you remember if there were any vehicles parked on the street that seemed out of place?"

"Out of place?"

"Cars you didn't recognise."

"I don't think so."

"Did you see anyone acting suspiciously? Perhaps they were walking quickly, or they had their head down."

"Nothing like that."

"What did you do when you got home?" Smith said.

"I took the shopping to the kitchen," Peter said. "That's when…"

"It's OK," Smith said. "I understand this must be difficult to talk about, but I need to ask these questions. Where was Sophie? Where was your daughter when you arrived in the kitchen?"

"She was on the floor next to Mum. She was holding her hand, and she was staring straight across the room."

"Did you ask her about what had happened?"

"What?"

"Did you ask Sophie what had happened?"

"Of course I didn't ask her. It was quite obvious what had happened. Did you see the blood?"

"I'm sorry," Smith said. "Did Sophie say anything to you?"

"She hasn't spoken a word since," Peter said. "And I'm afraid that she's never going to be able to speak again."

Smith was running out of questions to ask. He opted for the one they asked in every murder investigation.

"Can you think of anyone who would want to hurt your mother?"

"Of course not," Peter said. "She was a kind woman. She was a loving mother and grandmother."

"Did she have any enemies?"

"I've just told you that she didn't. Who would do such a thing?"

"I'm going to do everything I can to find out," Smith promised. "I won't take up any more of your time. Do you know if your wife has been informed?"

"Emily will be coming later."

"Is she not in the city?" Smith said.

"She's working, and she can't get away."

Smith thought this was rather odd, but he didn't share this with Peter Downing.

Something else occurred to him as he was on his way out of the hospital. Everything about this murder felt wrong. Not only did the killer carry it out during the light of day, in front of a witness, but he also left that witness alive. It was becoming clear that Janet Downing was the primary target here and Smith's initial thoughts were reinforced – this was not going to be a straightforward investigation.

CHAPTER EIGHT

Harriet Jordan looked left and right and decided that the coast was clear. She pushed the wheelie bin to its designated place at the side of the driveway and quickly returned to the house. Somebody would complain – of that there was little doubt, but Harriet didn't care. According to the rules, the wheelie bins should only be put out in the morning of collection. That was tomorrow, and Harriet knew that the refuse collectors came between eight and nine. She was planning on having a lie-in in the morning, and her husband Duncan was away on business until tomorrow evening.

Harriet had made arrangements with a man she'd met online, and she had the whole evening planned. She would make a delicious meal with plenty of wine and after that, who knew what would happen? One thing was for certain – Harriet did not intend to be up early in the morning. The neighbours could moan all they liked.

There was a knock on the door and Harriet groaned. She wondered which of the neighbours it was. It was probably Mr French from number 12. She was sure that Lionel French spent every waking hour observing the street, waiting for someone to break the unwritten rules of the neighbourhood. Harriet debated whether to ignore him, but the banging was persistent, and she knew from experience that Mr French wouldn't give up easily.

"I'm coming," Harriet shouted. "There's no need to bang down the bloody door."

She opened up and saw that it wasn't Lionel French. A young man in a courier uniform was smiling at her.

"Mrs Jordan?"

"That's me," Harriet said.

She couldn't remember ordering anything, but it could be something for her husband. They rarely communicated these days.

"Harriet Jordan?"

"Got it in one," she said.

Harriet thought he had an attractive face. He was a good few years younger than her but that had never stopped her before. His eyes were an interesting shade of green, and she liked the way he maintained eye contact when he spoke. Harriet realised that he didn't have a package with him. He spoke with an accent she couldn't place.

"Do you have something to deliver here?" she asked.

He nodded. "Perhaps it's better if I come inside."

Harriet recognised the accent now – it was Australian.

"What's going on?"

"I won't take up much of your time, Ma'am. Two minutes, tops."

"You'd better come in then."

She asked him to take a seat at the table in the kitchen.

"Could I get you something to drink?"

"No thank you. I'm here to deliver a message."

"Go on," Harriet said.

The courier reached inside his jacket and took out a large knife.

"Please don't scream. It won't change anything."

"What do you want? I've got money."

"Why do they always offer me money? Not everything is about money."

He examined the serrated blade of the hunting knife.

"Please," Harriet begged. "I don't understand."

Before she realised what was happening, a hand was clamped over her mouth, and she experienced an intense burn in her lower back.

"That was courtesy of James."

The second stab pierced the kidney on the other side. The pain was like nothing she'd ever felt before.

"Consider that a gift from Allan."

Harriet was instantly wide awake. His way of speaking was uncannily similar to how her husband spoke to her when they argued. It was subtly condescending, and it irritated the hell out of her.

Through the pain she thought about James Green. Their fling hadn't lasted long but it had been fun. Allan Rowntree had been on the scene for a bit longer. Harriet couldn't understand how her attacker knew so much. She felt him remove his hand from her mouth and she gasped. He helped her to the floor, and she placed her hand to her side. There wasn't as much blood as she'd expected there to be.

"Why?" Harriet managed.

"I'm far from finished."

"Is this Duncan's doing?" Harriet said.

"There is no Duncan on the list. Only Keith."

This was followed up with a jab to the face. Harriet's scream was cut short by a hard slap to her cheek.

"And Simon."

The blade of the knife entered her stomach and was yanked out so violently that Harriet lost consciousness for a moment.

"Last but not least," the courier stared right into her eyes.

Harriet guessed what was coming. He was going to say the name of her most recent affair. Paul Fowler was supposed to be coming round later. The ingredients for the lasagne were in the fridge, and the wine was ready to be opened. It was supposed to have been a memorable, exciting night.

The courier spoke Paul's name and Harriet's final thought as the serrated blade sliced her throat open was a strange one. She'd developed a new-found respect for her husband. There was little doubt that what was happening was down to Duncan, and as her life ebbed away, she regretted not being able to get the chance to get to know this new version of him.

CHAPTER NINE

Smith wasn't in any hurry to get back to the station. He knew he would probably face a barrage of abuse from DI Smyth for walking out of the briefing the way he had, and he lingered on the way back. He cursed when his phone started to ring. He activated the hands free and took the call.

"Where are you?" It was DI Smyth.

"On my way back from the hospital," Smith said. "The little girl isn't talking, and the doc doesn't think she will be for a while."

"Where exactly are you?"

Smith eased his foot off the accelerator.

"I'm on Hull Road, just before the Tang Hall Lane turnoff."

"Make a detour," DI Smyth said. "A call has just come in from a Mr Lionel French. He lives on Murton Way in Osbaldwick, and he thinks something has happened to his neighbour."

"What makes him think that?"

"He watched her push her wheelie bin out onto the pavement," DI Smyth said. "And then he saw a man arrive at the house. The woman answered the door, the man went inside, and he emerged five minutes later."

"Big deal. It could have been anyone."

"Mr French went to remind the woman that the wheelie bins are only allowed to go out on the morning they're collected, and she didn't answer the door."

"It doesn't mean that something has happened to her," Smith said. "He sounds like a pain in the arse, and she was probably avoiding him."

"That's what I would have thought," DI Smyth said. "If he didn't mention the fact that the man was wearing a courier uniform, and he had a balaclava over his face when he exited the house."

"I'm on my way," Smith said.

He turned right onto Tang Hall Lane and took the next right. DI Smyth had informed him that some uniforms were on their way, and he was to wait for them before he entered the property. Smith didn't think there was any danger still inside the house. The witness had spoken about a man in a courier uniform, but according to him, the man was long gone. Smith didn't know why, but he sensed that the woman was dead. He activated his hands-free and brought up Grant Webber's number.

The Head of Forensics answered on the second ring. "I've got nothing for you at the moment."

"I need you to get to a house in Osbaldwick," Smith told him. "Possible murder."

"Possible murder?" Webber repeated. "I don't know how many resources you think we have to spare in the Forensics department, but we do not come out for *possible* homicides."

"Forget I said that," Smith said. "We have a dead woman."

"Are you high on something?"

"Are you on your way or not?"

"You had better not be wrong about this," Webber said.

"I'm not wrong."

Smith parked his car outside number 12 Murton Way, got out and looked around. The wheelie bin on the pavement was the only one on the street. The door to one of the houses across the road opened and a short thin man walked across the road.

"Are you from the police?"

Smith showed him his ID. "DS Smith. Are you the one who called us?"

"Lionel French. Is there something you can do about that while you're here?" He pointed to the wheelie bin.

"I think that's a council matter," Smith said.

"The rules state that the bins can only be put out on the morning of collection," Lionel said. "What's the point of rules if nobody adheres to them?"

Smith couldn't care less about petty neighbourhood squabbles.

"You told the officer on the switchboard that you suspected that something had happened to the woman in number 12," he said.

"Harriet Jordan," Lionel said. "Hussy – that's what she is."

"Why do you say that?"

"I've seen them come and go," Lionel said. "Her husband works away a lot, and it's pretty obvious what she gets up to when he's not around."

"Are you suggesting that Mrs Jordan has a lot of male visitors?"

"It's been going on for months. There isn't much that goes on around here that I don't know about."

"Have you called the police about that before?" Smith said.

"Of course not. It's immoral, but it's not illegal, is it?"

"What makes this instance different?"

"I don't know," Lionel said. "Something about his mannerisms felt suspicious. And why was he wearing a balaclava when he came out of the house?"

"It's winter," Smith said. "A lot of people cover their faces in winter."

"Then why wasn't he wearing it when he arrived?"

Smith thought he had a very good point.

"You mentioned a courier."

"That's what his uniform looked like. He arrived at the house – they spoke for a while, and she invited him in. Why would someone invite a courier into the house?"

Smith wondered if he'd got this all wrong. It was possible that he'd jumped to all the wrong conclusions when he heard about the courier. It was the week before Christmas and there were plenty of couriers on the roads.

"Do you make a habit of keeping an eye on the street?" he said.

"It's not like I stand by the window, twitching the curtains," Lionel said. "I have cameras."

"CCTV?"

"Good ones. I can monitor them from my phone, and I have a big screen showing all four of them."

"Did you get the courier on camera?" Smith said.

"I just told you I did."

A police car pulled up and stopped. PC Simon Miller and a woman Smith didn't recognise got out.

"Could you go back inside your house now please?" Smith said to Lionel French.

"You can't make me do that," Lionel said.

"No," Smith said. "But I'm asking you nicely. We'll probably need to talk to you later."

"I have some really nice coffee."

"I'll bear that in mind," Smith said.

Lionel French nodded and made his way across the road.

"What have we got?" PC Miller said.

"Something that needs checking out," Smith said. "The woman's name is Harriet Jordan. A neighbour witnessed a courier coming to her house. He went inside the property, remained inside for a short while and left. The neighbour said she's not answering the door, and he thinks something has happened to her."

"Do you want us to go in and take a look?" the woman PC asked.

"Sorry, Sarge," PC Miller said. "This is Angie Bowler. She's recently joined us from Leeds."

"It's a pleasure to be working with you, Sarge," she said. "You're one of the reasons I applied for a transfer here."

Great, Smith thought. *Another fan*.

He really couldn't understand what the attraction was.

"Good to meet you," he said. "This might be nothing, but I want to wait for Forensics. Webber is on his way. In the meantime, I want you to speak to some of the other neighbours. See if anyone else saw anything. Then you can pay Mr French a visit. He caught the courier on CCTV, and he has some really nice coffee."

PC Bowler looked at him with wide eyes.

"Sounds good, Sarge," PC Miller said.

Smith took out his cigarettes and lit one. He wondered what was taking Grant Webber so long. He looked at the front of number 12 and it occurred to him that he could have made a huge mistake. He'd only spent five minutes in the company of Lionel French, and he'd got the impression that he was a pedantic nosy neighbour who probably complained about every little thing. It was quite possible that Harriet Jordan had simply ignored him. Smith wouldn't blame her - he would probably do the same.

He finished his cigarette and walked up the path to the front door of number 12. Webber was still nowhere to be seen. He knocked on the door and waited. After twenty seconds he knocked again, harder this time. He opened the letterbox and peered inside the house.

"Mrs Jordan," he shouted. "Police. Could you open up?"

The house remained silent.

"You'd better be right about this."

Smith turned around to see that Webber had crept up on him without him realising. The Head of Forensics was alone.

"I hope I'm not," Smith said. "But this feels wrong. Why isn't she answering the door?"

"Perhaps she went out," Webber said.

"Not according to the neighbour," Smith said. "And Lionel French sees everything that happens on this street. A courier came here not long ago. Mrs Jordan opened the door to him and then invited him inside. Shortly afterwards he exited the house, and she hasn't been seen since. Something's wrong."

"I would have appreciated it if you hadn't banged on the door just now," Webber said. "If this is a killer posing as a courier, you've probably just contaminated possible evidence."

Smith held his hands up in apology. "I tend to get a bit carried away when I'm waiting to be proved right."

Webber sighed deeply. "Let's take a look then."

Webber went in first. Even though it hadn't been confirmed that this was a crime scene, both he and Smith had donned SOC suits. The house was a semi-detached property with three bedrooms. Downstairs there were two similar sized rooms and a kitchen. The living room and dining room were both unoccupied. The door at the end of the hallway was closed. There was nothing so far to indicate that a serious crime had been committed.

"Mrs Jordan," Smith called out. "Harriet."

"She's not here," Webber said.

"She's here," Smith insisted.

He nodded to the kitchen door. Webber walked ahead of him. He opened the door and went inside.

Smith took no pleasure in being right. A woman he assumed was Harriet Jordan was lying face-down on the floor next to the washing machine. Smith stood completely still and took in the room. There were no obvious signs of a struggle, and Smith guessed that Harriet had been taken by surprise. Blood had spread outwards from her lower abdomen on either side. A much larger pool of blood had circled her face and neck.

"He slit her throat," Smith said.

Webber nodded. "The blood spatter on the window behind the washing machine suggests it. That's an impressive arterial spurt. If you've seen enough, I'd like you to leave please."

"I've seen enough. The man who did this was caught on camera, and I want to take a look at the footage."

CHAPTER TEN

"Lionel French has a camera pointing directly across the road from his property," DI Smyth said. "It captures the front of numbers 10,12, and 14."

"Isn't that illegal?" DC Moore wondered.

"Who cares?" Smith said. "At just before three this afternoon the camera caught Harriet Jordan pushing her wheelie bin onto the pavement outside the house. Mrs Jordan goes back inside, and soon afterwards we can see a man walking up the path to the front door. After a brief discussion the man goes inside, and he comes out six minutes later."

"Unfortunately," DI Smyth said. "We couldn't get a good look at his face. He approached the house from the direction of the A64, and he had his back to the camera when he walked up the path. When he emerged from the house he was wearing a balaclava."

"He was aware of the cameras," DC King said.

"He was," Smith said. "He didn't care about Harriet seeing his face because he was planning on killing her, but he knew the camera on our nosy neighbour's property would catch him coming out."

"If he knew about Lionel French's CCTV," Bridge said. "It means he's done some homework. This isn't the first time he's been to the street."

"We're already onto it," DI Smyth said. "Mr French was more than willing to cooperate. The footage from his CCTV cameras is stored on a cloud for twenty-eight days and we might get lucky."

"We won't," Smith said.

"Here we go," Bridge said.

"I'm not being a downer for the sake of it," Smith said. "But this bloke isn't your run-of-the-mill killer."

"He knocked on her door in the middle of the day," DC Moore said. "He was taking a huge chance doing that."

"He's brazen," Smith admitted. "But nothing he does is left to chance. That audacity is part of his MO. He left a witness alive at the scene of the first one."

"Hold on for a second there," DI Smyth said. "We don't know that the two murders are connected."

"They're connected. A courier knocks on the door, gains access to the property and it's all over in minutes."

"I'm inclined to agree," DC King said. "There are too many similarities to ignore."

"There is a certain professionalism on display here," Smith said.

"Are you suggesting we could be dealing with a pro?" DC Moore said.

"It's worth thinking about. Look at the facts. The CCTV shows what appears to be a friendly conversation on the doorstep. There's nothing there to suggest that Harriet Jordan felt threatened in any way."

"Do you think they were acquainted?" Whitton said.

"No," Smith said without thinking. "The timing doesn't fit for that. A friend turns up on your doorstep, you don't have a chat in the cold before inviting them in. You let them in straight away. It's freezing right now. I think Harriet truly believed that he was a courier."

"He wasn't holding anything in his hands," DC Moore pointed out. "And there was no sign of a van on the road. I would have smelled a rat."

"I'm just reading the camera footage, Harry," Smith said. "He didn't force his way in – Harriet let him in without question. And I reckon Janet Downing did the same."

"They didn't feel threatened," DC King said. "They didn't suspect a thing."

"According to the neighbour," Smith said. "Harriet Jordan had a lot of male visitors. Her husband works away a lot and Lionel French claims that men come and go all the time."

"Do you think the killer could be one of those men?" Bridge said.

"It's worth looking into," DI Smyth said. "If Lionel French is telling the truth, where did Mrs Jordan meet these men? We need to speak to her family and friends."

"Prioritise the friends," Smith said. "If Harriet was meeting other men, it's more likely she'd confide in a friend about it."

"What about her husband?" DC King said. "It's possible he's involved."

"It's always the husband," Bridge said.

"He may have known more about Harriet's indiscretions than she realised," DC King said. "It's a solid motive for murder."

"It certainly is," Smith said. "But something doesn't fit in this instance, especially when we add Janet Downing into the equation. We'll speak to the husband, but my money isn't on him."

"Moving on to the initial forensic findings," DI Smyth said. "It looks like Harriet sustained a number of injuries to her face, torso and neck but it was the laceration to her throat that probably killed her."

"The spatter pattern suggests it," Smith said. "She had her throat slit – the arterial spurt was pretty impressive, and I think he sliced her throat open from behind."

"I'm all ears," DI Smyth said.

"The CCTV footage tells us that he's a tall bloke. Taller than me. He will have been unable to avoid getting in the path of the arterial spurt if he was standing in front of her when he slit her throat."

"He would have been covered in blood," Bridge said.

"Not only that," Smith said. "The blood on the window was one long, uninterrupted splash, if you'll excuse the crude description. Webber is convinced that there was nothing in the path of the spurt as it left Harriet's arteries and hit the windowpane. If someone was standing in front of her, the spatter pattern would be irregular."

"So, he sliced her throat from behind," DC Moore said. "What does that actually tell us?"

"I'm convinced we're dealing with a pro," Smith said. "His actions are calm and collected, and the murders themselves are cold and calculated."

"Have you recently discovered alliteration, Sarge?" DC King dared.

"What?"

"Never mind."

"Are we definitely assuming the two murders were carried out by the same perpetrator?" DC Moore said.

"We are," Smith confirmed.

"A grandmother and a housewife," Bridge said. "Do we know if they were acquainted?"

"We know very little about either of them," DI Smyth said. "And I want to do something about that. It's early days, but I still believe that these murders will be resolved quickly."

"I disagree, boss," Smith said.

"I wouldn't expect anything less," DI Smyth said. "But whatever you believe is irrelevant. We have two cold-blooded slayings carried out in a very short space of time. The killer left a witness behind at the scene of the first murder, and he was caught on CCTV at the house of the second victim."

"Nothing he does is unintentional," Smith insisted. "Sophie Downing was left alive because she wasn't his target. He would have killed her without hesitation if he had to. He was aware of Lionel French's cameras, and that's why he put on the balaclava when he left Harriet Jordan's house. We haven't even scraped the surface of this one, but I know for a fact that there's more to it than we think – a hell of a lot more."

CHAPTER ELEVEN

Smith was about to leave for the day when he received a phone call from City Hospital. It was Dr Donna Frome.

"Please tell me you have good news," Smith said.

"I've got good news and bad news," Dr Frome said.

"Has Sophie's condition improved?"

"That's the good news. She's making remarkable progress, considering what she went through. She's displaying signs that she's open to outside stimuli and she's communicating."

"That's brilliant," Smith said. "That little girl could be the key witness in her grandmother's murder."

"That brings me to the bad news."

"She's refusing to talk about what happened?" Smith guessed.

"She has no memory of the event," Dr Frome said. "She keeps asking when her grandmother will be coming to see her."

"How can that be possible?" Smith said. "She was there when it happened."

"I believe the memory of the murder is being repressed. It's not uncommon for victims of extreme trauma to block out the initial cause of the trauma."

"Is there any way to help jog her memory?" Smith said.

"The only cure is time," Dr Frome said. "These things can't be forced. Sophie's brain has blocked out what happened for a very good reason."

"But it should come back to her?"

"Only time will tell. I have to go."

"Just one more thing," Smith said. "Do you believe there is any way to expedite the process? There must be something you can suggest that could help to jog her memory."

"I can't help you," Dr Frome said. "I'm not a psychologist and this really isn't my field of expertise."

"I understand," Smith said. "Thanks for letting me know."

Whitton caught up to him. "Problems?"

"Sophie Downing has no memory of the murder," Smith told her. "Her doctor doesn't know when what happened will come back to her."

"It's probably for the best. That poor little girl."

"She was there when it happened, Erica. She can help us catch him."

"She's six years old," Whitton said. "How would you feel if it was Laura who'd witnessed the murder of her grandmother?"

"We can't afford to think like that," Smith said. "It wasn't Laura, and even if it was, I know that she would want to help catch the person who did it."

"What else did the doctor say?"

"She said it's not her area of expertise, and she can't help me. Hold on."

"I get nervous when you say that."

"I might have an idea, but I need to think about it. I'll see you at home."

He checked in on DI Smyth before he left. The DI was looking at something on his laptop when he went into the office.

"I need to run something by you," Smith said.

"Hold on a second," DI Smyth said. "Come and take a look at this."

"What is it?"

"We've got some CCTV footage from one of the houses in Janet Downing's street in Heslington. Tell me if this is our man."

He shifted the laptop so Smith could see the screen.

"This is a house three doors down from Mrs Downing's."

"It's 12:15," Smith read. "The son left for the shops at noon."

"He'll be in the shot soon," DI Smyth said.

At 12:17 a figure appeared on the right of the screen.

"He's heading towards Janet's house," DI Smyth said.

"Pause it there," Smith said when the man was in the middle of the screen.

DI Smyth obliged. The quality of the footage wasn't great – it was impossible to make out the man's face, but it did tell them that he was tall. "It looks like he could be wearing a courier uniform," Smith said. "And he's carrying something in his hand. Is there any way to get this enhanced?"

"The tech team have a copy of the footage," DI Smyth said. "This has to be our man."

"Does he come back?" Smith said.

DI Smyth tapped the keypad, and the footage was now shown at five times the normal speed.

"Stop it there," Smith said when another figure came into the shot.

"It's not him," DI Smyth said.

It was a woman pushing a pram. She'd appeared from the direction of Janet Downing's house.

"We need to find her," Smith said. "It's possible she might have seen something."

"An appeal will be going out this evening," DI Smyth said.

The CCTV didn't capture anyone else until 12:28, and it didn't take Smith long to realise that this wasn't the man they were looking for either. It was an elderly man with a stick, and he was walking extremely slowly. Smith estimated that the distance from one side of the screen to the other was no more than twenty metres, but the clock told him that it took the old man almost a minute to cover it.

Five minutes later it was quite clear what had happened.

"He didn't leave the same way he arrived," Smith said.

"He didn't," DI Smyth said. "I'm debating whether to widen the search – carry out door-to-doors further afield. What do you think?"

"It's worth a shot, but I don't think anything is going to come of it. It's almost as if he doesn't care about being seen, and that makes me believe that he's not local. He's done a lot of homework beforehand – he knows the geography of the city, but anyone with Google Maps can do that."

"What was it you wanted to ask me?" DI Smyth said.

"Sophie Downing's condition has improved," Smith said. "She's communicating again, and the doctor thinks she should make a full recovery."

"That's good news. Has she spoken about her grandmother's murder?"

"That's where the problem lies," Smith said. "She has no recollection of it. Dr Frome explained that it's another one of the brain's coping mechanisms, but she couldn't elaborate. She said psychology isn't her field of expertise."

"We'll have to carry on without the girl's help then."

"Fuck that, boss. She saw what happened and I'm not going to let her memory loss stop her from remembering."

"That makes no sense whatsoever."

"I want to ask Porter Klaus to help us," Smith said. "I assume you and the giant German are still together."

"That's none of your business."

"I'll take that as a yes then."

"Do I have to remind you that Porter is no longer allowed to practice psychology?"

"That's a minor detail," Smith said. "And anyway, that's not what I need his help with. I want him to hypnotise Sophie Downing into remembering what happened to her grandmother."

CHAPTER TWELVE

Catherine Gordon pulled the curtains tight even though they wouldn't close any more. The only light inside the room was the artificial flicker of the laptop on the bed opposite the window. It suddenly occurred to her that she was acting excessively cautiously. There was little chance of being interrupted here on the fourth floor of the hotel.

It wasn't an ideal place to celebrate Christmas. The Grand Hotel in Holgate was impersonal and sterile but that was one of the reasons that Catherine had chosen it. She'd booked four nights, and she'd spent most of the first night gazing out of the window debating whether to jump. Two weeks ago, her husband had done precisely that at The Albert Hotel in Leeds. John had jumped from the 24th floor and if it wasn't for two unique gold teeth it would have been impossible to tell if the crumpled mess of blood and bones on the pavement below was actually him.

John had been taken for a ride by his business partner of ten years, and he'd lost everything in the process. While the partner became stupidly rich overnight, John was left with only the clothes on his back, and when he learned that there was nothing anyone could do to rectify the situation, John had taken to the air in a city he'd always hated.

Catherine's decision was helped along with a bottle of gin and at three in the morning she made up her mind not to go the same way as her husband. She'd made a considerable sum of money that John wasn't aware of. It was all virtual currency, and Catherine had never really thought about what to do with it before. Perhaps she could put it to good use now. Also, she wasn't quite sure if a leap from the fourth floor would be fatal, and she would hate to get it wrong.

Catherine turned on the light next to the bed and returned to her laptop. Using an OnionShare service she accessed her Tor browser and stretched out her arms. She carried out some deep breathing exercises she'd read about and got ready to start. Experience had taught her that this wasn't a quick process, and it was best to warm up beforehand.

It was going to take some time to find the website – it was designed with that in mind, but Catherine had nothing but time right now. After the numbness from John's suicide had died down, Catherine had been consumed with hate. She been told that this was common. Anger was generally known to be the second stage in the grieving process, but Catherine's rage had been deeply concerning. She felt like she could kill, and soon she began to contemplate self-termination. The view from the window of The Grand Hotel changed everything.

Catherine focused on the screen and readied herself. If she was going to locate the site, she was going to have to go deep. The Dark Web was forever evolving and navigating its depths was not as simple as the normal World Wide Web. This was a place you could get lost in, and if you weren't careful, you might never find what you were looking for.

The familiar screen popped up two hours into the search.

"The Graveyard," Catherine whispered.

This was no ordinary burial ground. There were no lost souls here – this was a place where the fate of the future dead was sealed.

Catherine's heart was beating dangerously fast as she reread the information on the screen. This was it. Once she'd signed the contract there was no going back. Time seemed to stand still as she started the process of selling her soul to an invisible devil.

Afterwards, Catherine was overcome with a sensation of pure relief, and she was also mildly amused. It was highly inappropriate given the circumstances but the steps she'd gone through in sealing the deal weren't unlike the process of purchasing a car. Payment had been settled – terms and conditions were discussed, and when Catherine had finalised the deal with a virtual signature, she felt no more emotion than she had when she was given the keys to her old Ford Fiesta.

There was no need to close the site. The images and words on the screen vanished shortly after the contract had been signed. Catherine Gordon would be contacted soon. That's all she'd been told.

* * *

"I agree with the DI," Whitton said.

Smith had told her about his idea to hypnotise Sophie Downing to try to help her remember what happened earlier.

"What if it works?" Smith said. "What if it can make her recall the events of her grandmother's murder?"

"It could have the opposite effect," Whitton said. "It could traumatise her even more."

"Since when were you an expert on hypnosis?"

"You're no expert either. I think it's a risky idea."

"I'm going to speak to Porter anyway," Smith said.

"He'll go along with what the DI wants. They're in a relationship; in case you've forgotten."

"I don't think that's even relevant," Smith said. "Porter is a man of science, and he will be able to explain to me the possible dangers and side effects. I have to try this."

"We're not going to have the Christmas we were hoping for, are we?" Whitton changed the subject.

"It doesn't look like it," Smith said. "And I'm sorry. I know how much you wanted it."

"You're not sorry at all."

"I am," Smith said. "I really am. I didn't think about it from your perspective. This is probably going to be the last Christmas with your dad."

Whitton didn't say anything. She didn't have to – the look in her eyes told Smith everything he needed to know.

Harold Whitton had been diagnosed with prostate cancer a few weeks ago and the prognosis was bleak. He'd known about it for a long time, and he'd done nothing about it. The cancer had now spread to his liver and, even with treatment, the doctors didn't think he would see another summer. Harold had refused treatment and everyone in the Smith household had accepted that.

"I'm going to speak to the boss," Smith said. "You're going to get your Christmas with your dad."

"What about the investigation?" Whitton said.

There were tears in her eyes now.

"Fuck the investigation," Smith said.

He wrapped his arms around her and pulled her close. He could feel the tears in his own eyes now.

"Fuck the investigation."

CHAPTER THIRTEEN

Smith decided that there was no time like the present and he was now in his car on the way to DI Smyth's house in Foxwood. He hoped that Porter Klaus would be there too – he could kill two birds with one stone. He was determined to make sure that Whitton got to spend Christmas Day with her dad and he was also hoping to persuade Porter to hypnotise Sophie Downing. He understood the risks. He didn't think that Dr Frome would give permission for this, and they would have to find some other way, but Smith decided that the benefits outweighed the risks, and he was willing to take his chances. He was certain that the six-year-old girl would be able to give them some answers.

He was in luck. There was a white 4x4 parked behind DI Smyth's car in the driveway. The German hypnotist was here. Smith walked up the path to the front door and rang the bell. Shortly afterwards the door was opened by a man who filled the doorway. Smith had forgotten how huge Porter Klaus was. He gave Smith a warm smile.

"Come in. Oliver is just showering. Have you eaten?"

Smith realised that he hadn't. "No, but I wouldn't want to put you out."

Porter rolled his eyes. "Come in."

Smith had brought some beers with him. He placed them on the table in the kitchen.

"You didn't have to bring your own drinks," Porter said. "I always keep some of my Belgium beer here."

"That's why I brought my own," Smith told him. "I remember the last time I had a few of those things. I'm sorry to pop round unannounced."

"What is it with the English and their obsession with making appointments for everything?"

"I'm Australian," Smith reminded him.

"You've been here too long. I'm making a winter stew. Pork of course."

"Of course," Smith said.

"What brings you here?" Porter said.

He opened the door of the oven and lifted the lid on the casserole dish.

Smith took a sip of his beer. "I'm glad I caught you on your own. I need your help with a witness to a murder."

"I'll help if I can," Porter said and closed the oven door.

"It's a little girl," Smith explained. "She's six years old and I think she witnessed the murder of her grandmother."

"Extraordinary."

"When I arrived at the scene of the murder," Smith said. "She was in a deep state of shock. Her doctor told me later that she'd suffered some kind of semi-catatonic episode as a result of the trauma she'd undergone."

"It's not uncommon," Porter said. "The brain often shuts down certain pathways to aid with the healing process."

"That's what Sophie's doctor told me," Smith said. "She wasn't responding to any outside stimuli, but she made a swift recovery and she's now communicating again."

"Do you want me to talk to her?"

"I don't think that will help."

"Because I need to remind you that I'm no longer allowed to practice."

"I'm aware of that," Smith said. "The problem is that the little girl has no memory of the event. She has no recollection of the murder of her grandmother."

"It's likely the memory has been repressed," Porter said.

"The doc said something similar. I want you to hypnotise the little girl."

DI Smyth's timing couldn't have been any worse. His entrance to the kitchen coincided perfectly with Smith's request to the German hypnotist. "This is out of order, Smith," he said.

"You smell nice, boss," Smith said.

"I gave you my answer," DI Smyth said. "And you chose to ignore it."

"I needed to get it from the horse's mouth. This is the only way – I understand that there are risks involved but we need to do this."

"This is not up for debate," DI Smyth said.

"Hear me out," Smith said. "Let's discuss the pros and cons first. There's something else I need to ask you, but that can wait until afterwards."

"Let's eat first," Porter said to DI Smyth. "I took the liberty of inviting your stubborn Australian if that's OK."

"Talk me through the process of hypnotism," Smith said.

He'd polished off a huge bowl of Porter's winter stew.

"Under hypnosis a patient is fully aware of everything around them," the big German said. "They're not asleep – in fact the opposite is the case and they're in a state of enhanced cognition."

"How would you go about digging out a memory that has been repressed?"

"When a person loses the ability to remember after severe trauma, it's what's known as dissociative amnesia. The brain's response is to alter how these memories are stored and processed."

"But you can get these memories back using hypnosis?" Smith said.

"It's possible, yes."

"She's six years old," DI Smyth reminded them.

"In theory," Porter said. "That ought to make her more susceptible to hypnosis. Her hypothalamus hasn't fully developed and..."

"Her hypo what?" Smith interrupted.

"It's the part of the brain responsible for, among other things wake-sleep function and emergency responses to stressors. Therefore, a girl her age will be more open to hypnosis than yourself, for example."

"We already know that Smith can't be hypnotised," DI Smyth said.

"I have a strange brain," Smith said.

"I won't comment on that," DI Smyth said.

"Will you do it?" Smith asked Porter. "Will you hypnotise the little girl?"

"Hold on," DI Smyth said. "We still haven't discussed the possible side effects."

"Hypnosis," Porter said. "When practiced by a trained professional, is generally safe. Some people may experience drowsiness or disorientation afterwards, but this usually only lasts for a short period of time. In the case of trauma victims, the adverse effects can be substantially enhanced. A person who has undergone severe trauma may recall memories they'd hitherto kept hidden."

"Isn't that the whole point of this?" Smith said.

"These memories can heighten anxiety and distress. And in rare cases the stress can lead to certain mental illnesses."

"Rare cases," Smith repeated. "How rare?"

"I can't give you an exact number," Porter said. "But roughly one percent."

"That's a risk I'm willing to take," Smith said.

"The risk isn't yours," DI Smyth pointed out.

"We need to help Sophie to remember," Smith said. "And we need to do that quickly. She was in the house when her grandmother was killed, and she can help us catch the man who did it."

"OK," DI Smyth said and drained the wine in his glass. "Let's say we're willing to give hypnosis a go – how are you planning on persuading the doctor?"

"Leave that up to me," Smith said. "You won't regret this."

"I'm already regretting it," DI Smyth said. "You mentioned something else that you wanted to ask me. I'd appreciate it if you could make it quick – Porter and I were planning on having a quiet evening together."

"No worries," Smith said. "I know this is a big ask but Whitton needs some time off."

"We're in the middle of a murder investigation," DI Smyth said.

"I'm aware of that, but this is important."

"How much time are we talking about?"

"One day," Smith said. "Christmas Day to be precise."

"We really need her on the team," DI Smyth said.

"I wouldn't ask if it wasn't important, boss."

"No," DI Smyth said. "No, you wouldn't. OK then. One day."

"Thank you. Don't you want to know why I'm asking?"

"You must have your reasons. That's good enough for me."

Smith stood up. "I appreciate this. I really do. I'll let you know when it's time to hypnotise Sophie Downing."

"Take your beers," DI Smyth said.

"I'll leave them here for next time," Smith said.

"There won't be a next time," DI Smyth said. "Take the beers and get out."

CHAPTER FOURTEEN

Christmas Eve dawned grey and wet. According to the bookkeepers, the odds on a white Christmas in York this year were a whopping sixty-to-one. Smith wasn't a gambling man, but he knew that they weren't going to get snow on Christmas Day. It looked like it was going to be a miserable, rainy festive season and that suited him just fine.

Whitton was already in bed when he got home last night so he wasn't able to tell her that she would get to spend Christmas Day with her dad. He let her know as soon as she came downstairs.

"Thank you for doing that," she said. "Did you tell DI Smyth the reason?"

"The boss didn't ask," Smith said. "He knows it's important, and that's as far as it went. He's a good bloke."

"Shit," Whitton said.

"What?"

"There's so much to do. I haven't even thought about the food."

"Get Lucy and Darren to help you," Smith said. "It's not like they've got anything else to do. And I'm sure Darren's mother will give you a hand. I still don't know where you're going to put them all."

Whitton did some quick mental arithmetic. "There'll be ten of us, including Andrew. I'm sure we'll find place for all of them."

"You're not officially off until tomorrow," Smith said. "Give Darren and Lucy the credit card and a list. Let them sort it out."

"It's not going to be the same without you," Whitton said.

"I'll be fine," Smith said. "I would much rather be at work on Christmas Day."

He hadn't been able to celebrate Christmas in over twenty years. He recalled Christmas Day when he was sixteen like yesterday. The day had started out well. Smith and his little sister had opened their presents and laughed with their parents. Afterwards, Smiths mother and his sister, Laura made a start on the food in the kitchen and Smith spent a while inspecting the presents he'd been given.

An hour or so later Smith recalled his mother asking him to go and find his dad. The food was almost ready, and she hadn't seen him for a while. Smith went outside to the large back garden. The sun was shining in a blue sky, and it was very hot. He called his dad's name, but he didn't reply.

He found him at the back of the garden. He'd hanged himself with a rope from one of the trees there. It was a defining moment in Smith's life, and the image of his father swaying in the gentle breeze was one Smith would never be able to erase.

He often wondered if he was being selfish for shunning Christmas altogether. He had a family now and it wasn't fair on them to suffer because of something that happened before most of them were born, but Smith couldn't bring himself to enjoy the festive season like he was supposed to.

He told Whitton that he would see her at work and left her to make a start on the last-minute Christmas preparations. The roads were quiet as Smith drove through the persistent drizzle. It really was a miserable day, and Smith wondered what lay in store for him. He made a mental to-do list as he drove. The priority for the day was to come up with a way to hypnotise Sophie Downing. He didn't think the pink-haired doctor would allow it, so Smith needed to figure out a different approach.

It came to him when he parked his car outside the station. He realised that he didn't actually need Dr Frome's permission. He would persuade Sophie's father that it was extremely important to help Sophie remember what happened. Smith was sure that Peter Downing would agree when Smith explained that it could give them a clue about who killed his mother. Smith tapped out a message to Porter Klaus and asked him if he would be available later today, to which the German hypnotist replied that he was free all day. Smith sensed that they were going to make progress today.

He grabbed a quick coffee in the canteen and headed for the small conference room. Bridge and DC Moore were already seated.

"We're going to hypnotise the little girl today," Smith told them.

"How did you manage to get the DI to agree to that?" Bridge said.

"Gentle persuasion. Sophie Downing is going to give us something – I know she is."

"What about the doctors?" DC Moore said. "How are you going to get round them?"

"I don't need their permission, Harry. They can't stop us from hypnotising Sophie if her father agrees to it."

"I hope you know what you're doing," DC Moore said. "This could backfire. What if she goes mental or something?"

"She's not going to go mental or something," Smith said. "Although I don't really know what that means."

DI Smyth came in with DC King. They joined the others at the table.

"Where's Whitton?" DI Smyth said. "I was under the impression that she'd only requested one days' leave."

"Her car battery was giving her shit," Smith lied. "I'm sure she'll be here soon."

"We'll make a start without her," DI Smyth said. "We had quite a response to the appeal that went out last night. A number of people remember seeing a man wearing a courier uniform yesterday, in both Heslington and Osbaldwick and they'll be working with a police artist during the course of the day."

"Are we going to release a photofit of him?" Bridge said.

"Let's see what the witnesses can come up with first," DI Smyth said. "

"Have we managed to locate Harriet Jordan's husband?" Smith asked.

"We have," DI Smyth confirmed. "Duncan Jordan has a watertight alibi for the time his wife was murdered. He was attending a conference in Harrogate."

"What kind of conference?" Smith said.

"What does that matter?" DC Moore said.

"It's Christmas, Harry," Smith said. "What kind of company organises a conference at this time of year? Is the alibi legit?"

"It is," DI Smyth said. "Mr Jordan has produced credit card receipts and there are dozens of witnesses who can put him at the hotel in Harrogate. And there's more – according to the uniforms who spoke to him, Mr Jordan is no more than five foot six. He's not the man in the CCTV footage."

"That means nothing," Smith said. "He could have paid someone to carry out the murder. His wife was a bit of a slut, and she wasn't exactly subtle about it. I wouldn't discount Duncan Jordan just yet. It might be an idea to sift through his bank records to see if he's made any unusual withdrawals or payments."

"We'll do that, of course" DI Smyth said. "If only to make you happy."

"I've figured out a way to bypass the doctor treating Sophie Downing," Smith said.

"I thought you might," DI Smyth said.

"We don't actually need her permission to hypnotise the little girl," Smith said. "Not if her father says it's OK."

"What if he doesn't?"

"I'll make sure he does."

"Is he still in hospital?" DC King said.

"I reckon we'll find him there," Smith said. "Sophie isn't going to be discharged any time soon, and he wouldn't leave her there by herself."

"What about the mother?" Bridge said. "Where's she been hiding?"

"That's a very good question," DI Smyth said. "Mr Jordan mentioned something about his wife having to work late yesterday, but who puts their job before their daughter's welfare?"

"More people than you think," Smith said. "I'm going to head over to the hospital to persuade Sophie's dad that it's in everybody's best interests for her to be hypnotised. I'll pick up your German on the way."

"That's a bit presumptuous, isn't it?"

"That's the way I roll, boss."

"And Porter is not my German," DI Smyth added.

"I'll let you know how it goes," Smith said.

CHAPTER FIFTEEN

The view from the window of the penthouse of the New Tower Hotel was truly extraordinary. The thirteenth-floor suite offered its guests a panorama, stretching from the Minster all the way to Walmgate Bar across the river. Tom Lowe had been reluctant to book the suite at first – he wasn't a full blown triskaidekaphobic, but he'd always shied away from anything involving the number thirteen. He'd been surprised that the New Tower even had a thirteenth floor – he'd always assumed that hotels were somewhat superstitious about it, but the New Tower clearly wasn't.

"What's happened to the room service?" the woman on the bed asked. Her name had slipped Tom's mind. He'd picked her up in the hotel bar last night and she'd lingered longer than he would have liked.

"I have some work to do," he lied.

"I'm hungry. I thought we were going to eat something."

"I'll chase them up," Tom said. "But I think it would be best if you left me in peace. I really need to finish off an urgent presentation."

"You're just like the rest of them."

"I never pretended that I wasn't." Tom picked up his wallet and took out a wad of notes without bothering to count them. "Go and get yourself something to eat."

"I'm not a fucking whore," the woman said.

She took the money, nevertheless. She got off the bed, picked up her handbag and left the room without a backwards glance.

Tom turned on his laptop and waited for it to warm up. He picked up the phone next to the bed to find out what had happened to the room service and at the same time there was a knock on the door.

"About time," Tom said.

He opened the door to a young man in a hotel uniform.

"Room service."

He had an accent that Tom couldn't place.

"What took you so long?" Tom said.

"Will you be dining alone?"

Tom thought he had a friendly, open face and he was wearing latex gloves on his hands. Tom wondered if they were part of the hotel uniform. He knew what the accent was now – it was definitely Australian.

"My friend has left," he said. "It's just me. Are you going to bring the food inside or not? It's going to get cold."

"Where do you want it?"

Tom pointed to the table next to the bed.

The food trolley was pushed inside, and the hotel employee closed the door behind him. He glanced at the laptop on the table and looked at Tom.

"Are you right or left-handed?"

"What?"

"It's a simple question."

"I'm right-handed," Tom said.

He didn't know how a man could move so quickly. Before he realised what was happening, the other man was behind him, and something was stuffed inside his mouth.

"This will hurt."

Tom felt a tight grip on his left wrist, and he screamed a silent scream when his hand was slammed down on the table and the thumb was severed just below the knuckle. The pain was intense, and the initial spurt of blood made him feel ill. The grip on his wrist was incredible.

"It will be over soon." The man's voice was calm and oddly reassuring. Tom's ring finger was next, and he was starting to feel lightheaded. A slap to his face made him forget about the pain in his hand for a moment.

"Will you scream if I take the rag out of your mouth?"

Tom shook his head.

"Can I trust you not to make a sound?"

This was answered with a nod.

The cloth was yanked out of his mouth and Tom gasped.

"What do you want?" he managed.

"Two things. Is your laptop ready to rock and roll?"

"What?"

"I'm going to bandage your hand. Then I want you to log into your online banking for me."

"Fuck you."

The rag was quickly stuffed back into Tom's mouth, and the renewed grip on his wrist told him what was about to happen.

"Do you think we could start again?" the man asked after the hunting knife had made quick work of Tom's middle finger.

The rag was pulled out again.

"Who the hell are you?" Tom gasped.

"I want you to take a few deep breaths, and then you're going to log into your online banking. You still have seven fingers left."

Tom was directed to the laptop with the blade of the knife at his back.

"You won't get away with this."

"Quickly please."

Tom woke the screen of the laptop and keyed in the login details. His right hand was shaking, and he was unsuccessful on the first try.

"Concentrate."

"You won't get away with this," Tom said once more.

"You have more than one account."

The balance on the screen was a little over seven thousand pounds.

"This is the only one I can access without outside authorisation," Tom said.

"Give me your hand please."

"OK," Tom said. "No more. No more."

It took fifteen minutes for Tom Lowe to empty his bank accounts. He lost another two fingers in the process and at one stage the one-time-pin was problematic when it necessitated access to his mobile phone. The phone was unlocked using one of his severed digits, and Tom almost passed out when he watched as the bloody finger was held against the screen of the phone. The sum of almost two million pounds left Tom's accounts and was transferred to various other accounts. Tom didn't know where the money had ended up, but if he was privy to this information, he would see that the majority had been donated to dog shelters and animal charities all over the city.

"What now?" he said. "You've got your money, so what now?"

"One more thing."

The cloth was shoved back inside Tom's mouth, and he gagged. A hand was pressed against his throat, and he reacted by lashing out. The man's grip was too strong, and Tom could feel himself weakening. Red dots were coming and going in front of his eyes, and he could hear his heartbeat in his ears.

Tom lost consciousness soon afterwards and he was unaware that he was now lying on his back on the floor of the room. He also couldn't hear the crash of the glass as the table was smashed through the window. A blast of icy air came into the room. The rag was removed from Tom's mouth, and he was dragged towards the broken window. One good shove and the man with the Australian accent watched as gravity did its thing. It took precisely seven seconds for Tom Lowe to plummet downwards and land on the pavement below. There was no sound as he hit the ground.

The Australian picked up Tom's phone and put it in his pocket. He put on a green balaclava and had a final look around the room. He lifted the lid of the tray on the trolley, raised the balaclava, took out a prawn tail and popped it in his mouth. He chewed thoughtfully for a moment, left the room and closed the door behind him. With his elbow, he smashed the emergency fire alarm panel on the wall and soon afterwards the wailing siren filled the air. He followed the signs for the stairs and made his way down the thirteen floors to the ground.

CHAPTER SIXTEEN

Smith got out of his car and lit a cigarette. Porter Klaus got out of the passenger side and rubbed his hands together.

"Your car smells funny."

"You're not the first person to notice that," Smith said. "It's always smelled a bit weird, and I don't know why."

They'd discussed the plan of action during the drive to the hospital. Porter had admitted that he'd never done anything like this before. He'd hypnotised many people, but he'd never been involved in a police investigation before.

"That's not strictly true," Smith reminded him.

"That was an unofficial, off the record thing," Porter said. "And it didn't involve a little girl."

He'd asked Smith what particular questions he was to put to Sophie Downing – Smith outlined what he wanted to know and told the big German to play it by ear. He had every faith in his abilities.

"We still have the father to get through," Smith said. "But I'm sure we can persuade him."

"Perhaps I should hypnotise him too," Porter suggested.

"That's not a bad idea."

"It was a joke."

"I'm sure we won't have too much trouble with him."

Peter Downing wasn't the only obstacle in their way. When Smith and Porter Klaus found Sophie's father, he wasn't alone. A big woman with a fierce stare was with him. Peter introduced her as his wife, Emily.

"How is she?" Smith asked. "How's Sophie doing?"

"She still doesn't remember a thing about yesterday," Peter said. "Dr Frome explained that her reaction isn't uncommon in patients who've suffered extreme trauma, and her memory should come back in time."

"That's what we need to talk to you about," Smith said.

He introduced Porter Klaus and explained what they wanted to do.

"Absolutely not." It was Emily. "You want to use my daughter like an exhibition in a freak show. I won't allow it."

"Please, Mrs Downing," Smith said. "Sophie witnessed the murder of her grandmother. Your husband said it himself – the memory of what happened yesterday will come back in time, but we don't have time to wait. The man who killed Janet is still out there somewhere and it's possible that he will kill again."

"You're only saying that to get me to change my mind."

"I'm not," Smith said. "I'm not supposed to talk about the details of an ongoing investigation, but the man who killed Janet killed another woman shortly afterwards. He will carry on until he's caught, and Sophie can help us catch him. I would appreciate it if this information went no further."

"What do you think?" Peter asked his wife. "It's up to you."

"Why does every damn decision have to be mine?" Emily said.

"That's not fair," Peter said. "And where were you when Sophie needed you yesterday? Who had to pick up the pieces as usual?"

"Who had to go out and earn the money, as usual?"

"Please," Porter said. "I appreciate that this is an extremely difficult time for you, but now isn't the time for petty bickering. You'll have plenty of opportunity for that later."

Emily glared at him. "You're a hypnotist?"

"I'm a psychologist," Porter corrected her. "And I've used hypnosis successfully many times. It's completely safe, and Sophie will be able to end it whenever she feels she can't carry on. You and your husband will be with her the entire time."

"I think we should give it a try," Peter said. "I want the bastard who did this to Mum to pay."

"We all want the same thing," Smith said. "And Sophie will be completely safe."

Porter explained the process. He told Sophie's parents that he would induce hypnosis in the old-fashioned way. He would ask her to picture a staircase with warm carpeted steps. Then he would start the countdown, and they would go downstairs together as he counted down. Sophie would be assured that she was utterly safe the whole time, and she wouldn't have to worry about anyone hurting her.

"How are you planning on retrieving her memory of yesterday?" Emily wondered.

"I'm going to try to help her piece together the fragments by talking about the events that led up to the man entering the house," Porter explained. "Before we get to the time of the murder itself, I'll ask her questions about what she was doing. I'll ask her to tell me if there are any smells she can remember, and what she had to eat. Often sensory memories are stronger, and they can help to restore the other recollections."

"Let's do this then," Peter said.

Emily's phone started to ring. She glanced at the screen and sighed.

"I have to take this," she said and walked away down the corridor.

"No prizes for guessing what that's all about," Peter said.

"Work?" Smith said.

"She's never not at work."

"What does Emily do?" Porter asked.

"Finance," Peter said. "I've given up trying to remember her job title, but she's some high-flying financial adviser."

"Don't the financial markets close over Christmas?" Smith said.

"The Nasdaq closes on Boxing Day, but that's the only day there's no trading. I've got used to Emily's hectic hours, and the money's great."

"Money isn't everything," Smith said.

"So, I've come to realise."

Emily returned and informed them that she needed to get some work done.

"Can't someone else do it?" Peter said. "You're not the only finance guru in the company."

"No," Emily said. "But I'm the most senior. There's a rumour that the Greenberg-Hillman stock is about to tank, and I need to offload before that happens."

"And it can't wait?"

"It can," Emily said. "If I want to see sixty million go down the plughole. You don't need me here for this anyway. I'll get away as soon as I'm finished."

Her swift exit told them that the matter wasn't up for debate.

"Sixty million?" Smith said.

"Silly money," Peter said.

"Shall we go and speak to Sophie's doctor?" Porter said.

"I thought we didn't need her permission," Peter said.

"No," Smith said. "But she needs to be aware of what we're planning on doing, out of common courtesy."

He expected Dr Frome to be difficult, but he didn't anticipate what she told them. The pink-haired doctor refused to allow them to hypnotise Sophie Downing in her hospital room, and Smith realised that the only way this was going to work was if she was discharged and allowed to go home. Dr Frome advised against it – Sophie was still very weak and according to the doctor, she needed to stay in hospital for at least another two days.

In the end it was Peter Downing who made the final decision. He didn't want Sophie to have to spend Christmas in a hospital bed and he asked Dr Frome to bring him the necessary paperwork to have his daughter discharged. One thing was clear – Sophie wasn't going to be hypnotised any time soon, and Smith had no choice but to wait until she was taken home.

CHAPTER SEVENTEEN

Bridge and DC Moore were en-route to Duncan Jordan's second property in Holgate when Bridge's phone started to ring. He asked DC Moore to answer it. The man from London took the call, listened carefully and uttered the three words that always heralded something nasty.

"On our way."

"What is it?" Bridge said.

"We've got a jumper, Sarge," DC Moore said.

"A jumper?"

"Suicide. Bloke took a leap from the penthouse of the New Tower Hotel."

"I wish you wouldn't call them that," Bridge said. "*Jumper* is so American. What has a suicide got to do with us anyway? We've got bigger fish to fry than some rich bloke who decides to end it all at Christmas."

"I didn't get much info," DC Moore said. "But it looks like he didn't act alone – he had a bit of help with his failed base jump."

The scene outside the hotel was chaotic. Officers in uniform were fighting a losing battle trying to keep the people away from the entrance. Bridge estimated there to be at least fifty people. Some of them were wearing identical uniforms and when they got closer, he saw that it was the uniform of the employees of the hotel. He'd spotted Grant Webber's car further down the street, but the Head of Forensics was nowhere to be seen.

There was an ambulance parked directly outside the hotel and Bridge wondered what they were hoping to achieve. A leap from the thirteenth floor was bound to be fatal, so what were the paramedics doing there?

"I thought hotels were suspicious about the thirteenth floor," DC Moore said.

"The New Tower obviously isn't," Bridge said. "Thank God, they've already covered him up."

He nodded to the blanket on the pavement outside the hotel. A cordon had been set up and the police tape was blowing in the breeze. PC William Griffin was standing in front of it, preventing anyone from getting any closer.

"What now?" DC Moore said.

"I'll go and find someone in charge," Bridge said. "Go and give the uniforms a hand. There's far too many people trampling around out here."

He walked towards the entrance of the hotel to look for someone who could shed some light on what happened.

After speaking to one of the receptionists he was pointed in the direction of the woman who was one of the assistant managers of the hotel. Joss Hatton was a short woman in her thirties. She suggested that they get away from the mayhem and talk in the room the hotel used for conferences.

"What happened?" Bridge said.

"I was checking the Christmas bookings behind the reception desk," Joss said. "When something caught my eye. I didn't know what it was at first, but then the screaming started. I went outside and that's when I realised what had happened. I've never seen anything like it. He was so broken, and the blood..."

"I know this is hard," Bridge said. "Take your time, and perhaps it might be an idea to get yourself checked out by the paramedics outside."

"I'm fine," Joss said. "It was just such a shock."

"Do you know who the dead man is?"

"I didn't at first," Joss said. "But one of the porters spotted the broken window in the penthouse when he looked up at the hotel."

"He must have good eyes," Bridge said.

"She," Joss corrected. "I checked the register, and his name is Tom Lowe. Your forensics team are up in his room now."

"Do you know if Mr Lowe was alone in the room?" Bridge said.

Joss shook her head. "We value our guests' privacy."

"That's not what I asked. When he booked the penthouse, did he stipulate how many guests would be staying?"

"The penthouse sleeps four people," Joss said. "The price is the same whether it's one person or four."

"So, it's possible there was someone else with him?"

"It is."

"Can you talk me through the events before you saw him fall," Bridge said.

"I didn't see him fall."

"Before you caught his landing then."

"It all descended into chaos very quickly, if you'll excuse the inappropriate pun. I saw him land outside and shortly afterwards the fire alarm went off. The emergency alarm was activated on the thirteenth floor."

"How do you know that?"

"All the emergency alarm points are monitored, and when one of them is activated, a signal is sent to the control room behind reception."

"Interesting," Bridge said. "How soon after the man landed did the alarm go off?"

"Not long. Probably no more than a minute."

"What's the procedure when the fire alarm is activated?" Bridge said. "I imagine you have to evacuate the hotel."

"That's right. It's a logistical nightmare. We need to be absolutely sure that nobody is left inside and that can be problematic if guests are not in their rooms. We have to check the spa and the gym, and we need to make sure that the restaurant and bar are cleared."

"Do you do a role call?" Bridge said.

"Eventually. People are justifiably irritated when something like this happens, and often we have guests who refuse to cooperate."

"Did you check to see if there was actually a fire?"

"Everything here is monitored remotely," Joss said. "All the rooms have smoke detectors, as do the public areas. None of the detectors sensed anything out of the ordinary. The fire department are automatically notified, but they were advised to stand by and then they were given the all clear. Someone activated that emergency alarm on purpose."

"OK," Bridge said. "I assume the hotel has CCTV."

"Of course," Joss said. "There are cameras in all of the hallways, and in the general areas. We have two cameras over the entrance too."

"We're going to need that footage. Could you arrange that for us please?"

"Sure. Do you think he was pushed?"

"We don't know anything yet," Bridge said. "You said the porter noticed that the window of the penthouse was broken."

"I assumed it was done so the man could jump," Joss said. "Regulations stipulate that the windows can't be opened enough to allow this sort of thing to happen, but that didn't make a blind bit of difference here, did it?"

CHAPTER EIGHTEEN

"It's like a torture chamber in there," Billie Jones told Bridge in the corridor outside the penthouse on the thirteenth floor.

"Does it look like he definitely had some help with his final leap of faith?" Bridge said.

"That's really morbid. But yes, he did not voluntarily jump out of the window. There's blood all over the room, and we've found five severed fingers so far."

"Bloody hell."

"That's one way to describe it. Do you want to have a look?"

"Is Webber OK with that?" Bridge said.

"You know the drill."

"I'll just take a quick peek."

He regretted it as soon as he set foot inside the room. He registered the smell first – it was the unmistakable metallic tang of fresh blood, mixed with something sickly sweet. It reminded Bridge of the odour from a seafood platter he'd once eaten. It was freezing inside the room – the cold air was blowing in through the shattered window.

Grant Webber was examining something on the floor next to it.

"Webber," Bridge said. "What the hell happened here?"

"He was tortured," the Head of Forensics said without looking up. "And when Dr Bean examines what's left of him, he'll discover that he's missing all of the fingers on his left hand."

"Good God. Is that what smashed the window?"

He pointed to the upturned table on the floor.

"It looks like it. Hotels make it hard for suicidal individuals – the windows only open so far, but that didn't stop this one."

"The assistant manager told me that it was the emergency fire alarm on this floor that was activated," Bridge said. "It might be an idea to give the panel a once over."

"Thanks for the heads-up. What do *you* think happened here?"

Bridge took in the room. The penthouse took up the entire top floor of the hotel, and it looked like there were two bedrooms. There was a mini bar at the back of the room, and a bathroom off to the right. Bridge spotted the trolley in the corner. There were two trays on it.

"He ordered room service."

"The food was left untouched," Webber said. "Tempura prawn tails and a side order of chips."

"That's what I can smell," Bridge said. "We need to find out when this was ordered."

"You're especially sharp this morning."

"I slept well. Why chop off his fingers?"

"If we examine it from a torture perspective," Webber said. "What we have here is a prime example of inflicting pain to extract information. This method has been practiced since time began."

"Extracting information," Bridge pondered. "And the final act suggests that he was successful. He got what he came for and sent Mr Lowe on a final flight into the unknown."

"That's a bit dramatic," Webber said. "But, yes – I too believe that's what transpired here. I can also tell you that his laptop was switched on. The screensaver had kicked in but when I woke it up it was logged into an online banking website. The session had expired but I took some photos of the screen."

"That's our answer."

"I believe it is," Webber said. "Someone came here to kill him, but before they did that, they needed him to access his banking. If I were to speculate, I'd hazard a guess that this was all about money – as simple as that."

"Thanks, Webber," Bridge said. "I'll let you carry on."

He left the room and stopped when he spotted the broken glass of the emergency fire alarm. He turned around and his eyes came to rest on the blinking red eye of the CCTV camera directly opposite. This camera will have captured the torturer entering the penthouse and it will also have caught him smashing the alarm panel. He made his way to the lift and summoned the elevator.

After speaking to the man in charge of the security operations in the hotel, Bridge was asked to take a seat in front of the screen in the small control room behind the reception area. DC Moore sat down next to him.

"You can leave us now," Bridge said.

"The system can be a bit tricky to navigate," the security operative said.

"If we get stuck, we'll give you a shout," DC Moore told him.

"It was some sick bastard who did that," Bridge said when they were alone in the room. "He had five of his fingers cut off before he was thrown through the window."

"Why would someone do that?" DC Moore said.

"There was a laptop with an online bank website open on it. The session had expired, but I think he was tortured into giving out his banking logins."

"It's about money then?"

"Murder and money have been in bed together since the dawn of time," Bridge said.

"True, so all we need to do is follow the money, and we've got him."

"Let's see what he looks like first, shall we?"

He'd learned that Tom Lowe ordered room service at 10:36. He'd chosen tempura prawn tails with a side order of chips.

"Who eats prawns in the middle of the morning?" DC Moore said.

"The rich have different ways to us," Bridge said. "According to the kitchen, the food was sent up twenty minutes later."

He started the footage from the camera in the hallway at 10:50

Nothing happened for a few minutes then, at 10:53 the door to the penthouse opened and a woman with black hair emerged.

"We need to find out who she is," Bridge said.

They watched as she stuck something inside a handbag and walked towards the lift.

"Do you think she's involved?" DC Moore said.

"I don't know, Harry," Bridge said. "The room service hasn't arrived yet."

At five minutes to eleven a man appeared in the shot. He was pushing a trolley with two trays on it. He stopped outside the penthouse and knocked.

"There's the room service," DC Moore said.

"Something doesn't feel right," Bridge said.

"You sound like Smith."

"The timescale is bothering me. Tom Lowe went out of the window not long after this. I think this is our man."

"He's wearing a hotel uniform," DC Moore pointed out.

"That means nothing. The door's opening."

The man with the trolley stood in the doorway for a while and after a brief conversation Bridge and DC Moore couldn't hear, he pushed the trolley inside the room and closed the door.

Ten minutes went by, and the man still hadn't come back out.

"I think you could be right," DC Moore said. "He's been in there too long. It's a shame we can't see what's happening in there."

"Take it back to when he arrived," Bridge said.

"You couldn't see his face."

"Rewind it anyway."

DC Moore had been right. The man pushing the trolley kept his face hidden from the camera the whole time.

"He knew the camera was there," Bridge said. "Can you speed up the footage?"

DC Moore soon figured it out and now the clock at the bottom was moving at four times normal speed.

At 11:16 the door was opened, and a figure emerged. DC Moore returned the speed to normal. This time the man didn't seem to care about the CCTV camera, and he turned to look right at it. It didn't matter – he was now wearing a green balaclava over his face.

"Bloody hell," Bridge said. "It's the same bloke as the others."

They watched him approach the emergency fire alarm panel and calmly smash through the glass with his elbow.

CHAPTER NINETEEN

"And now we have three," DI Smyth said. "Two women and a man have been brutally slain in the space of twenty-four hours. A man wearing a green balaclava was seen at the scene of two of the murders and he posed as a courier in the first two. We have the identity of the man who took flight from the thirteenth floor of the New Tower Hotel. Tom Lowe was forty-two. Mr Lowe booked the penthouse for three days."

"The CCTV showed a woman leaving his room," Bridge said. "Not long before the fake hotel employee arrived. It's possible she was involved."

"Do we know who she is?" DC King said.

"Not as yet," Bridge said. "According to the assistant manager, the penthouse sleeps four, and the price is the same regardless of how many people occupy the room."

"Is that even allowed?" DC King said. "What about in the event of a fire? I thought the hotel was required to know how many people are in the hotel at all times."

"That's irrelevant, Kerry," DI Smyth said. "We need to find out who the woman is."

"The CCTV caught her leaving the room," DC Moore said. "And it gives us a good shot of her face."

"The timing is bothering me," Bridge said. "Mr Lowe ordered room service at 10:36. According to the kitchen it was sent up twenty minutes later. The woman was caught on CCTV leaving the room at 10:53 and two minutes later the camera showed the room service arriving."

"How many lifts are there?" DC King asked.

"That's what got me wondering. There is only one elevator. If the mystery woman left the penthouse at 10:53, it means she will have probably bumped into the fake hotel employee when he exited the lift to deliver the room service."

"If she wasn't booked into the hotel with Mr Lowe," DI Smyth said. "It's going to be difficult to find out who the woman is."

"We have her on CCTV," DC Moore said. "I say we get the hotel staff to take a look to see if any of them recognise her. Even if she wasn't officially booked into the room, it's possible that one of them might know who she is."

"How did the killer manage to pull it off?" DC Moore wondered. "I don't mean the murder itself – how did he know that the room service had been ordered?"

"According to the assistant manager," Bridge said. "The food was picked up where it usually is. The New Tower has a high staff turnover, and they always hire extra staff at this time of year, so nobody thought anything of a bloke they didn't recognise picking up the room service order. As for how he got hold of a uniform, the assistant manager didn't know. All the uniforms are cleaned by the hotel, and he could have swiped one from the laundry."

"He did a lot of homework," Whitton said.

"Where's Smith?" DC King said.

"He's still convinced that a six-year-old girl holds the key to the investigation," DI Smyth said. "The doctor treating Sophie Downing has refused to allow her to be hypnotised at the hospital, so Smith persuaded the father to have her discharged. Porter is going to hypnotise her at home."

"Why is Smith so obsessed with this?" DC Moore said.

"Don't even bother trying to understand," Whitton said. "When Smith gets an idea in his head, it's pointless trying to change his mind."

"What did we get from the friends of Harriet Jordan?" DI Smyth said.

"I spoke to her best friend," DC King said. "Gail Brown has known Harriet since they were in junior school. She was reluctant to open up at first, but I finally got it out of her. Harriet and Duncan's marriage was a mess. He worked away a lot and they barely had anything to do with each other."

"Plenty of marriages are a mess," Bridge said. "But it doesn't make a spouse want the other spouse dead."

"Gail knew all about Harriet's affairs," DC King said. "There have been plenty of other men in Harriet's life."

"Did you ask her if she thought Duncan was aware of these flings?" DC Moore said.

"She didn't think he knew about it," DC King said. "But I think he knew exactly what was going on."

"The nosy neighbour saw the men come and go," Whitton said. "It's possible that Duncan heard about it from someone on the street."

"It doesn't mean he wanted her dead," DI Smyth said.

"And he has an alibi for the time of the murder," Whitton said.

"He certainly does," DI Smyth said. "Mr Jordan is the CEO of a construction company. His firm builds high-end commercial properties – hotels and the like and he was indeed at a conference in Harrogate at the time Harriet was killed. Some architect soiree."

"We can't rule out a hired hit?" DC Moore said.

"How soon before we can access his bank accounts?" Bridge said.

"If Mr Jordan refuses to let us see them, we're going to need a court order," DI Smyth said. "And so far, nothing about Harriet's murder points to her husband."

"Bridge and me were on our way to speak to him," DC Moore said. "When we got the call about the jumper."

"Will you please stop calling them that?" Bridge said.

"Anyway," DC Moore said. "We were on our way to his second house when we got the call."

"He's got a second house?" DC King said.

"In Holgate," Bridge said. "God knows why he needs two houses. We'll pay him a visit after the briefing."

"Ask him for permission to access his banking," DI Smyth said. "Ask nicely – we all know how frustrating going the court order route can be."

"I say we just ask him for the account information," DC King said. "Why would he refuse to give us that information if he's innocent?"

"OK," DI Smyth said. "It's worth a try."

His phone started to ring on the table in front of him.

"It's Smith," DI Smyth said and turned the speakerphone on.

"We're on our way to Peter Downing's house," Smith said.

"How is Sophie doing?" DI Smyth said.

"She still has no memory of yesterday, but apart from that she seems to be fine. When I spoke to her dad, he said he's making her something to eat."

"This had better not backfire on us, Smith."

"It won't."

"If anything happens to that little girl because of the hypnosis," DI Smyth said. "Heads are going to roll."

"Trust me, boss."

"You persuaded a little girl's father to have her discharged, against the advice of her doctor," DI Smyth said. "And you also coerced a psychologist who just happens to have been struck off, to hypnotise her into recalling the horrific events of the murder of her grandmother."

"You make it sound much worse than it is," Smith said. "We're going to get some answers from this – I just know it."

"You'd better be right."

"I hope to God that I am," Smith said.

CHAPTER TWENTY

Smith wasn't sure what to expect from Peter Downing's house, but when he parked his car outside the property in Heslington the quaint detached building didn't strike him as something a high-flying finance expert would choose to live in. Smith thought Emily would have opted for one of the modern apartment buildings overlooking the river, but this house was nothing like that.

The five-bedroom period property looked like it belonged in the countryside. The ivy that covered half of the walls on the front was dead now, but Smith imagined it would be quite a feature when it came to life again in the spring. The property was a stones' throw from the golf course in the west and the university campus to the north, and when Smith got out of the car, he couldn't believe how quiet it was.

"What a beautiful house," Porter exclaimed.

"I never expected a finance guru to live in a place like this," Smith said. "Are you ready to do this?"

"Of course. I hope I can help you."

"Me too," Smith said.

He'd debated whether to take Sophie Downing back to the scene of the murder and hypnotise her there, but Porter had advised against it. He'd suggested somewhere where she would feel safe, and the house in Heslington was the perfect place.

Peter Downing opened the door and invited them in. Smith and Porter followed him through a spacious hallway into a huge kitchen. Sophie was sitting at the breakfast bar in the separate snug. She was eating a sandwich and Smith decided to let her finish eating.

The kitchen wouldn't look out of place in a restaurant. The stovetop was enormous, and Smith counted nine gas burners. He wondered why a family of three needed such a huge oven. The double-door fridge looked like it was big enough to climb inside. Smith estimated there was more than enough space to store a couple of bodies in there. All of the counter tops were marble and the lighting inside the kitchen was provided by subtle spotlights inside the ceiling. There was a separate room off to the side that looked like a pantry. It was almost as big as Smith's entire kitchen.

"This is quite a house," he said.

"I love it," Peter said. "Sophie does too."

"It's a rather unusual place," Porter said. "The exterior and the interior don't quite match, yet the contrast seems to work."

"It was built in the 1800s," Peter said. "I think it's actually listed – the building itself is, I mean. But the interior has been renovated extensively."

"Did you carry out the alterations?"

"It was like this when we bought it. I'm not much of an interior designer."

"What is it you do for a living?" Smith said.

"I'm a teacher," Peter said. "Part time. We agreed when Sophie was born that I would carry out the lion's share of the household duties. Emily's job is extremely demanding, and I won't even go into the difference in our salaries."

"That's a commendable attitude," Porter said.

"This is the twenty-first century. Just because women have to be the ones who give birth, it doesn't mean the burden of parenthood should be theirs alone."

"You have my utmost respect," Smith said.

"I love spending time with Sophie. Sometimes I wonder if there will come a day when Emily will walk through the door and Sophie won't know who she is anymore."

Smith thought that it was a good thing that Emily Downing wasn't here – it was quite obvious that Sophie was much more relaxed in her father's company.

"I appreciate you agreeing to this," Smith said to Peter. "I know it must be a difficult time for you."

"I'm willing to do anything to help find the man who killed my mother," Peter said. "How is this going to work?"

"Where does Sophie feel most relaxed?" Porter asked. "It's important that she is completely calm before we begin. Does she have a favourite place to go in the house?"

"She loves the second living room at the back," Peter said. "She sits there for hours, reading on her tablet by the fire."

"Could you make a fire now?" Porter said.

"It's a wood burner."

"Could you start it for us?" Porter said. "It really will help."

Peter nodded and left the room.

Sophie had finished eating and she'd got off the chair in the snug. She walked past Smith and Porter without saying anything and soon afterwards they could hear the sound of a piano. It was a simple tune, and half of the notes were wrong, but it made Smith smile.

"That's a good sign," Porter said.

"You think so?"

"She's a terrible pianist, but it's clear that she's comfortable with us here."

"Talk me through this again," Smith said.

"Once I'm sure Sophie is in a hypnotic state, I'm going to build up to what happened yesterday. I'll ask her questions about the events leading up to the murder of her grandmother. If you think I've left anything out, you can ask your own questions."

"Won't that distract her?" Smith said. "Hearing my voice, I mean."

"Not at all."

Peter Downing came to tell them that he'd got a fire going in the back living room. Sophie was still playing the piano.

"She's not bad," Smith said.

Peter smiled. "She's got a long way to go. Is there anything else I need to know before we begin?"

"We're going to record the session," Porter said.

"On video?"

"No, just the audio. It'll help us if we're able to review the footage, bit by bit afterwards."

"Makes sense. I don't have a problem with that."

"It's probably going to be unpleasant for you," Porter said. "And there will be moments where you'll want to stop it, but I need you to be strong. If it gets too much, you can leave the room. I have to ask you one more time if you're absolutely sure you want to go ahead."

Peter nodded. "If Sophie can help find the person who did that to my mum, then it's worth it, because I want him to rot in hell."

CHAPTER TWENTY ONE

"Is this where you usually like to sit?" Porter asked.

Sophie Downing was seated in the corner of the three-seater sofa. The fire opposite her was burning nicely and the room was already warm.

Sophie nodded.

"Give me a hand with this." Porter pointed to what looked like a low upholstered table.

He started to push it towards where Sophie was sitting.

"We don't allow anyone to use it as a footrest," Peter said. "Emily would have a hernia if she were here."

"Come on," Porter said. "Help me."

Peter helped him push the table closer.

"Good," Porter said. "Sophie, lie back a bit and put your feet up."

He gave her a wink, and she reciprocated with a shy smile.

"It's good to break the rules once in a while," he told her.

She looked at her father, Peter nodded, and she stretched her feet out.

"That looks comfortable," Porter said. "Sophie, I want you to look at the fire."

"What for?"

Peter Downing looked like he was going to cry. Smith wondered if these were the first words Sophie had spoken since she witnessed the murder of her grandmother.

"Look at the fire," Porter said. "And we'll begin. I want you to listen to my voice. There will be other sounds, but you'll hear only my voice. Your dad may speak, as will the policeman, but all you'll hear is me. Are you OK?"

Sophie nodded and shuffled on the sofa to get more comfortable.

"The fire is warm," Porter said. "And the flames are soothing. You're relaxed now and you're completely safe. In a moment I'm going to start counting backwards. I want you to listen to my voice and as I count down, you'll feel more and more relaxed. The fire is making you feel sleepy, but you're not asleep. Imagine yourself at the top of a carpeted staircase. It's soft under your feet and you can feel the warmth of it on your soles. Slowly, we're going to walk downstairs together. Ninety-eight, ninety-seven. I'm still here and you're completely safe. Nothing can hurt you here. Ninety-six."

A log on the fire popped but Sophie didn't seem to notice it.
"Eighty-five," Porter said. "You can close your eyes, or you can keep them open. Eighty-four. The carpet on the stairs is warm, and you may be finding it harder to walk. We can stop at any time. Do you want to stop?"
The shake of her head was so subtle it was barely noticeable.

"Forty," Porter said. "We're over halfway there now, and you've never felt so warm and cosy. The fire will keep burning, even if you close your eyes."
Sophie did just that.

"Twenty-one. You're doing so well, and you're still completely safe. The only thing you need to worry about is the carpet on the stairs. When we reach the bottom, you'll feel more relaxed than you've ever felt. I'll be there with you."
A mobile phone started to ring somewhere close by and Smith gasped. He'd forgotten where he was for a while, and he wondered if he'd been dragged down by Porter's words too. Peter Downing soon silenced the phone and Sophie's face told them that she hadn't even been aware of it.

"I'm counting down from five now," Porter said. "And when I get to zero, we'll be right at the bottom."
He finished the countdown and observed the little girl on the sofa.
"All you can hear is my voice. Nothing can hurt you here. I want you to tell me about decorating the Christmas tree yesterday."

He'd come here armed with a bit of background information. Based on what the forensics team found inside the house, he had a vague idea of what Sophie did at her grandmother's house. The box of Christmas decorations in the living room suggested they were in the middle of decorating the tree when the killer knocked on the door.

"The fairy has lost her wings."

Sophie spoke the words quietly.

"Oh dear," Porter said.

"I put her on top of the tree," Sophie said. "The wings might grow back."

"That's entirely possible."

"The balls on the tree look wrong." Sophie put a hand over her mouth. "Baubles, I mean. Nan said they weren't balls."

"What's wrong with them?" Porter asked.

"Too many silver ones. It needs more red."

"Good idea. I hate a tree with too much silver. Is your nan helping you?"

Sophie shook her head. "I can do it. Nan is going to make some sandwiches."

Forensics had also informed Porter that there was a bread knife on a breadboard in the kitchen. Next to it were four slices of bread and butter.

"What's your favourite sandwich?" he asked.

"Cheese and ham," Sophie said. "But no tomatoes. Tomatoes are horrid."

"I agree. Are you still decorating the tree?"

Another nod.

"While you're making the tree look pretty," Porter said. "Do you hear anything?"

"I'm singing a song."

"What song are you singing?"

"Vivo," Sophie said. "The one about the drum."

"It's a film we went to see," Peter explained when he saw Porter's bewildered expression.

"Are you going to go to the kitchen?" Porter said.

"I'm hungry."

"It's OK. You want to see why the sandwiches are taking so long. What do you find in the kitchen?"

"A song is playing."

"Do you know the song?"

"No," Sophie said. "It's a silly song."

"A lot of them are. What's the song about?"

"African snow. Africa is hot – it doesn't snow there."

"What else do you see?" Porter said.

"There's a man in the kitchen," Sophie said.

Porter cast a glance at Smith and turned back to Sophie.

"Do you know the man?" he asked.

"He's saying hello."

"You're completely safe," Porter said. "Nothing will hurt you down here. Do you say hello back?"

"He has a nice voice."

"Do you know him?" Porter asked again. "Have you seen him before?"

"No."

"What does he look like?"

"Big."

"What's he wearing?"

"A blue jacket," Sophie said. "And he has a mask on his face."

Porter can see Smith shuffling his feet out of the corner of his eye.

"What does the mask look like?" he asked Sophie.

"It's green, and it's covering his face."

"I wonder why he's wearing that inside the house."

"He says he doesn't like people looking at his face."

"That's odd."

Sophie's eyes shot open, and Porter wasn't expecting it.

"You're safe here, Sophie. Nobody is going to hurt you."

"The pain won't last long."

Her eyes didn't blink.

"Nan is hurt."

"It's OK," Porter said. "Tell me what you can see?"

"The man is helping Nan to the ground."

"Why is he doing that?"

"Her spider column has been severed."

Peter Downing caught Smith's eye and left the room.

"What's happening now?" Porter said.

"Screaming. Nan is on the floor. I'm calling the police."

"Do you call the police?"

"Not yet. He says not yet."

"The man tells you not to call the police yet?" Porter said.

Sophie nodded. "We still have thirty-two minutes."

"I don't understand."

"I'm not hungry," Sophie said. "The man tells me to make a sandwich, but I'm not hungry. The silly song has started again."

"The man can't hurt you," Porter said. "What is he doing now?"

"Nothing."

"Nothing at all?"

"Four minutes," Sophie said. "Thirty-six minutes for thirty-six years is…"

"It's OK," Porter told her. "We're going to go back up in a minute. When we get there, you'll feel sleepy, but you'll be completely fine."

Sophie's eyes closed again.

"Are you ready to climb back up the stairs?" Porter said. "The fire is still burning and it's warm."

"Who are you?" Sophie said.

"My name is Porter, and I'm…"

"I'm not going to hurt you," Sophie interrupted. "He's telling me he's not going to hurt me. I have to call the police."

"Does he tell you to call the police?"

"But not an ambulance. I have to stand facing the door."

Smith was starting to feel sick. This wasn't what he was expecting at all. Sophie's breathing was more rapid now, and he was worried that pushing her any further could do some damage. He tried to get Porter's attention to try and get him to stop but the big German wasn't looking.

"We'll be going back up soon," Porter said. "You're standing facing the door."

"Thirty-six minutes," Sophie said. "One for every year. You'll feel what he felt."

"I don't understand."

"And now you will feel nothing."

"Jesus." Smith couldn't help himself.

"He's smiling," Sophie said.

"He's wearing a mask," Porter said.

"I can see his eyes. I know he's smiling."

"I'm going to start counting again," Porter said. "One, two, three. We'll go back up quickly. Four, five, six."

"What colour are his eyes?" Smith asked.

Sophie's breaths were coming in quick bursts.

"Seven, eight, nine," Porter said. "Ten."

"Can you see his eyes, Sophie?" Smith said.

"No! No! No!"

Her eyes shot open, and she let out a shriek so loud that Smith had to cover his ears. Peter Downing was inside the kitchen in a flash.

"What the hell are you doing to her?"

"I'm trying to bring her out of it," Porter said.

"You killed her," Sophie screamed.

"You're totally safe," Porter said. "We're almost at the top of the staircase."

"What colour are his eyes, Sophie?" Smith asked again.

"You killed her. You killed her."

"Detective Smith is trying to help you," Porter said.

"Why do you think I killed her?" Smith said.

"I want to go home," Sophie said. "I want my dad."

CHAPTER TWENTY TWO

"What the fuck just happened?"

Smith was outside the house in Heslington. He was smoking a cigarette, and his hands were shaking.

"She was doing so well," Porter said. "She was open and receptive, and she was clear and descriptive, but something about you really spooked her."

"Is that a psychology term? Why would she react like that?"

"I really don't know. Is today the first time you've met her?"

"I saw her briefly at Janet Downing's house just after she was killed but Sophie had already shut herself away from the world."

"Well, there was something about you that triggered a reaction while she was under."

"I thought you said she would only be able to hear your voice."

"I really don't know what happened," Porter said. "I've never seen anything like it before."

"Is she going to be alright?"

"After you left, she seemed perfectly fine. She asked her father if she could watch some television. Let me listen to the footage of the session, and I'll see if I can come up with an explanation for Sophie's reaction at the end."

"I'll get you a copy," Smith said. "Thanks again for doing this. I thought it went pretty well apart from the freak out at the end. Do you need a lift back to your place?"

"I think I'll take a walk. I only live about a mile from here, and I'd quite like to take a stroll around the university campus."

"The term has finished," Smith reminded him.

"Even better. Email me a copy of the session footage and I'll get onto it this afternoon."

Smith didn't head straight back to the station. He sat in his car outside Peter Downing's house and brought up the recording of the Sophie Downing hypnosis session. He fast-forwarded it to the bit where she'd reacted to his words and listened to it three times. He still couldn't understand what had got her so rattled. The only thing he'd done was to ask her the colour of the man's eyes. It didn't make any sense.

The mystery was cleared up shortly afterwards. Someone rapped on the window of the car and Smith saw that it was Peter Downing. He wound down the window.

"I think I know why Sophie reacted like she did," Peter said.

"Get in," Smith said. "It's freezing out."

It wasn't much warmer inside the old Ford Sierra but at least it was sheltered from the wind that was now blowing.

"Is Sophie OK?" Smith said when Peter had made himself comfortable on the passenger seat.

"She's watching TV."

"What can you tell me?" Smith said.

"When I switched the television on it was still tuned to the last thing we watched – a travel channel I enjoy, and there was a documentary on. It was all about the Great Barrier Reef and when the narrator began talking Sophie reacted in a similar manner to how she did with you. The narrator was Australian, and I think the man who killed my mother is too."

"An Australian?" Smith said. "I've spent most of my life in York – I didn't think I had much of an accent left."

"You probably can't hear it," Peter said. "But it's still very obvious. I'd better get back inside. I don't want to leave Sophie on her own for too long."

He got out of the car and Smith watched him as he walked up the driveway to the house and went inside.

He wondered if there was some truth in Peter Downing's words. Could the person they were looking for really be a fellow Australian? Smith started the engine and pulled away from the side of the road. He listened to the entire recording of the hypnotism as he drove, and he knew instinctively that there were some answers there. Janet Downing's killer had been extremely kind to her granddaughter, and this made Smith believe that he had no intention of hurting the little girl.

A song had been playing the entire time. And Sophie had led them to believe that it had been played on repeat. This was also something to look into. Smith had no idea what Sophie had meant by African snow, but it was possible that someone on the team could shed some light on that. The killer had talked about thirty-six years more than once. Smith wondered whether this could be a reference to something that happened thirty-six years ago. The more he thought about it, the more he had his doubts. If the man who killed Janet Downing was the same killer as the man who'd slaughtered Harriet Jordan and Tom Lowe the thirty-six-year thing didn't quite fit. Harriet wasn't even born thirty-six years ago, and Tom Lowe would have been a small child.

The killer told Sophie to call the police after he was gone. What kind of murderer asks a witness to do that? Did he think Sophie was too young to be able to explain to them what had happened?

You'll feel what he felt?

That part had made Smith shiver. Those five words left little doubt that this was personal, but Smith couldn't think of what Janet Downing had done to justify someone coming into her home and killing her like that.

"You'll feel what he felt," Smith spoke the words out loud to see if this made it any clearer.

It didn't – if anything it confused things even more. Janet was stabbed in the upper back. Her spinal column was severed, and she would have been paralysed immediately. The killer left her to suffer for more than half-an-hour before he put her out of her misery by severing the arteries in her throat.

"This was a revenge killing," Smith decided as he parked his car in the car park at the station.

But if that was the case, where did the pieces that were Harriet Jordan and Tom Lowe fit into the puzzle?

CHAPTER TWENTY THREE

Mary Lions raced along the walkway next to the river as though someone was chasing her. It was just after three and the pedestrian path was busy with people taking a stroll before the sun bid its farewells for the day. The lights beyond the river were coming on as the mid-afternoon half-light was about to fade to black.

Mary banged into a woman walking with some friends and received an earful of expletives for her trouble. She didn't care. She was on her way to the playhouse behind the Millenium Bridge, and she needed to get there quickly.

"Watch where you're going, you dumb bitch."

Mary didn't turn around to face her abuser.

The lights were on in the playhouse. The York Amateur Dramatic Society was getting ready for the performance that afternoon. It was a Christmas Eve tradition and this year they were putting on their own rendition of *The Winter's Tale*. Mary's fiancé, Annie, had been cast in the role of Hermione, the wife of Leontes. Annie was ecstatic when she landed the role. She'd declared it an act of the gods – she and Mary were soon to be married, and Annie had agreed to take Mary's name. Lions – Leontes, it really did seem as though fate had stepped in.

Mary didn't believe in fate. She was a firm advocate of creating your own destiny, and she thought the concept of fate was reserved for poets and dreamers. She was also aware that Annie's fate was supposed to have been sealed this afternoon. That is, until Mary began to have doubts. The doubts had crept in until they were all-consuming, and she had to do something to throw a spanner in the works of Annie's destiny.

The stage was set and a couple of actors in full costume were running through their lines. Annie was nowhere to be seen. Mary asked a woman in a clown costume if she'd seen her and she was pointed in the direction of the backstage area. It was three-thirty and time was running out. Mary pushed through a couple of amateur actors and headed for the dressing rooms.

Annie Drew was applying some last-minute makeup in front of a small mirror. Mary observed her reflection for a moment. She really was beautiful, and she could understand why what had happened had happened. Annie could have any woman she wanted. Mary walked over to her and kissed her on the back of the head.

"Hey," Annie said. "You gave me a fright."

"I don't want you to go on this afternoon."

Annie turned to face her. "What's brought this on?"

"I have a bad feeling about it."

"I thought you didn't believe in stuff like that. My fiancé, the realist."

"Please," Mary begged. "Just do what I ask."

"I've been working my butt off for this," Annie said. "I can't just quit now without a good reason."

Mary thought for a moment. Then she told Annie the truth.

"You're going to die on stage."

Annie laughed. "No shit, Sherlock."

"I'm serious."

"And I'm Hermione," Annie said. "Everyone knows that Hermione dies in The Winter's Tale."

"Five minutes," a woman's voice shouted.

"I need to go," Annie said. "Are you going to say break a leg?"

"Please," Mary said. "Something bad is going to happen up there."

"I can't feel it, and you know how sensitive I am to things like that. I'll keep an eye out for you in the audience."

"You're going to die," Mary said. "Trust me."

"Everybody involved in the first scene," the woman said. "Action stations please."

"I'm not on until the second scene," Annie said. "Why are you so spooked?"

"I can't tell you," Mary said. "Please don't go out there."

"I have to go," Annie said.

She got up and flung her arms around her fiancé. Then she marched out of the room with her head held high.

Mary watched her go.

"You shouldn't be back here." It was the stage director.

Mary looked her in the eye. "Fuck you."

"What did you say?"

"You heard me," Mary said. "This is all your fault."

"I'm calling security."

"Go for it," Mary said. "I'm leaving anyway."

The stage director was a woman called Penelope. Mary didn't know her surname. She did know that Penelope had almost destroyed Mary's future with Annie. Annie didn't know that Mary knew about the affair – she hadn't confronted her about it but the evening she'd come to the playhouse unannounced had been the worst evening of her life. Annie and Penelope were alone in the dressing room – both of them were naked and the image of them together had stayed with Mary for a very long time.

Mary was leaving the dressing room when an idea started to take shape in her head. It was the boxes on the floor that gave her the idea. She walked past the stage and stepped behind the edge of the curtain. She waited for Penelope to emerge from the dressing room. The stage manager passed her, and Mary retraced her steps back to the dressing room.

The indoor fireworks were to be used after the final act, when the players came on stage to accept the applause. Mary counted five boxes of them. She opened the first box and stuffed as many fireworks as she could inside her coat. She picked up one of the other boxes, ripped open the lid and scattered the contents all over the floor of the dressing room. She could hear the music that announced the onset of the first scene. Camillo and Archidamus were about to go onstage.

Mary took out her lighter, ripped off some cardboard from the box and set fire to it. She waited for the flame to spread and threw it inside one of the full boxes. She repeated the procedure with another box and quickly left the dressing room. She made her way to the side of the stage, took a firework from her coat and lit the end. When it started to spark, she hurled it onto the stage. She did this with all of the fireworks in her coat.

Somebody screamed onstage. Mary didn't stick around. She headed for the exit just as a loud bang sounded. This was followed by a number of other explosions and Mary could smell smoke. The first sprays from the sprinkler system could be felt and a wailing alarm went off. Mary ran outside, turned left and hurried along the walkway. She stopped a safe distance away and watched as the theatregoers and actors piled out of the playhouse.

Her heart was beating fast, and she was finding it difficult to breathe. She wondered if she'd done enough. She didn't know then that her actions inside the playhouse had actually made matters worse. Mary had neglected to read the fine print in the contract she'd signed, and the consequences of this were dire. Neither Mary nor her fiancé, Annie were going to live long enough to celebrate Christmas together.

CHAPTER TWENTY FOUR

"What do you think?"

Smith looked at the faces of his colleagues around the table in the small conference room. They'd just listened to the recording of Sophie Downing's hypnosis session.

"She doesn't like you very much," Bridge stated the obvious.

"It's the accent," Smith explained. "She didn't freak out until I started to speak. Sophie's dad told me she reacted the same when she watched an Australian documentary. I think Janet Downing's killer is Australian."

"That'll be a first," Bridge said.

"You're forgetting the Fulton twins," Smith said.

"Boomerang," Bridge remembered. "But we haven't had any Aussie psychos since then. Present company excepted of course."

"Of course."

"Could we please carry on," DI Smyth said.

"I believe what Sophie recalled from yesterday will get us a step closer to figuring out the motivation behind the murder," Smith said.

He walked up to the whiteboard at the back of the room.

"Thirty-six years."

He wrote this on the board.

"Something happened thirty-six years ago – something involving Janet Downing."

"1985," DC King calculated.

"How old was Janet when she was killed?" Whitton asked.

"Fifty-two," Smith said.

"That would make her sixteen in 1985," DC Moore joined in. "What could a teenager have done to justify what happened to her?"

"That's what we need to find out, Harry," Smith said. "Something happened in 1985. We'll come back to that."

"What was the song she spoke about?" Whitton said.

"She didn't know," Smith said. "She said it was a silly song because it mentioned African snow."

"It doesn't ring any bells," Bridge said.

"I'll see what my mate Google can tell us," DC Moore said.

He woke his laptop up and keyed *African snow* into the task bar.

"Yes, it does snow in Africa," he read. "Especially in certain regions and at higher altitudes. Nope, that's not it."

"Try *African snow* and *song*," DC King suggested.

DC Moore added the word *song*.

"There are a few songs that match," he said. "Hold on..."

"What is it?" Bridge said.

The team watched as DC Moore tapped a few keys.

"This has to be it."

"The suspense is killing us, Harry," Smith said.

"Sorry, Sarge. It's Band Aid."

"There won't be snow in Africa this Christmastime," DC King remembered.

"I remember hearing it," Smith said. "When was the song released?"

"1984," DC Moore said.

"That was thirty-seven-years ago," Bridge said.

"Live Aid was in 1985," DC Moore added. "The concert itself was in 1985."

"It doesn't make sense," Smith said.

"Come on, Sarge," DC King said. "Snow in Africa and 1985. That has to be it."

"I'm not debating that," Smith said. "Where does Janet Downing come into the equation?"

The small conference room was silent.

"What else can we glean from the hypnosis session?" DI Smyth said.

"Sophie mentioned something about Janet feeling like he did," Smith said. "The killer told her she would feel what he felt for thirty-six minutes. One minute for every year. Any thoughts on that?"

"If we look at it from a revenge perspective," DC King said. "We can translate it to mean Janet was involved in the suffering of someone for thirty-six years."

"Are we assuming the motive is revenge?" DI Smyth said.

"It's the logical assumption to make, boss," Smith said.

"You seem to be forgetting Harriet Jordan and Tom Lowe."

"Let's analyse the murders as separate incidents for the time being."

"You were the one who convinced us that they're connected," DI Smyth said.

"I still believe they are, but not in the way we think."

"Your brain is going off on a tangent again," Bridge said.

"Forget about that," Smith said. "Janet Downing was sixteen in 1985. Her killer played a song on repeat, and it looks like it was the song from the Live Aid thing. It could simply be a reference to the year of the concert, but I think there's more to it than that."

"The year has already been referenced," DC King said. "The killer mentioned thirty-six years."

"Exactly, Kerry. That song means much more than we know right now."

"Any other thoughts before we wrap things up for the day?" DI Smyth said.

"It's only five o'clock," Smith reminded him.

"And it's Christmas Eve," DI Smyth said.

"What's your point?"

"The answers we seek will still be there tomorrow."

"We need to find them now," Smith said.

"Go home," DI Smyth told him. "Enjoy some time with your family."

"Fuck that."

"Charming," Whitton said.

"I didn't mean it like that," Smith said. "We're getting close – I can feel it, and I can't stop when we're this close."

"I can," Bridge said. "I have a date with the forensic technician with the finest arse in Yorkshire."

"Bridge," Whitton said. "Stop it."

"I only do it to wind you up."

"Let's call it a day," DC Moore said.

"I'm fine with that," DC King said.

"Well, I'm not," Smith said. "The solution to the mystery is out there somewhere, and I'm going to find it before I go anywhere."

"Suit yourself," DI Smyth said. "I'll see you in the morning."

CHAPTER TWENTY FIVE

Smith smoked a cigarette in the car park and stopped in front of the camera above the entrance to the station. He raised his arm and gave the blinking eye the middle finger before going back inside. Earlier that month, during a pointless meeting of the people with the pips, the discussion had turned to the hours that were lost due to unauthorised smoke breaks. A new initiative was implemented that was aimed at curbing unauthorised cigarette breaks and the broken camera above the entrance had been replaced with a functioning one. Smith liked to express his indifference to it every time he went outside for a cigarette. He didn't even know if the camera footage was monitored, but he hoped it was.

"Working late?" Smith said to Baldwin.

She was manning the front desk as usual.

"You know what it's like?" she said.

"Don't you have somewhere better to be?"

"I don't, no. I'll be spending Christmas alone, so I may as well be at work."

"Can I ask you to check something for me?" Smith said.

"Of course. What is it?"

"It's a long shot, but something happened in 1985, and I'm convinced that the first victim in the investigation is dead because of it."

"You're going to have to give me a bit more than that."

"Her name is Janet Downing," Smith said. "She was sixteen at the time, so her surname will be different, but I know for a fact that something significant happened in that year. Janet's killer played a song, non-stop during the murder."

"What song?"

"The one from Live Aid," Smith said. "The snow in Africa one."

"Do they know it's Christmas."

"Do who know?"

Baldwin laughed. "It's the name of the song, Sarge."

"Oh. Shit, I was three years old in 1985."

"I wasn't even born."

"Now you're making me feel old."

"What else can you give me?" Baldwin said.

"That's about it. Hold on..."

"What is it?"

"Something," Smith said. "That I haven't quite figured out. I'm going to grab a coffee from the canteen. Can I get you anything?"

"I'm fine, thanks. I'll see what I can find."

"Look for any link between Janet Downing and something that happened that resulted in someone getting hurt."

"Could you be more specific?"

"Not really," Smith said. "I've got the feeling that Janet's murder was a revenge killing, so her injuries could be symbolic of something."

"It's not much to go on," Baldwin said. "But I'll see what I can come up with."

Smith thanked her and went upstairs to the canteen. There wasn't a soul inside, and he wondered if everybody had gone home for Christmas. He remembered when he first started in the job – Christmas always seemed to consist of bar brawls and petty violence carried out because of too much Christmas spirit, but times seemed to have changed. Perhaps he'd just become immune to it.

He got a strong coffee from the machine and took it to his usual table. He opened his laptop and waited for it to warm up. He brought up his Internet browser a couple of minutes later.

"Fuck."

There was a sponsored advert on the screen for a half price sale on one of the online shopping sites, and Smith suddenly remembered that he hadn't got round to buying Whitton a Christmas present. He didn't even have an idea of what to get her. He took out his phone and tapped a short message to her, explaining his problem. She replied shortly afterwards, telling him that she didn't want anything. Smith answered with a thumbs-up and told her he would be home soon.

He thought back to Sophie Downing's words under hypnosis. The man who killed her grandmother had spoken about thirty-six years. He'd told Janet that she would feel what he felt – for thirty-six minutes she would feel what he felt for thirty-six years.

"She was paralysed."

Smith happened to say these words just as a woman in uniform came in. It was the new PC from Leeds – PC Angie Bowler.

"They reckon it's the first sign of madness, Sarge," she said. "But I disagree. I've been having conversations with myself for as long as I can remember. Who was paralysed?"

"Janet Downing," Smith said. "The first victim. She had her spinal column severed and it means something."

"I'm sure you'll figure it out," PC Bowler said with a smile. "You usually do." She selected a coffee from the machine and left him alone.

"She was paralysed for a damn good reason."

Smith thought about what that reason could be. He didn't believe that Janet Downing had done something that resulted in someone suffering paralysis, but after a brief internal debate he wondered if that was exactly what she'd done.

"What can cause paralysis?"

There were only a few things he could think of. A fall from a great height was one, as was a car crash, and Smith thought the latter seemed more likely.

He found a site that documented every road traffic accident since 1982 in the UK. He was shocked to discover that the number of road accidents had declined dramatically in the past forty years. Last year there were 115,000 accidents on the roads in the whole of the UK – resulting in 20,000 serious injuries and 1500 deaths. Back in 1985 the number was more than double that. This was going to be a greater task than he initially thought.

He took a sip of his coffee and rubbed his eyes.

"Where do I even start?"

He knew that the song the killer played was important. He vaguely remembered it. He was too young to recall the Live Aid concert, but he'd heard the song plenty of times. He decided to start there.

According to the information on the Internet, the event was a two-venue concert that took place on the 13th of July 1985. Two concerts were held simultaneously at Wembley Stadium in London and the JFK Stadium in Philadelphia. This was where Smith would begin his search. He minimised the page and looked for road traffic accidents on the 13th of July. There were 912 in total on that particular Saturday and Smith didn't hold out much hope of finding what he was looking for.

He scrolled down the page, looking for accidents that resulted in serious injuries, but the website didn't go into much detail. There were thirteen fatal accidents that Saturday, all across the UK, but that was all Smith could get. He wondered if he was looking in the wrong places.

He was ready to admit defeat when Baldwin came into the canteen, and the expression on her face told him she was the bearer of good news. He should have expected nothing else.

"You've found something."

"I think I've got some answers."

She sat down next to him and Smith caught a whiff of her perfume. It brought back a memory he'd kept buried for good reason, and he pushed it to the back of his mind.

"There was a car accident on the day of the Live Aid concert," Baldwin said.

"That was about as far as I'd got," Smith said. "But I couldn't get any details."

"The accident occurred on the A1 just south of Pontefract. There were four people in the vehicle."

"Was anyone paralysed in the crash?"

"I'm getting to that," Baldwin said. "The car was travelling in the fast lane and the driver pulled over too soon after overtaking a truck. The vehicle spun round and slammed into a car about to overtake the truck too. There were no fatalities, but two of the passengers were injured. One of them, an eighteen-year-old man suffered spinal trauma and that's all I could get from the traffic records."

"But…"

"But," Baldwin humoured him. "There are many ways to skin a cat. I found out who the paralysed man is. His name is Brian North. The other injured passenger was Donna Blake. Her injuries were less severe. I got this info from a news report at the time. Unfortunately, the other two people in the car were sixteen and because of the law, the press weren't allowed to release their identities. That's when I had to get creative."

Smith realised he was smiling. "I like the sound of this."

"I looked up Donna Blake," Baldwin said. "She's Donna Brown now, but she was easy to track down. I gave her a call, and she told me something very interesting."

"Janet Downing was in that car, wasn't she?" Smith guessed.

"Not only that," Baldwin said. "Janet was the one who was driving."

CHAPTER TWENTY SIX

July 13th, 1985

"Can we please listen to something else?"

Jack Wilson took a long drink from the bottle of cider.

"I'm going to dream of that song for months," he added.

"Ladies and gentlemen," Brian North said. "We witnessed history today. We were a part of something exceptional."

"You're drunk," Donna Blake stated the obvious.

"And you're not?" Brian said.

"Should you even be driving?" the fourth member of the group asked.

Janet Miller was the only sober one.

"I drive better when I've had a few drinks," Donna said. "Besides, the adrenalin from the concert is keeping me alert. What a fucking concert."

The song started again from the beginning and Jack sighed.

"It's Christmas time," he sang.

"It's not even fucking Christmas," Janet said.

"It feels like it is," Donna said. "Shit."

She slammed her foot on the brake when she realised that she was far too close to the car in front.

"You really shouldn't be driving," Janet said. "What if we get stopped by the cops?"

"Do you want to get home, or not?" Donna said.

"I can drive," Brian offered. "I'm only half-pissed."

Jack laughed. "You've been pissing it up since we set off back."

The sound of a car hooter behind them caused Donna to slow down. She'd veered into the fast lane without realising it.

"I think we should pull over," Janet said. "You're in no state to drive. I'll take over."

"You can't even drive," Jack said.

"I can too," Janet said. "I've been driving my brother's car since I was fourteen."

"You're sixteen," Brian said. "You're not old enough to drive. What if we get stopped by the cops?"

"That's the cool part," Janet said. "If the police pull us over and find out that Donna is over the limit, she'll be in big shit. If I'm driving, all that will happen is I'll get a fine or something. They can't take away a license that I don't have."

"I'm perfectly capable of driving," Donna said and belched.

"It sounds like it," Jack said. "Janet might have a point."

Donna pulled into the service station at Woodall and swapped places with Janet. She insisted on making Janet do a circuit of the car park before they joined the motorway again.

"Have I passed?" Janet said.

"Not bad," Brian said. "For a novice."

"Arsehole," Janet said.

She turned onto the A1 and kept her speed to a steady sixty miles per hour. *Do they know it's Christmas* came over the speakers again and nobody complained. Jack and Donna were fast asleep in the back, and Brian North was close to joining them in the passenger seat. Janet turned up the volume and smiled as she heard about snow in Africa for the umpteenth time that day.

A sign on the side of the road told her she was six miles from Pontefract and Janet knew they didn't have far to go to get back to York. She eased her foot off the accelerator when a truck driving incredibly slowly appeared up ahead. Janet checked her mirrors and indicated that she was about to overtake. She moved across, making sure to leave a decent gap between her and the truck. The heavy-duty vehicle chose this moment to increase its speed, and Janet had no option but to do the same. The speedometer read: 75mph.

When she was sure there was enough space to move over to the slow lane, Janet indicated and turned the wheel. A car was approaching quickly in the fast lane and the sight of it in the rearview mirror caused Janet to become distracted for a moment. She turned the wheel harder and realised her mistake too late. The truck didn't have time to brake, and Janet gasped as the rear end of Donna's Ford Fiesta made contact with the front of the truck. The impact sent the Ford into a spin and Janet panicked. Instead of taking her foot off the accelerator and applying the brake, she slammed her foot hard on the gas and the car flew into the path of the car in the fast lane. The last thing Janet remembered was looking across and realising that Brian North wasn't wearing his seat belt.

CHAPTER TWENTY SEVEN

"According to the accident report," Baldwin said. "The driver misjudged the distance between her and the truck – the rear of the car hit the front of the truck, and she was sent spinning into the path of an oncoming car. The passengers sitting on the left side of the vehicle came off worst. Brian North went through the windscreen and landed on the tarmac fifteen feet away. Donna Blake suffered injuries to her face when she was flung forwards. She broke her collarbone and sustained a number of other minor injuries. The other passenger in the back, a sixteen-year-old called Jack Wilson sustained nothing more than a bit of whiplash."

"What about Janet Downing?" Smith said.

"She was Janet Miller then," Baldwin said. "She suffered some concussion, but other than that she walked away from it relatively unscathed."

"What happened to Brian North?" Smith said.

"It wasn't in the accident report," Baldwin said. "But Donna Brown told me about his injuries. He suffered severe spinal trauma. His back was broken in four places, and the prognosis wasn't good."

"He was going to be confined to a wheelchair?"

"Correct."

"This is the link we've been looking for," Smith said.

"I've got more for you."

"Why the hell are you not on our team?"

"I was under the impression that I was, Sarge," Baldwin said.

Smith's phone started to ring. The annoying whine of Meatloaf told him it was Whitton, and he let it go to voicemail.

"Donna Brown told me that the accident was a big deal back then," Baldwin carried on. "The press made a big thing out of it because the driver was only sixteen, even though Janet's name was never released. The tragedy was made even worse because Brian North's girlfriend was six months pregnant at the time. She gave birth to a baby boy in the October of that year. His name is Callum and he's now thirty-six."

"Thirty-six," Smith repeated. "Why does that number keep coming up? We have our motive. Thanks, Baldwin."

"Would you believe that I'm still not finished?"

"You are a machine, mate," Smith said. "You should consider a change of career."

"I'd miss the scenery," Baldwin said.

She gave him a smile, which Smith was unable to interpret.

"Go on then," he said.

"This part was easy to come by," Baldwin said. "I got thinking about the details of Janet Downing's murder and I wondered, why now?"

"If she was murdered because of what happened all those years ago, why wait so long?" Smith said.

"Exactly. If this is someone exacting revenge for Brian North's paralysis, what made them wait until now? And a quick look at births and deaths gave me the answer."

"Brian North died recently," Smith guessed.

Baldwin nodded. "Two weeks ago."

* * *

"What is wrong with you?"

Annie Drew hadn't even taken off her coat. She'd stormed into the house, slammed the front door and gone to find her fiancé.

"What are you talking about?" Mary Lions said.

"I know it was you," Annie said. "Somebody could have been killed."

"I really have no idea what you're going on about."

"The fireworks. You ruined the whole performance. Penelope is talking about getting the police involved. You could have burned the place to the ground."

"Nonsense," Mary said. "They were indoor fireworks."

"So, you admit it now, do you?"

"I had to do something to stop the play from going ahead."

Annie took off her coat and opened the fridge. She reached for the bottle of wine in the back.

After pouring two glasses, she turned to face her fiancé.

"Why? Tell me why you did that."

"I can't," Mary said. "You'll just have to trust me when I tell you it was the only way. I love you."

"And I love you too. But I can't forgive you for what you did this afternoon. You know how hard I've worked for the play, and you ruined it. I can't forgive you for that."

"I forgave you for what you and Penelope did."

Annie's mouth opened wide, but no words came out.

"I saw you," Mary said. "I wanted to surprise you by taking you out for a meal after the rehearsal, and I saw you. There was no rehearsal, was there?"

"I'm sorry," Annie said. "Why didn't you say anything?"

"I was too angry. You shattered my heart that night and I hated you."

"I'm really sorry. It was a stupid, drunken thing and it meant nothing."

"Penelope of all people," Mary said. "Do you know how that made me feel?"

"Is that why you set off the fireworks?" Annie said. "To get back at me and Penelope?"

"Of course not."

"Why then?" Annie said. "I don't understand. That was a really stupid thing to do."

"I can't tell you."

"You can tell me anything."

"You'll hate me," Mary said.

"Try me."

Mary topped up their glasses and sighed. She took a long drink of wine. "Talk to me," Annie said.

"Promise me that you won't hate me," Mary said.

"Nothing will make me hate you. You know that. In a few months we're going to be married, and I'm looking forward to growing old with you."

"I want to spend the rest of my life with you," Mary said.

The doorbell sounded.

"Who the hell is that now?" Annie said.

"Whoever it is," Mary said. "I'll get rid of them."

"Then you can tell me what's on your mind," Annie said. "And we can move past it and start planning our future."

Annie's and Mary's future had already been decided. They would realise that as soon as Mary opened the front door to the man with the Australian accent.

CHAPTER TWENTY EIGHT

"How much did you pay to have Janet Downing killed?"

This was exactly what DI Smyth had warned Smith *not* to do. Smith had promised him that he wouldn't go in with his teeth bared, but he had no intention of keeping that promise. He hadn't even explained who he was when Callum North opened the door to him. He was convinced that Callum was behind the murder of Janet Downing, and he needed to gauge his reaction when he was confronted with the accusation.

The reaction wasn't what Smith had been expecting. The man inside the house started to laugh. Callum was a short man with thinning hair. He looked older than his thirty-six years and Smith wondered if the recent death of his father had contributed to this. The house in Murton was a four-bedroom detached property and Smith knew that the houses in this estate weren't cheap. It was clear that Callum North had the wherewithal to be able to pay for a hired killer. He introduced himself and DC King.

"Did I say something funny?" Smith said.

"Were you even listening to yourself?" Callum said. "You think I paid someone to kill Janet?"

"You know about her murder then?" DC King said.

"It was on the news."

"No, it wasn't," Smith said. "Mrs Downing's details haven't been released to the press."

"It must have been social media then," Callum said.

"Can we come inside for a quick word?" Smith said.

"I'd prefer it if you didn't. My mother is still very upset after my dad's death."

"Does your mother live with you?" DC King said.

"I live with her," Callum said. "It's her house. It's not against the law, is it?"

"Not as far as I remember," Smith said. "We really would appreciate a little chat."

"It's Christmas Day."

"I'm aware of that," Smith said. "We'll try to keep it brief."

Callum reluctantly let them in. It was immediately clear that someone confined to a wheelchair had lived here. Everything inside the house had been modified to accommodate a wheelchair-bound person. The doorways were wider than normal, and all of the light switches were at waist height. Smith wondered if Callum and his mother would change things now that Brian was dead.

Callum told them to take a seat in the living room. He didn't offer them anything to drink.

"Make it quick," he said. "This is the first Christmas without Dad and I'd quite like to make it as painless as possible for my mother?"

"Where is she?" DC King said.

"She's upstairs having a nap. Dad's death has really hit her hard."

"How did he die?" Smith said.

"What's that got to do with anything?"

"It's a simple question."

"My father has been in a wheelchair for thirty-six years," Callum said. "He was eighteen at the time of the accident. I'd say he did well to last this long."

"Do you know about the accident?" Smith said. "Did your dad talk about it much?"

"Never," Callum said.

"But you must know what happened?" DC King said.

"Of course. My mother told me about it when I was very young, but we rarely spoke about it."

"It must have been hard," Smith said. "Growing up with a wheelchair-bound father."

"You wouldn't understand," Callum said.

"Help me then. I couldn't help noticing that the house has been modified."

"My grandfather paid for all of it. My mother's father, that is."

"It can't have been cheap," DC King said.

"I wouldn't know about that."

"Is it just your mother and you now?" Smith said. "No brothers or sisters?"

"It's just the two of us. You have no idea how hard it was for us. Looking after a paraplegic is a full-time job."

"I imagine it is," Smith said. "Did you not get any outside help?"

"Mother wouldn't hear of it. She didn't want some stranger prodding and poking my dad."

"And now he's dead."

"What is it you really want?" Callum said. "You come here on Christmas Day and accuse me of paying someone to kill a woman I've never met."

"You never met Janet Downing?" DC King said.

"Maybe once or twice."

"You just said you'd never met her," Smith said.

"I really don't know what you want me to say. Why would you think I had anything to do with her murder?"

"The timing seems a bit suspicious," Smith said. "Shortly after your father passes away, the woman who was responsible for destroying his life ends up dead. I don't believe in coincidences."

"You are so far off the mark. I did not play any part in her death."

"Did you hate her?" Smith said.

"Of course not," Callum said.

"She caused the accident that resulted in your father being confined to a wheelchair for the rest of his life. You must have resented her for that."

"It was an accident," Callum said. "A terrible accident, nothing else."

"She walked away from it without a scratch," DC King said. "That must have stung a bit."

"It didn't."

"I think your lying," Smith said. "If that was my dad, I would despise the person who was responsible. Even if it was just an accident – it's human nature to feel resentment."

"It's clear that you and I are nothing like each other," Callum said. "If there's nothing else, I'd quite like to check up on my mother."

"We'd like to take a look at your bank accounts," Smith said.

"Absolutely not."

"Are you afraid we'll find something that you don't want us to find?"

"I believe you need some kind of warrant for that."

"That's true," Smith said. "But if there's nothing untoward there, why deny us?"

"Because I don't like you."

"I have that effect on people."

"It's Christmas Day," Callum said.

"So, you keep saying. Does the song *Do they know it's Christmas* mean anything to you?"

"I've heard it."

"Your father suffered the injuries on the way back from the Live Aid concert, didn't he?"

"Apparently."

"He did. Janet took over the driving because everyone else, including your father, was too drunk to drive. They were in high spirits after the concert, and they were all drunk. Perhaps the accident wouldn't have happened if Janet hadn't had to take on the responsibility of driving."

"I want you to leave now," Callum said.

"In a minute. Did I say something to upset you?"

"I'm calling my lawyer."

"What for?" DC King said.

"Because this is bordering on police harassment."

"We'll be on our way in a minute," Smith said. "I'm starting to get a picture of what happened. Thirty-six years. For thirty-six years you and your mother were lumbered with the burden of your father. You probably missed out on a lot because of it. You're knocking on for forty and you still live with your mother. It's understandable that you'll be resentful. Then, your old man goes and dies, and it's probably left some kind of vacuum in your lives. You think back on how much you and your mother sacrificed for over three and a half decades, and you start thinking about revenge. You're hoping to reset the balance somehow."

"Get out of my house now," Callum said.

"I thought it was your mother's house," Smith said. "Will you be moving out, now you're no longer needed here?"

"Sarge," DC King said quietly. "I think we should go."

"Listen to your colleague," Callum said.

Smith got to his feet. "You're involved in the murder of Janet Downing. I know you are, and when I come back here with a piece of paper telling you to give me access to your bank records, it's going to tell me I'm right."

"You're going to be sorely disappointed," Callum said.

"It can't have been cheap," Smith carried on. "The man who killed Janet was a pro. Were you aware that Janet's six-year-old granddaughter was there when she was butchered? She witnessed the whole thing."

"The poor girl. I feel for her."

"I bet you do. She's not going to forget what happened that day – not for the rest of her life. Perhaps she'll contemplate revenge one day, just like you did."

"That is enough," Callum said. "Get out of my house before I have to call your bosses."

"They don't like me very much," Smith said. "Come on, Kerry. Let's leave Mr North in peace to have a think about everything that we've said."

CHAPTER TWENTY NINE

"Callum North has lodged a formal complaint against you."

Smith hadn't even made it up to the canteen when he was pounced upon by DI Smyth.

"I thought he might," he said.

"Have you forgotten that you're currently under investigation for the professor thing?"

"How could I forget?" Smith said. "Callum is rattled. He's involved in the murder of Janet Downing, and he's spooked because I told him that we're onto him."

"I expressly told you not to go in like a bull in a China shop, and you blatantly ignored me."

"It'll blow over."

"This is serious, Smith."

"I'm getting a bit sick of not being able to ask the questions I want to ask without having to put up with this kind of bullshit afterwards. The scumbags have more rights than we do these days. Callum North is a suspect in a murder investigation, and I won't treat him with kid gloves because I'm worried about him getting a bit upset. He's involved in this, boss."

"I think you should go home," DI Smyth said.

"Fuck that."

"It's not up for debate."

"Are you suspending me?"

"Of course not. Go home and enjoy the day with your family. I'll see if I can smooth things over with Mr North, but in the meantime, I think it would be better if you're not here."

"What about the investigation?" Smith said.

"The investigation will still be here tomorrow."

"I'm right about this, boss. Callum North paid someone to kill Janet Downing."

"If that's the case," DI Smyth said. "We will make him pay for it, just not today."

"We need a warrant to get access to his bank accounts."

"Smith," DI Smyth said. "Go home."

Smith observed the expression on the DI's face and admitted defeat. He was not going to win this argument. He got up and left the office without another word. It was still mid-morning, and he knew that Whitton and the rest of the Smith clan were preparing the Christmas dinner. Harold and Jane would be arriving at lunchtime and Darren's parents had been told to get there around then too. Smith really didn't feel like getting roped into the preparations, so he went upstairs to the canteen to grab a cup of coffee and think about his next move.

Bridge was sitting at a table with the DCs King and Moore.

"Haven't you got work to do?" Smith said.

He walked over to the coffee machine and selected his usual.

"I heard about your interrogation of the grieving son," Bridge said. "Kerry thinks you were a bit hard on him."

Smith looked right at her. "Is that right?"

"You were a bit cruel, Sarge," DC King said.

"What the hell is wrong with all of you?" Smith said. "Since when did we have to tiptoe around murder suspects because we don't want to risk hurting their feelings?"

"The bloke has just lost his dad, Sarge," DC Moore said.

"Which gives him a rock-solid motive for the murder of the woman who was responsible for him being in a wheelchair for thirty-six years. Am I the only one who can see that?"

"I'm on the same page as you," DC King said. "But if he is involved in Janet Downing's murder, I don't think an aggressive approach will work."

"What do you suggest?"

"See what the evidence tells us first. You have to admit that you were a bit aggressive."

"That's the way I operate, Kerry," Smith reminded her. "When I know someone is hiding something, I go straight for the jugular."

"Where do we go from here?" Bridge said.

"I've been told to go home," Smith said. "Callum North has lodged a complaint, and the boss has told me to fuck off while he sorts it out."

"What are you still doing here then?" DC Moore said.

"Avoiding getting roped into the Christmas Day preparations," Smith said. "I reckon Whitton and the rest of them should have everything done in an hour or so, and I'll head home then."

"That's so mean," DC King said.

"Do I look like someone who cares, Kerry?" Smith said. "Are there any shops open today?"

"Not many," Bridge said. "You've left it a bit late for last-minute Christmas shopping."

"It slipped my mind."

"Have you not bought any presents?" DC Moore said.

"Nope."

Smith's phone started to ring. It was Whitton.

"Shit," he said.

"Meat Loaf is telling you to go home, Sarge," DC King said.

"Meat Loaf can fuck off," Smith said.

He let the phone go to voicemail.

"Do we know anything else about Tom Lowe?" he said.

"The jumper?" DC Moore said.

"What have I told you about calling them that?" It was Bridge.

"His bank accounts were cleaned out," DC King said. "We still don't have an exact figure but we're talking over a million."

"Where did the money go?" Smith said.

"We're still waiting on that too," DC King said. "It's a difficult time of year to get any answers quickly."

"What about the bank records of Harriet Jordan's husband."

"Same thing, Sarge. Our hands are tied."

The wail of *Bat out of Hell* started again and the three pairs of eyes on Smith told him he needed to answer it.

"I suppose I'll see you all tomorrow then," he said.

He left the canteen, leaving his coffee untouched on the table.

"Where are you?" Whitton said when Smith had answered the call.

"Still at work."

"The DI said you were on your way home."

"He did, did he?" Smith said.

"He also told me about Callum North," Whitton said. "Come home. Forget about everything for one day and come home. It won't be the same without you."

"I'm on my way," Smith said. "I'll be there in ten minutes."

CHAPTER THIRTY

Smith opened the door to the sound of music playing inside the house. It was a Christmas song he was familiar with, but he couldn't recall who the singer was. Whitton and the others had been busy in his absence. The hallway was decorated with tinsel and a row of Christmas lights had been hung on the pictures hanging on the walls. The smell of something cooking in the kitchen filled the house.

Smith had no sooner taken off his coat when he was pounced upon by two giggling eight-year-olds. Laura and Fran were wearing identical Christmas hats and Smith noticed that Laura was holding one out to him.

"You have to wear a hat," Laura informed him.

"Not just now," Smith said. "Let me get in the house first."

"You're in the house," Fran said.

Smith couldn't argue with an eight-year-old's logic.

Laura handed him a felt hat with reindeer horns sticking out of the top.

"Put it on."

Smith obliged and he could feel the material irritating his skin immediately.

"Are Nanna and Granddad here?"

"They're on their way," Laura said. "Mum said you didn't get her a present."

"I did send a reminder to Father Christmas," Smith said. "He must be busy."

"There's no such thing as Father Christmas," Laura said.

"Since when?"

"Timothy Green told us," Fran said.

"The Australian kid?"

Laura nodded.

"You shouldn't pay any attention to that wombat. Timothy Green doesn't know his arse from his elbow."

"What's a wombat?" Fran said.

"Google it."

Smith managed to free himself from the two excitable girls and made his way to the kitchen. He removed the reindeer hat and walked over to give Whitton a hug.

"Sorry about your present."

"It's fine," she said. "Having you here with us is enough."

"No," Smith said. "It's not. I tell you what – how about you choose your own present. I'm shit with stuff like that anyway. Anything you want."

"Anything I want?"

"Within reason. Do we have any beers?"

"Of course."

"Do you need me to do anything?" Smith asked.

"It's all done. Lucy and Darren have been brilliant."

"Where are they?"

"Next door. Andrew is having a nap, but they should be here shortly."

Darren Lewis's parents arrived at the same time as Whitton's mum and dad. Smith sorted out some drinks and went outside for a cigarette. The sky was grey and overcast but it wasn't too cold. There was no chance of a white Christmas this year. He lit the cigarette, and his thoughts turned once more to the investigation. He couldn't help himself. He was convinced that all of the victims were taken out by a hired gun, and he knew from experience that in cases like these it was extremely difficult to catch the people responsible. Professional killers did not advertise their services in the conventional way – they didn't go door to door posting flyers through letterboxes, and Smith wondered how they were going to find this man.

He considered what they knew about him so far. Sophie Downing's reaction to his voice suggested he was a fellow Australian, but even that didn't help much. There were plenty of Australians in the country and Smith didn't think that this man would be careless enough to use his real identity when he travelled.

He was motivated and he was driven. That was quite clear, taking the murder of Janet Downing into account. Janet was his target and only Janet. Smith thought he'd been given detailed instructions on how the murder should be carried out and he'd followed them to the letter. He'd severed her spine and left her alive for thirty-six minutes. One minute for every year that Brian North was confined to his wheelchair.

He'd tortured Tom Lowe in order to extract his banking logins from him, and then he'd emptied his accounts. Smith wondered where the money had ended up. And why did he push Tom out of the window? It would have been much easier to kill him inside the hotel room. Why did there have to be so much drama involved?

Smith knew why. And that's why he took out his phone and called DC King. She answered on the third ring.

"Kerry," Smith said. "I need you to check something for me."

"I thought you'd been ordered to go home," DC King said.

"I'm here now, but something occurred to me. We dropped the ball with the Tom Lowe murder, and we shouldn't have."

"I'm listening."

"Find out if there have been any suicides recently," Smith said. "Specifically, people who have chosen to end their lives by jumping from tall buildings."

"It should be easy enough to check. He was pushed to his death for a reason, wasn't he?"

"He was. Why not just slit his throat in the hotel room? The leap from the window was dramatic, and it was also risky, but it was necessary. This bastard is working to strict instructions and so far, he's managed to pull it off."

"Perhaps it's worth liaising with the NCA."

"The National Crime Agency?" Smith said.

"This killer is obviously a pro," DC King said. "He's highly trained and it's possible he might be on the radar of the NCA."

"I'd rather not get them involved unless it becomes absolutely necessary."

"I'm not sure if we have the experience to deal with someone like this, Sarge," DC King said.

"The bloke's a killer," Smith said. "We've got more than enough experience of killers. Find out about those suicides. I'd better go – if Whitton catches me on the phone to you, I'm history."

"Will do," DC King said. "Oh and, Sarge."

"Yes."

"The DI managed to persuade Callum North to drop the complaint against you."

"Looks like I owe the boss again."

"Enjoy your Christmas."

"I reckon I'm going to," Smith said and hung up.

CHAPTER THIRTY ONE

"Why didn't someone do this yesterday?"

PC Griffin looked at the information in his notebook.

"We only got the witness statements late last night," PC Miller explained. "It was pretty chaotic at the scene, and it took a while to get a clear picture of what happened. What difference does it make?"

"It's Christmas Day."

"That means nothing to the criminals," PC Miller said. "You'll soon come to accept that. What's the address again?"

"Hawthorne Terrace. Number 17."

They were travelling north towards Heworth. Officers had been called out to a fire at the playhouse on New Walk yesterday afternoon and after speaking to a number of witnesses, it was clear that the fire had been started deliberately. It wasn't much of a blaze - the damage had been limited to the dressing room behind the stage, and the sprinkler system had extinguished the fire before the fire department even arrived. It didn't take long to figure out that someone had set off a large quantity of indoor fireworks and the stage manager claimed to know exactly who the culprit was.

"Nobody was hurt," PC Miller said. "And the fire didn't spread, so that's something."

"It's still arson though," PC Griffin said. "And arson is against the law."

"What are we supposed to do?" PC Miller said. "There's no concrete proof that this Mary Lions woman actually did set off the fireworks. The stage manager didn't see her do it, and it's all going to boil down to one woman's word against another's. We don't even have a warrant for her arrest."

"All we can do is have a word with her," PC Griffin said. "See what she has to say about it. We can arrest her if we have reasonable grounds."

"Without proof, we have nothing."

"Let's see what she has to say for herself," PC Griffin said.

"For what it's worth," PC Miller said.

He parked as close as he could get to the house on Hawthorne Terrace. All of the parking spaces in front of the house were taken, so he had to park some distance away.

"What are your plans for later?" he asked PC Griffin.

"Plans?" the shifty-eyed PC said.

"It's Christmas. Will you be spending time with your family?"

"Not if I can help it. We don't exactly get on."

"Why not?"

"That's none of your business," PC Griffin said.

"Easy, mate," PC Miller said. "I was just making conversation."

After ringing the bell three times, it was clear that there was nobody home at number 17.

"Does she know we're coming?" PC Griffin said.

"I don't think so," PC Miller said. "It can wait for another time."

PC Griffin pressed the bell again. He opened the letterbox.

"Police. Could you open the door please?"

PC Miller rolled his eyes. "It's not a raid. She's probably spending Christmas with some family somewhere. Let's get out of here."

PC Griffin ignored him. "Miss Lions. Mary, open the door. We know you're in there"

"She's not home," PC Miller said.

"I think she is. I'm sure I saw some movement inside."

"We'll come back another time. It's not like she's going to leave the country because we want to have a chat about some indoor fireworks."

PC Griffin wasn't listening. His face was glued to the letterbox.

"There's definitely someone in there."

"Move over," PC Miller said. "Let's have a look."

He saw it straight away. Something was moving in the middle of the hallway.

"Call it in," he said to PC Miller. "We need an ambulance here now."

He was an experienced officer, but he disregarded everything he'd ever been taught about protocol at a potential crime scene. He placed a hand on the door handle and tried the door. It was unlocked.

"What are you doing?" PC Griffin said.

PC Miller wasn't listening. His focus had been taken by the figure on the carpet next to the door to the living room. The woman let out a low groan and stopped moving.

"We need an ambulance," he said.

He went inside the house while PC Griffin made the call.

"Ma'am. An ambulance is on the way."

He hadn't realised how much blood there was. It was on the carpet surrounding the woman and it was on the walls. More blood had splashed onto the mirror in the hallway.

"You're going to be OK," PC Miller said. "Is there anyone else here?"

He didn't get an answer to this.

"Ambulance is on its way," PC Griffin called from the doorway. "ETA ten minutes."

"I don't think she's got ten minutes," PC Miller said.

He crouched down next to the woman. She was curled into the foetal position and her hands were clutching her throat.

"Help is on the way."

There was a lot of blood on her hands, and PC Miller saw that there were deep lacerations on her right hand. One of the fingers was gone, and another was attached only by a thin flap of skin.

"Can you hear me?" PC Miller asked.

The woman coughed and her eyes opened. She tried to speak but the only sound that came out of her mouth was a horrible rasp. Bubbles of blood popped from her lips.

"You're going to be alright. Just hold on."

PC Miller was trained in first aid but none of it came back to him now. He placed a hand on the woman's shoulder and recoiled when he felt something cold and sticky. He removed his hand and saw that it was covered with blood.

The woman stirred and PC Miller felt a grip on his arm. She said something and pulled him closer. Her strength was surprising.

"Don't try to talk," PC Miller said.

She coughed again and PC Miller caught a whiff of something sour.

"I did this."

"Don't talk," PC Miller said. "The ambulance will be here soon."

"Graveyard."

That was the last word she would ever utter. As PC Miller was trying to make some sense of what was happening something caught his eye in the living room. There was another figure on the floor in there and this one was definitely beyond help. The woman's eyes were fixed on his, even though the light in them had gone out long ago. The sirens of the ambulance could be heard but when the woman next to PC Miller exhaled a long breath of fetid air, he knew instinctively that they were too late.

CHAPTER THIRTY TWO

"Cheers," Harold Whitton held up his glass to make a toast.

Harold, Jane and Smith were sitting on one side of the table. Whitton sat opposite them with Darren's parents, Frankie and Jenny. Whitton had decided that there wasn't enough space for everyone around the table in the kitchen and Darren and Lucy had drawn the short straw and were eating their Christmas dinner in the living room with Laura and Fran.

"This spread is fantastic, love," Harold told Whitton. "You've done yourself proud."

"I had a lot of help," Whitton said. "Darren and Lucy did most of the food."

"Well, it's a feast fit for a king."

Harold drained the beer in his glass and let rip with a loud belch.

"How many have you had?" Jane said.

"Not nearly enough," Harold said.

"You really shouldn't be drinking."

"Leave him be," Frankie Lewis said. "Christmas comes but once a year, and all that shite."

"Language," Jenny said.

Smith had eaten more than he should. The turkey had been cooked just the way he liked it, and Whitton had told him he had Darren Lewis to thank for that. The meat was moist, and the skin was crisp, and Smith had helped himself to a huge portion.

Whitton had insisted they turn their phones off for the day. It had taken a bit of persuading, but Smith had reluctantly agreed. There would be no distractions today. Neither of them were aware of the brutal double murder in the house in Heworth, and they were both blissfully ignorant of the fact that the dying words of one of the victims was going to muddy the investigation to such an extent that they were going to wonder if this would be the first murder case to beat them.

After smoking a cigarette, Smith offered to wash the dishes.

"Laura and Fran are taking care of it," Whitton told him.

"How did you manage that?" Smith said.

"My mum and dad and Darren's parents brought presents for the girls, but I said they're only allowed to open them when the dishes have been done."

"You're a cruel woman, Erica," Smith said. "But good plan. Have you thought about what I'm getting you for Christmas?"

"I have, and just having you here is enough."

"You're not going to get all soppy now, are you?"

"I'm a Yorkshire girl," Whitton said. "And us Yorkshire lasses are allowed to be soppy on Christmas Day. Are you OK?"

"Never been better. Your dad seems chirpy."

"He's putting on an act," Whitton said. "Mum said he's not doing too well. He has good days and bad days, but the bad ones are starting to be more frequent."

"Should he be drinking?" Smith wondered.

"Apparently, a few beers aren't going to hurt this late in the day. Mum was especially pissed off when she heard that straight from the doctor's mouth."

"I can imagine."

"I'm worried about her," Whitton said. "She's woken up next to him for over fifty years, and I don't know how she'll cope when he's not around anymore."

"We'll worry about that when it happens. Today is all about forgetting the other shit. Today is for nothing but the family."

"Aren't you tempted to switch your phone back on?"

"Actually," Smith said. "I'm not. Whatever else is happening out there can be someone else's problem for once."

* * *

"You do realise you've caused us a whole lot of extra work?"
Grant Webber was furious. Not only had he been interrupted in the middle of his Christmas dinner for one, when he'd arrived at the crime scene, he'd been informed that the scene of the double murder had been seriously contaminated by PC Simon Miller's actions.

"Did you suddenly forget everything you'd ever been taught?" Webber wasn't finished.
PC Miller wasn't in a great place either, and even though he'd always been slightly intimidated by the Head of Forensics and he held him in high regard, the image of the dying woman in the hallway still consumed his thoughts. And that was why he was about to offer a reply that Webber couldn't have expected in a million years.

"I was trying to save a woman's life."
"You trampled all over a..."
"I'm not finished," PC Miller interrupted. "I didn't consider any minor consequences for the forensics team – my mind was focused on saving the life of another human being. Fat lot of good that did. She still fucking died, didn't she?"

Bridge intercepted PC Miller before things got any more heated.
"Go and get yourself checked out by the paramedics."
"I'm fine," PC Miller said.
"At least get some sweet tea inside you. Come on, mate – you did your best."
PC Miller glanced at Webber, turned around and walked over to the waiting ambulance.

"Give him a break," Bridge said to Webber. "If it makes you feel any better, it could have been worse – it could have been Smith arriving first on the scene."

Webber nodded. "I'll apologise to PC Miller later. I'm always a bit more on edge at this time of year. I really don't know why people even bother with Christmas. It's promoted as a time of joy, when in reality all it achieves is to remind those of us who live a lonely existence, how joyless we really are."

"Do you fancy a few pints after work?" Bridge said.

"Excuse me?"

"A couple of drinks," Bridge said. "It might remind you that you're not actually alone, no matter how miserable you might pretend to be."

"Have you been studying Philosophy on the sly?"

"I've got a pair of eyes in my head. Billie and me will be in the Lion on Grant Street later if you're interested. I'll let you get to work."

CHAPTER THIRTY THREE

"How are you feeling?" Smith asked Harold.

The sun had set, and the house was quiet. Darren and Lucy had gone next door with Lucy and Fran. Darren's parents had gone home, and Whitton was chatting to her mother in the living room. Even the dogs were still. Theakston and Fred were suitably fed on the leftovers of the turkey, and they were busy sleeping it off on the sofa. Smith was alone with Whitton's dad in the kitchen.

"I'd be a whole lot better if people stopped asking me how I'm feeling," Harold said. "I've been told by someone who trained for years to know what they're talking about, that I'll be dead long before Christmas next year, so asking me how I'm feeling is tantamount to asking a turkey how he's doing a week before Thanksgiving."

Smith laughed. "Fair enough."

"I want you to do something for me, son," Harold said.

Smith didn't like where this was going.

"Of course," he said anyway.

"I want you to promise me that when my time is near, you'll keep the girls away."

"I can't promise that, Harold," Smith said.

"I'm not asking for much. I don't want them to remember me like that."

"I think that should be their decision," Smith said.

Harold slammed his fist on the table and Smith flinched.

"Sorry about that," he said. "I've done some reading, and I know the score. This bastard is eating me alive from the inside out. It's going to consume me until I'm nothing more than a shell – a shrivelled mess. I'm going to stink, and I'm going to be unpleasant to look at. I don't want the girls' last memories of me to be some dying old man in a hospital bed. When it's time, you have to keep them away."

"You'll still be their grandfather, no matter what. Those kids are tougher than you think, and I won't let you make that decision for them."

"Are you defying the last wishes of a dying man?"

"I'm asking you to think of yourself for once, Harold," Smith said. "I understand where this is coming from, but you have to start thinking about yourself. Don't worry about the girls – they'll want to be there for you no matter what you look like. That's how family works."

He got another two beers from the fridge, mainly to occupy himself during the ensuing silence. He opened them both and handed one to Harold. "Happy Christmas," he said.

"Aye." Harold took a sip of beer. "You're not a big one for this time of year, are you?"

"I used to love it," Smith said. "Christmas in Australia is nothing like it is here. It's warm for a start. We'd sometimes head down to the beach in the afternoon and stay there until the sun went down."

"Erica told us about your dad."

"I thought she might."

"We didn't give her much choice," Harold said. "Jane wondered why you could never enjoy Christmas like everyone else, and Erica told us why. That must have been tough."

"It was a long time ago."

"Don't give me that shite, son," Harold said.

"Did Erica tell you the details?" Smith said.

"She said you found your old man hanging in the garden."

"That's about all there is to it."

"Do you know why he did it?"

"That was the worst part," Smith said. "I was sixteen years old, and I couldn't figure out why he would leave us like that. What had we done to make him do it?"

"He must have had his reasons, and none of it was your fault."

"Try telling a sixteen-year-old that," Smith said. "I think it was worse because of how he did it. He killed himself in my garden, knowing full well that one of us would find him. I suppose it could have been worse – it could have been Laura who found him, swinging there from the tree. She was a lot younger than me."

"That was your sister?"

"I adored her," Smith said. "She was a real pain in the arse, but little sisters are supposed to be, aren't they. She's dead too now. In fact, the only family I have left are Erica and the girls."

"And they're an incredible bunch of ladies," Harold said. "Every last one of them."

"They are," Smith agreed.

"I never much cared for you at the beginning," Harold said.

Smith laughed. "I wouldn't have guessed."

"I thought you were a jumped up, arrogant fool."

"I probably was."

"*Probably* doesn't come into it," Harold said. "You're a good man, Jason. You still have your moments, but you step up to the plate when it really matters. And I couldn't imagine a better husband for my little girl."

"Can we talk about something else now?" Smith said. "I know it's Christmas and all that, but all this blokey heart-to-heart stuff makes me feel a bit uncomfortable."

Whitton came into the kitchen, and Smith was glad. The talk with her father had drained him.

"Saved by the bell," he said.

"What have you two been talking about?" Whitton said.

"Really deep shit," Smith said.

"The Queen's speech is about to start," Whitton said. "Are you going to come and watch it?"

"Is she not dead yet?" Harold said.

"Dad, that's terrible."

"I thought she was. I'll be right through – I want to see what the decrepit old bint has to expound on this year."

CHAPTER THIRTY FOUR

"This is a copy of the CCTV footage from the camera outside the house owned by Mary Lions and Annie Drew," DI Smyth began the afternoon briefing.

He'd promised to keep it short, and Bridge, DC King and DC Moore were hoping he would be true to his word. All three of them were looking forward to going home to enjoy what was left of Christmas Day. DI Smyth started the tape.

"At 16:25 we can see Mary Lions arriving home," he said. "And an hour or so later, her fiancé, Annie Drew goes inside the house too."

The footage was black and white, but the quality was good. The team could make out the faces of the women quite clearly. DI Smyth had already seen the footage – he knew that nothing happened for another twenty minutes, so he fast-forwarded it.

"Just before six," he said. "A man knocks on the door, and I think you'll all agree that he is aware of the camera."

"Bloody hell," Bridge said. "That's our bloke."

His face was obscured by the green balaclava, but they could gauge his height and build, and he did bear a striking resemblance to the man caught on camera at the scenes of two of the previous murders.

They watched the footage in slow motion and all of them came to the same conclusion. This was definitely the man who killed Harriet Jordan and Tom Lowe and there was a strong chance that he was the one responsible for Janet Downing's murder too. Nothing happened outside the house for fifteen minutes then, at 18:13 the camera caught the back of the man as he walked calmly away.

"Right," DI Smyth said. "It's getting late, and I'm going to let you decide whether you wish to carry on or press on with a vengeance tomorrow morning."

"I'm all for carrying on," DC King said.

"I'm not too bothered either way," DC Moore said.

"Then I'll be the deciding vote," Bridge said. "I say we leave it for tomorrow. Until we know more about the two women, there's not much point in speculating. Plus, Smith and Whitton will be back tomorrow, so we'll have a full team."

"Before we go," DI Smyth said. "PC Miller spoke of something one of the women said before she died. Mary Lions managed to tell him that she did this, and she also mentioned a graveyard. With that thought, let's call it a day."

"A graveyard?" DC King said.

"What part of let's call it a day didn't you understand, Kerry?" Bridge said. He got to his feet to indicate to her that he didn't expect her to comment. DC Moore did the same, and both of them left the small conference room.

"Off you go then," DI Smyth said to DC King.

"There's something Smith asked me to look into," she said. "I've made no plans for Christmas Day, so I think I'll carry on here."

"When did Smith give you this task?"

"A few hours ago. I don't think he can let the investigation go."

"That sounds like Smith," DI Smyth said. "What was it he wanted you to check?"

"It's actually quite obvious when you think about it, sir. Janet Downing was left paralysed for thirty-six minutes because she was responsible for a man being in a wheelchair for thirty-six years. Tom Lowe's murder was equally dramatic. We still don't know where all his money ended up, but why throw him out of the window of a hotel?"

"Damn," DI Smyth said. "Mr Lowe was responsible for the suicide of someone, wasn't he?"

"Smith thinks he was," DC King said. "Or at least someone holds him responsible. I need to look into recent suicides, and specifically ones where someone jumped from a tall building."

"There's a pattern forming here, isn't there?" DI Smyth said.

"Definitely," DC King said. "These are all revenge killings. Janet Downing was driving the car that resulted in a man's life being ruined – Harriet Jordan made a fool out of her husband by openly inviting men into her house when he was away, and I think Tom Lowe was responsible for someone taking their own life. This has been about revenge all along."

"Where do Mary Lions and Annie Drew fit here?"

"I don't know yet," DC King said. "But it's the same killer, so it's safe to assume that someone hated them enough to want them dead."

"Do you need a second pair of eyes?" DI Smyth said.

"That won't be necessary, sir. I work better by myself."

"Smith has definitely rubbed off on you, Kerry."

"Is that such a bad thing, sir?" DC King said.

"Hmm," DI Smyth said. "And that's all I'm going to say on the subject."

DC King decided to work in the canteen. She booted up her laptop and got a cup of coffee from the machine. She had a suspicion that Tom Lowe's murder was the result of a suicide that happened recently. It made sense, taking the murder of Janet Downing into account. Janet was killed just two weeks after the man whose life she destroyed died.

According to the records there had been more than five thousand suicides so far that year. Contrary to popular belief, the month with the highest suicide rate is not December. More people do not take their own lives around Christmas time – statistically, the most popular month for self-termination is April.

DC King focused on the suicides for the month of December. There were three hundred registered deaths by suicide, and only six of those occurred in Yorkshire. As DC King dug deeper, she realised there were no suicides in York in December. A woman had hanged herself in Bradford, there were two intentional overdoses – one in Harrogate and another in Pontefract, and a man had fired a bullet through his temple in Sheffield. The fifth Yorkshire suicide involved a woman who'd driven her car into a wall in Rotherham, and DC King was starting to wonder if she was looking in the wrong places. It was quite possible that the suicide that Tom Lowe was involved in didn't happen anywhere near York.

Then she found it. On the thirteenth of that month, John Gordon had taken a leap from the thirty-fourth floor of a hotel in Leeds. John was forty years old. That was all DC King could find out about the incident, so she closed the page she was on and checked for websites for the local newspapers. The Leeds Herald ran an article on the suicide two days after John jumped.

DC King read the article carefully. It wasn't clear what John Gordon was actually doing in Leeds. His wife, Catherine was unaware of it, and that's about as much as the Leeds Herald could get out of her. There was speculation about the reason for John taking his own life and financial stresses seemed to be the general consensus. The article didn't elaborate on this.

DC King keyed John Gordon and Tom Lowe into the task bar and she knew she'd hit the jackpot when the results appeared. She clicked on the first page and everything slotted into place. John Gordon and Tom Lowe were partners in a web design company. They had a worldwide client list, and the turnover for the previous financial year ran into tens of millions. According to the web page, Tom Lowe had bought John Gordon out. The deal was all above board according to Mr Lowe, but John had claimed that he had been swindled out of the money that was owed to him. The matter was investigated and lawyers got involved, but Tom Lowe came away squeaky clean.

There were very few other details about what transpired, but DC King already had a good idea about what went down. It was clear that Tom Lowe had taken John Gordon for a ride and left him with nothing. John had seen no other way out and he'd jumped from the hotel in Leeds. DC King knew that this was another link in the chain of the investigation, and she also knew that John's wife Catherine needed to be located. Catherine had an extremely strong motive to want Tom Lowe dead.

DC King took out her phone and stared at the screen while she debated whether to phone Smith to tell him what she'd found. The clock on the phone told her it was almost seven, so she decided against it. Even if she had called his number, she wouldn't have been able to talk to him – his phone was still switched off.

CHAPTER THIRTY FIVE

"It would have been my sister's birthday today," Smith said.

He was sitting in the passenger seat of Whitton's car, on the way to work. He'd let Darren Lewis borrow his car. Darren had promised to help his brother move into his new flat.

"She would have been thirty-one," Smith added.

"Do you think we're going to crack this one?" Whitton changed the subject. She knew that if she engaged Smith in the topic of his sister, he would be maudlin all day and there had been enough of that yesterday. When everybody had gone home, Smith had cracked open the bottle of Jack Daniels' and soon afterwards his mood turned sombre. He wasn't often a melancholy drunk but when he did get that way, Whitton couldn't bear it. She'd eventually told him to shut up or go to bed. She wondered if he could remember that part of the night.

"My brain hurts," Smith said.

"I'm not surprised," Whitton said. "I hope you've got it out of your system."

"I have no idea. I can't really remember much after everybody left yesterday. It was a good day."

"It really was. My dad seemed to enjoy it. You and him were as thick as thieves."

That was one part that Smith did remember. The conversation with his father-in-law was very clear in his head, and he decided not to mention any of it to Whitton.

They went inside the station and headed upstairs to the canteen. Bridge and DC King were already there. Smith thought Bridge looked more hungover than he did. His skin was pale and there were bags below his eyes.

"You don't look well at all," Smith said.

"I don't feel well," Bridge said. "I had no idea that Webber could drink so much."

"He's full of surprises. What were you doing with Webber?"

"It seemed like a good idea at the time. I invited him for a few pints at The Lion on Grant Street. The man's an animal."

"I could have told you that," Smith said. "The only person I know who can drink Webber under the table is Chalmers, and he's a legend in the sport."

DC Moore came in and joined them at their table.

"Have you seen the DI this morning?" DC King asked him.

"Not yet," DC Moore said.

"I'll fill him in later. I found something significant last night. A bloke called John Gordon killed himself earlier in the month by jumping from the thirty-fourth floor of a hotel in Leeds."

"Interesting," Smith said.

"John just happened to be Tom Lowe's business partner," DC King said. "And it also appears that Tom Lowe took him to the cleaners in a dodgy buyout deal."

"What do we know about the people John Gordon left behind?" Smith asked.

"I didn't get much further than his wife, Sarge."

"That's as far as we need to go, I reckon. We're closing in on this bastard, I can feel it."

DI Smyth came into the canteen and DC King brought him up to date with the new developments.

"Catherine Gordon is definitely worth looking into," Smith said.

"She certainly is," DI Smyth said. "You and Kerry can pay her a visit this morning after the briefing."

"Do we really need another briefing?" Smith said.

"What are you thinking?"

"I'm getting a bit sick of discussing ways forward and not actually implementing them."

"I'm not following you."

"We can talk amongst ourselves until the cows come home, boss," Smith said. "But we should be talking to the people responsible for these murders."

"That's the whole point of the briefings – to pinpoint possible suspects. Only then will we know we're talking to the right people."

"Callum North is involved in the murder of Janet Downing," Smith said. "And as far as I can see nothing has been done about it. I don't see a warrant allowing us access to his bank records, and I don't see him in the back of a police car on the way to an interrogation."

"There is nothing linking Mr North to Janet's murder," DI Smyth said.

"That's because we're not looking hard enough. At least have him hauled in for questioning."

"Firstly," DI Smyth said. "We're still waiting on the court order to gain access to his bank accounts. Those things take time. And secondly, you're obsessing again."

"I am not."

"You are," DI Smyth said. "You're getting blinkered by the most obvious scenario and you're shutting yourself off to any others."

"If you can come up with an alternative scenario," Smith said. "I'm all ears. Callum North's old man just happens to die two weeks before Janet Downing is murdered. She wrecked their lives, and she needed to pay for it. Callum will have had time to ruminate. The death of his father will have sent him into emotional turmoil, and all rational thoughts will have gone out of the window."

"Are you suddenly a shrink?" Bridge said.

"It's common sense. Callum North is our man."

"We'll come back to that line of discussion," DI Smyth said. "Yesterday, the bodies of two women were found in a house in Heworth. It was two of our officers who made the discovery. One of the women was still alive when PC Miller went in, but she died before the ambulance arrived. Her name was Mary Lions, and she spoke to PC Miller right before she died. She told him that she did this, and she also mentioned a graveyard."

"A graveyard," Smith repeated. "Did PC Miller get anything else out of her?"

"Nothing. She said she did this, and she spoke the word, *graveyard*."

"Very weird," DC Moore said.

"Any thoughts?" DI Smyth said.

Nobody spoke up.

"Hold on," Smith said after a moment had passed. "What were the uniforms even doing at Mary's house?"

"There was a fire at the playhouse on New Walk on Christmas Eve. The blaze was soon extinguished, but the stage director called the police because she was convinced that Mary Lions was responsible for starting the fire."

"Why would she think that?" Smith said.

"She told the officers that she and Mary had an altercation moments before the fire started. There were boxes of indoor fireworks in the dressing room, and she claims that Mary set them off."

"I'd say it's irrelevant now," DC Moore said. "She's dead."

"It's extremely relevant, Harry," Smith argued. "Do we have the details of this stage director?"

"We do," DI Smyth said.

"Excuse me if I'm being a bit slow on the uptake," DC Moore said. "But how can the fire be connected to the murders?"

"I don't know," Smith said. "But it is. I'll speak to the stage director myself."

"I thought you and Kerry were going to see Catherine Gordon," Bridge said.

"We'll speak to her first," Smith said. "Come on, Kerry."

CHAPTER THIRTY SIX

Smith was instantly suspicious when he walked up the path to Catherine Gordon's front door. The house in Knavesmire was a large, detached property that wouldn't have come cheap.

"I thought her husband got cleaned out by his business partner," he said to DC King.

"That's what the reports claimed," she said.

"It doesn't look like Mrs Gordon is short of cash, does it?"

"This place must have cost a fortune," DC King said.

Catherine Gordon opened the door dressed in a pair of jeans and a T-Shirt. Smith explained who they were, and Catherine invited them in and told them to take a seat in the living room.

"Is this about Tom?" she asked.

"What makes you think that?" Smith said.

"What else could it be? I heard about it on the news. He took the easy way out in the end then."

"Easy way out?" DC King said.

"Tom Lowe destroyed our lives," Catherine said. "He was the reason why John ended his life."

"That was two weeks ago, wasn't it?" Smith said.

Catherine nodded. "I didn't even know he was in Leeds."

"He didn't mention it?"

"There was no reason for him to be there." Catherine rubbed her eyes. "Although perhaps there was. I don't know – it all came as such a shock."

"John and Tom Lowe were business partners, weren't they?" Smith said.

"For ten years," Catherine said. "They started out together."

"What sort of business was it?" DC King said.

"Corporate web design. It was John's idea. Anyone with a bit of IT savvy can churn out a half-decent website, but John knew there were massive opportunities to cash in on the huge conglomerates. It was a lot of work – long hours and travelling all over the world, but it paid off."

"I believe Tom bought John out," Smith said.

"Don't believe everything you hear," Catherine said. "A buy-out implies a two-way transaction. Oh, Tom got the company, but John wasn't paid for it."

"How did he get away with something like that?" DC King said.

"I don't know the full story," Catherine said. "John wouldn't tell me, but I got the sense that a lot of it was due to negligence on his part."

"Negligence?" Smith repeated.

"He didn't read the fine print. He put his signature on contracts that he shouldn't have signed in a million years."

"Did he try to rectify things?" DC King said. "You can't get away with something like that. There are regulations in place to prevent that sort of thing from happening."

"We got our lawyers involved," Catherine said. "Fat lot of good that did. Not only did John lose the business and the money he'd invested, we were landed with a hefty legal bill into the bargain."

"It must have been a difficult time for you," Smith said. "But I was under the impression that John lost everything."

"He did lose everything," Catherine said. "The apartment on the river, and the holiday place in Whitby all went up in smoke."

"You didn't lose this house though," Smith said.

"I'm renting."

"I don't understand," Smith said. "I don't know much about rentals, but this place can't be cheap."

"I have some money that John didn't know about. Perhaps if he was aware of it, he wouldn't have done what he did."

She wiped her eyes again, even though there were no tears.

Smith wasn't fooled.

"Why did you keep this from your husband?"

"Excuse me?" Catherine said.

"He was under the impression that you were both broke," Smith said. "How could you hide the money from him?"

"I don't like what you're implying."

"I'm not implying anything," Smith said. "It's a simple observation. You hid money from your husband."

"I didn't hide anything," Catherine said. "I'd forgotten all about it."

"You forgot you had some money stashed away?" DC King said.

"It's all crypto, and I hadn't realised how much it had grown."

"Cryptocurrency?" DC King said. "As in Bitcoin?"

"I invested ages ago," Catherine said. "And the returns have been massive."

"Excuse my ignorance," Smith said. "But how does that work?"

"It's not exactly legal tender," DC King explained. "But it can be exchanged for legal tender."

"I'm still not grasping this."

"You can use it for online purchases," Catherine said. "And you can convert it into currency quite quickly. Using an online exchange service like Kraken or Coinbase you can complete the transaction in hours."

"How much of this bit stuff did you forget about?" Smith said.

"Bitcoin," Catherine said. "I purchased seventeen in 2003 for forty-six dollars each."

Smith did some quick mental arithmetic. It wasn't an awful lot of money.

Catherine was about to give him an education on the weird and wonderful ways of cryptocurrency.

"Earlier in the year," she said. "Elon Musk added the Bitcoin hashtag in his Twitter profile and the currency soared overnight. In retrospect, I should have sold it then, but I wasn't paying attention."

"How much is it worth now?" Smith said. "A few hundred dollars a coin?"

Catherine laughed. "Hardly. When I exchanged it shortly after John's death Bitcoin was trading at a little over thirty-five-thousand dollars a unit."

CHAPTER THIRTY SEVEN

Smith had made an excuse to leave Catherine Gordon's rented house in Knavesmire. His head was spinning from her revelation about Bitcoin, and he needed to process it away from her. Smith and DC King were in her car on the way to the stage director's house a short distance away in Fulford.

"Was she being serious?" he said. "She paid less than fifty dollars a pop for seventeen of those bit things in 2003, and now they're worth thirty-five thousand each."

"It's insane, isn't it?" DC King said. "I bet the people who thought it would never take off are kicking themselves now. Do you think Catherine was involved in Tom Lowe's murder?"

"I don't know, Kerry. But we will be talking to Mrs Gordon again – of that there is little doubt. Seventeen times thirty-five grand is about half a million, isn't it?"

"Five hundred and ninety-five, Sarge," DC King said. "Dollars."

"What's the exchange rate now?"

"About zero point eight," DC King said.

"So, Catherine Gordon has just pocketed close to half a million pounds. More than enough to pay for a professional killer, wouldn't you think?"

"Definitely. She had motive and we now know she had the means to make it happen."

"We're going to need another court order," Smith said. "I doubt Catherine is going to let us see her bank details without one."

"There's far too much money around these days," DC King said.

"I hate money," Smith said. "I really fucking hate money."

It was obvious from the terraced house in Fulford that Penelope Swan wasn't particularly well off. The two-bedroomed property was in dire need of some TLC. The brick work needed attention, and the window frames looked like they hadn't been painted since the turn of the century. The doorbell wasn't working so Smith banged on the door, knocking off a chuck of old paint in the process.

Penelope opened the door and eyed Smith and DC King with suspicion. The stage director was in her mid-thirties, and she looked like she'd only just woken up. Her hair was unbrushed and she was still wearing her pyjamas.

"Mrs Swan?" Smith said.

"Miss," Penelope corrected.

Smith showed her his ID. "DS Smith and this is DC King. Can we come in?"

"I'm not dressed."

"We can wait while you put some clothes on," DC King said.

"Inside, if that's OK," Smith added. "It's not warm out here."

Penelope invited them in and asked them to take a seat in the living room while she got dressed. The interior of the house was at odds with the neglect outside. The carpet was spotless and there wasn't a speck of dust to be seen on any of the surfaces. There wasn't much furniture inside the room – two two-seaters and a coffee table was about it. A large TV was attached to the back wall. There were no pictures on the walls. Smith deduced that Penelope lived alone.

She came into the living room five minutes later, dressed in a pair of tracksuit pants and a woollen jumper. She sat down on one of the sofas. "You'll have to excuse the mess."

"I can't see any mess," Smith said.

"I was making a joke," Penelope said. "I'm rather anal about keeping the place tidy. The exterior is a different thing altogether."

"I didn't notice," Smith said.

"Liar. The landlord has been promising to do something about it for months. I'd fix it up myself if I had the cash. What do you want?"

"You're the stage manager at the playhouse on New Walk," Smith said. "Is that correct?"

"Stage director," Penelope said.

"I believe you were there on Christmas Eve when the fire broke out."

"That had nothing to do with me."

"I wasn't suggesting that it did. You accused Mary Lions of starting the fire with indoor fireworks."

"Is that why you're here?"

"Sort of," Smith said. "What made you think that Mary was responsible?"

"We had an argument shortly beforehand," Penelope said. "She stormed out, but she must have come back when I'd left. I know it was her."

"What was the argument about?" DC King said.

"That's none of your business."

"We'll decide on that," Smith said. "What were you arguing about?"

"I told her to leave, and she told me to fuck off, if you'll excuse my language."

"Why would she be so rude?" DC King said.

"She hates me."

"Could you elaborate on that?" Smith said.

"Mary knows exactly how I feel about her."

"Which is?" DC King said.

"I suppose you could say the hatred is reciprocal. She's not right for Annie, and I don't pretend otherwise."

"Annie Drew?" Smith said.

"Soon to be Annie Lions," Penelope said. "It's a joke. What is this really about."

Smith thought it was quite clear that Penelope Swan had no idea that Mary and Annie were dead – she'd referred to them in the present tense throughout. He didn't think it would hurt to tell her what happened.

"Mary and Annie are dead, Miss Swan."

Penelope's facial expression didn't change.

"They were murdered on Christmas Eve," Smith added.

"Are you having a laugh?" Penelope said.

"I never joke about murder," Smith said.

Penelope's eyes closed and she took a few deep breaths.

"Are you sure?"

"Positive," Smith said. "We believe that someone gained access to their property on Friday evening. The CCTV camera showed a man knocking on the door at around six."

"That wasn't long after the fire at the playhouse," Penelope said.

"We don't believe the two events are connected."

"I can't believe they're dead. Who would want to kill Annie?"

"How long have you known Mary and Annie?" DC King asked.

"A few years," Penelope said. "Annie is a talented actor. She really is special."

"Did you and Annie have more than just an actor-stage director relationship, Miss Swan?" Smith said.

Penelope didn't reply, but that in itself was enough to tell Smith everything he needed to know.

"Just a few more questions," he said. "And we'll leave you in peace. Just before Mary died, she said some rather odd things."

Penelope nodded.

"She told one of our officers that she did this. Can you think of what she could have meant by that?"

"She killed Annie?" Penelope guessed.

"We know she didn't," DC King said.

"Then I don't know."

"She also spoke about a graveyard," Smith said. "Does that mean anything to you?"

"No."

"Are you sure?"

"A graveyard is a graveyard," Penelope said. "How am I supposed to know why she mentioned it?"

"Thank you for your time," Smith said and got to his feet. "We might need to speak to you again."

"Whatever for?"

"You were one of the last people to see Mary and Annie alive, by all accounts," Smith said. "Don't get up – we'll see ourselves out."

CHAPTER THIRTY EIGHT

An hour later, Smith was writing names on the whiteboard in the small conference room.

"Catherine Gordon," he said as he wrote. "Not only did she have a classic motive for wanting Tom Lowe dead, but she also had the money to pay someone to do it."

"Her husband lost everything because of Tom Lowe," DI Smyth said. "It's as good a motive as any, but if they were broke, where did she get the cash to pay a pro?"

"Bitcoin," Smith said. "It's probably the craziest concept I've ever heard of. Catherine bought a few in 2003 and they're now worth stupid money."

"I was thinking of investing in Bitcoin," DC Moore said. "But I didn't fancy the risk. I should have done."

"Anyway," Smith said. "Regardless of her husband's financial woes, Catherine Gordon netted close to half a million when she cashed in her virtual money."

"What else do we know about the woman?" Bridge said.

"She claims to have no idea why her husband went to Leeds to do what he did, but I think she was lying."

"Why?" DC Moore said.

"It's a talent of mine, Harry. I have a built-in lie detector. Once again, we need to follow the money. Catherine Gordon paid someone to kill the man who drove her husband to kill himself. And that brings me to the next name on the list."

He wrote Callum North's name underneath Catherine's.

"It's another case of letting the money trail tell the story. I'm convinced that Callum paid the same people to arrange the extravagant murder of Janet Downing. We know that he's not short of funds, or at least his mother isn't."

"Money and motive," DC King mused. "As simple as that."

"As simple as that, Kerry," Smith said. "We find proof that Catherine and Callum paid a large sum of money to the same person and we're a step closer to figuring this out."

Duncan Jordan's name was next, and Smith outlined the motivation behind the murder of his wife, Harriet. Once again, Duncan had the wherewithal to pay for a professional killer. He'd denied them access to his financial records and Smith knew there was a reason for this.

"Can I say something?" DC Moore said.

"You're not in Kindergarten, Harry," DI Smyth said. "How many times do I have to remind you?"

"Sorry, sir," DC Moore said. "I just want to clarify something. Are we after the people who took out the contracts, or are we going for the ones who provided the service?"

"Both," Smith said without thinking. "But we need to concentrate on the ones who paid for the murders first. Once we hook them in, the bigger fish should be easier to catch."

"I never had you pegged for a fisherman, Sarge," DC King said.

"I'm not," Smith said. "The analogy just came to me. We're going to nail these bastards – it's just a matter of time."

"I hate to put a dampener on things," DI Smyth said. "While you're clearly on a roll, but where do Mary Lions and Annie Drew fit into this puzzle?"

"Right now," Smith said. "I haven't got a fucking clue, and I'm going to come back to them when I've finished assembling the easier pieces of the puzzle – the straight ones on the outside of the jigsaw."

"That's two analogies in the space of a minute, Sarge," DC King dared. "Don't overdo it now."

"I may have a few more up my sleeve yet, Kerry."

"I'm going to see if I can expedite the court orders to allow us access to the bank accounts we need," DI Smyth said.

"How long are we talking about?" Smith said.

"I know it's frustrating, but it's the silly time of year and everything slows down."

"Get Uncle Jeremy involved," Smith said. "He might be able to speed things up."

"That's not a bad idea," DI Smyth said. "And it's Superintendent Smyth to you."

"We have a good idea what these murders are all about," Smith said. "It's a simple case of exacting revenge by hiring someone to carry out a murder for you. The way the killing has been carried out suggests we're dealing with an exceptional assassin. Some of the murders have bordered on the outright bizarre and pulling that off is not easy. There's an important question we need to ask ourselves."

"How did the people who took out the contracts even find these people," DC King said.

"Got it in one. This is not a service you advertise on the Yellow Pages. How the hell did they make contact in the first place?"

"Internet?" DC Moore speculated.

"I very much doubt that, Harry," Smith said. "The Internet would not allow someone to advertise something like this."

"Word of mouth?" DC King guessed.

"It's worth considering," DI Smyth said.

"No," Smith said. "For that to be the case it would suggest that these people are somehow acquainted, and we haven't found any connections yet."

"And I doubt you'd hear about this kind of specialist service down the local pub," Whitton joined in.

"I'm going to see what I can do about those court orders," DI Smyth said.

He got up and left the room.

"What now?" Bridge said.

"We need to focus our attention on how the hits were arranged," Smith said. "Once we have an idea about that, we'll be a step closer. Look at what we have – Janet Downing was left alive for thirty-six minutes. She was paralysed and left to suffer for over half an hour. The Live Aid song was playing the entire time and that was to make her aware of why she was being attacked. The person who took out the hit gave detailed instructions about how the murder should be carried out."

"The MO was different in the Harriet Jordan murder," DC King said. "Harriet was simply stabbed multiple times."

"We don't know exactly what went on during the murder," Smith said. "We didn't have a fly on the wall for that one."

"Fly on the wall?" DC Moore said.

"It's a figure of speech, Harry. There is little doubt that Tom Lowe's staged suicide is connected to John Gordon's leap from the hotel in Leeds, and it was also stipulated in the instructions that his bank accounts had to be cleared out beforehand."

"Hence the torture," DC King said.

"Do we actually need a warrant to sift through the bank accounts of a dead bloke?" DC Moore said.

"As far as I'm aware," Smith said. "Tom Lowe had no dependents. He wasn't married, and I'm not sure what happens to his assets under those circumstances."

"Bona vacantia," DC King said.

"Do what?" It was DC Moore.

"It's a process where an estate passes to the Crown in the event of someone dying without a will or any relatives. The Treasury Solicitor will then handle the estate."

"If his accounts were flattened," DC Moore said. "He won't have had much left, will he?"

"He still had the business," Smith said. "Hold on."

"Here we go," Bridge said. "You're going to let us know when you've figured it out, aren't you?"

"It'll come to me," Smith said.

   DI Smyth came back inside the room.

"Good news. The Super just happens to be having lunch with Nigel Judd this afternoon."

"Nigel Judd?" Smith said.

"He and Superintendent Smyth are members of the same country club, and he just happens to be a magistrate. He's agreed to fast-track the court order requisitions, and fingers crossed, we should have them within the hour."

CHAPTER THIRTY NINE

After the lengthy wait for the court orders to allow the team to access the bank records of Callum North, Duncan Jordan and Catherine Gordon, the results were rather anticlimactic. According to the records, there was nothing suspicious about any of them. The team couldn't see any evidence of unusual spending at all. There were no large transactions that couldn't be explained, and Smith wasn't the only one who felt dejected.

"We also managed to track the money that was transferred out of Tom Lowe's bank accounts before he was thrown from the window," DI Smyth said. "And this is as bizarre as it gets."

"Everything about this investigation has been bizarre," Smith said. "Who pocketed the cash?"

"Close to two million pounds was distributed to a dozen animal charities and dog centres in the county."

"You're kidding me?" DC King said.

"It's no joke, Kerry. Every penny of that money was donated to charity."

"At least the dogs and cats in the city will have a good Christmas now," Smith said. "This is a tough time for animals."

"Will they even be able to keep the money?" DC Moore said.

"I hope so," Smith said. "At least there's some kind of happy ending to one of the murders."

"The funds will probably have to be returned," Bridge said.

"The press will have a field day if it is," Smith said. "I say let the dogs and cats get fat this Christmas."

"Let's move on," DI Smyth said. "This discussion is getting us nowhere."

"That was the only possible lead we had," Bridge said.

"I know all of them paid to have someone killed," Smith said. "But that's not what the bank records say."

"It's possible they have offshore accounts," DC King said.

"All of them?" Smith said. "I don't buy that."

"Or they could have completed the transaction using some other method of payment," DC Moore put forward.

"What other method of payment would a firm specialising in contract killing accept, Harry?"

"Cryptocurrency," DC Moore said. "It's easily converted to hard cash and transactions carried out using virtual money are notoriously difficult to trace."

"Surely there must be some way to monitor when cryptocurrency is changing hands," Smith said.

"It's extremely difficult to track," DC Moore said. "Especially if the currency is buried deep."

"I have no idea what you're talking about."

"How do you think people pay for stuff on the black market, Sarge? You don't buy a container full of human slaves by asking the seller for their banking details and transferring the cash."

"A container full of human slaves?" Bridge repeated.

"It was the first thing that came to mind. It's highly likely that this hired gun was contracted out from somewhere in the depths of the Dark Web."

"I think Harry might have a good point there," DC King said.

"The Dark Web," Smith said. "Fucking brilliant. We've been here before, haven't we?"

"And look how complicated that was," Whitton said.

Smith turned to Bridge.

"I'll give Barry a call," Bridge got in first.

"How did you know what I was going to say?" Smith said.

"What were you going to say?"

"I was going to ask you to give Barry Stone a call."

Barry Stone was an IT expert they'd called upon a few times in the past. What Barry didn't know about computers wasn't worth knowing. If the people who offered murder for hire operated from somewhere deep in the realms of the illicit Dark Web, Barry was the only person Smith could think of to assist. York Police had a team of IT technicians at hand, but Barry Stone knew more than all of them put together.

"We're missing something," Smith said.

"We're always missing something," Bridge said.

"No, this is something right in front of our faces. Look at the names on the whiteboard."

"Catherine Gordon," DC Moore read out. "Callum North and Duncan Jordan. What about them?"

"All of them are well off enough to be able to afford to hire a professional killer," Smith said. "And all of them have a strong motive for it. But we still don't know how they contacted the person who carried out the murders. That's bothering me."

"I thought we'd already decided that they probably found the guns for hire somewhere in the Dark Web," Whitton said.

"How?" Smith said. "It's possible that one of them stumbled across it that way, but all three of them?"

"With respect, Sarge," DC Moore said. "I think you're looking at this the wrong way round."

"It's the only way I work, Harry," Smith said. "What are you thinking?"

"You're working on the assumption that it's unusual that three people in the city have hired the same hitman, but it's not really, is it? I'm not claiming to know the ins and outs of hiring a pro to kill someone, but I bet there's a geographical element to it. You don't bring someone in from America to carry out a hit in York, do you?"

"Our man is Australian," Bridge reminded him.

"But the company he works for doesn't necessarily have to be Australian," DC Moore pointed out. "I'd say we're looking for a company offering guns for hire who are based in York."

"And you think they'd advertise that fact on the Internet?" Smith said.

"No," DC Moore said. "But the Dark Web isn't exactly the Internet, is it?"

CHAPTER FORTY

Barry Stone was happy to speak to Smith and Bridge. They were sitting next to him in the room he used as a home office of sorts. Smith had been here before, and it was like no home office he'd ever seen before. It reminded him more of a control room from a Sci-fi movie. He was sure there were even more screens attached to the walls now, and he wondered why Barry needed three laptops. Surely one was sufficient.

"We need your help with something," Smith said.

"That part is obvious," Barry said. "Nothing illegal, I hope."

"I wouldn't dream of it. What do you know about the Dark Web?"

"How long have you got?"

"We're in the middle of the most complicated case we've ever had," Bridge told him. "I don't know how much I'm allowed to tell you."

"Tell him everything," Smith said. "We can trust him."

"Sounds intriguing," Barry said. "Do you want something to drink? Beer?"

"We'd better not," Smith said.

"You don't mind if I have one?"

The question was rhetorical. Without getting up from the chair, Barry slid across the room, opened the small bar fridge and took out a bottle of Fosters.

"I didn't think anyone drank that shit anymore," Smith said.

"I thought you were Australian," Barry said.

"I am, but I've been in Yorkshire long enough to know the difference between beer and piss."

"Well, I happen to like it," Barry said. "Talk to me."

"We've got a professional killer out there," Bridge said. "Five people are dead so far, and we believe the services of this bloke were found somewhere on the Dark Web."

"Let me show you something," Barry said.

They watched as he leaned over to some kind of electrical device and flipped a couple of switches. Then he tapped the keypad of one of the laptops and the screen in the middle of the wall came alive. He closed his eyes and waited a few seconds.

"Count to ten."

"What for?" Smith said.

"Just humour me," Barry said.

Smith did. When he was finished, he looked over at Barry. Bridge's IT friend was grinning like an idiot.

"While you were counting," Barry said. "The random encryption I've enabled meant that the signal given off by my servers bounced between random servers all around the world. If anyone was monitoring my activity they would have been directed to Cairo, Santiago and Singapore in the blink of an eye. I call it cyber ping-pong."

"I have no idea what you're talking about," Smith said.

"A VPN is all very well," Barry said. "But even the latest versions are full of backdoors if you know what you're doing. The random encryption makes the system absolutely secure, and I suspect that'll be important for what you're asking me to help you with."

"Tell us about this dark web," Smith said.

"Prepare to be amazed," Barry said.

He drained his bottle, turned his head and let out a silent belch.

Smith watched as his fingers flew across the keypad. The screens on the wall flickered and then all of them turned blue.

"You're interested in hired guns," Barry said. "Take your pick."

One by one, the screens came to life. The options were limitless. Barry clicked on the first one and a web page that reminded Smith of a poster for an action movie appeared on the screen in the centre.

"Hitmen R Us," Bridge said. "Seriously?"

In the top lefthand corner was a picture of a woman in black. She was holding a gun across her face, and she was staring at them with menacing eyes. Smith read the words on the page next to her.

"We are a team of three contact killers operating in the US and Canada. Once you've made your *purchase*, you will be contacted within three days. Contract will be completed within two weeks, depending on target."

"This is incredible," Bridge remarked. "They even have rules."

"No children under ten," Smith read. "And no important politicians. What the hell constitutes an important politician?"

"Welcome to the deep, dark web," Barry said. "For ten-thousand dollars you can arrange an assassination from the comfort of your living room. You can hire a hitman dressed only in your Y-Fronts if you're that way inclined."

"As fascinating as this is," Smith said. "It doesn't really help us if all of this is untraceable."

"The Dark Web relies on the anonymising of technology," Barry said. "And the very nature of cryptocurrency is that it cannot be traced, but..."

"I hope that pause was for dramatic effect," Smith said.

"I need another beer," Barry said.

"You were about to tell us something," Smith said.

"You're going to have to give me more info," Barry said.

"We think the killer is Australian," Bridge told him. "And he's over six foot tall."

"I very much doubt there will be a photo of the hitman anywhere – even in the realms of the Dark Web."

"One of the victims mentioned something about a graveyard," Smith remembered. "It might not be important, but we don't really have much else at this stage."

"Graveyard," Barry repeated.

"We still have no idea what it means," Bridge said. "The victim said it just before she died."

"Leave it with me," Barry said. "I'll see what I can come up with."

"We can't pay you," Smith said. "This is off the books."

"I wouldn't expect anything else," Barry said. "And it's probably for the best. Some of the technology I use isn't exactly legal."

"We didn't hear that," Bridge said. "Thanks for your help."

"I haven't helped you yet."

"I thought you computer people had a load of contacts to call upon at times like these," Smith said. "Likeminded hacker geeks with weird nicknames."

"You watch far too many dodgy movies," Barry said. "I'm on my own with this one."

"We really appreciate your help," Smith said.

"I told you, I haven't helped you yet."

"I reckon you have," Smith said. "This has been quite an education."

CHAPTER FORTY ONE

"You're going to give yourself eyestrain."

Whitton was speaking to Smith's back. He'd been staring at the whiteboard in the small conference room for quite some time.

"What are you thinking?"

"Something," Smith said. "I don't know. There is definitely something here that we should be seeing."

"We've gone over it again and again and nothing has changed."

Bridge came in with DC King.

"What are you staring at?" Bridge said.

"The MO was different for the murders of Mary Lions and Annie Drew," Smith said.

"His MO changes depending on the circumstances," Bridge said.

"No," Smith said. "The double murder was totally different. I've seen the CCTV footage."

"He knocked on the door and went inside the house," Bridge said.

"He didn't. He knocked on the door and forced his way inside when it was opened. You can see that quite clearly in the footage. He wasn't dressed in a courier uniform – he didn't pose as a hotel employee, and he was in a hurry. There was an urgency to this one that he didn't display in the others."

"What does that tell us?" Bridge said.

"I have no idea."

"Brilliant."

"The timing is bugging me," Smith said. "There's something really wrong with it. The fire at the playhouse started at just before four. The stage director is convinced that Mary started it. Mary arrived home at just after four."

"16:25," DC King corrected.

"16:25 then. What time did Annie get home?"

"About an hour later."

"And the killer appeared on the doorstep at just before six," Smith said.

"That's the bit that's bothering me. The play was cancelled because of the fire, but how did he know this?"

"He could have been watching them," Whitton said.

"He was," Smith said. "Damn it."

"It's quite simple if you ask me," Bridge said. "The killer knew they would be at the playhouse – he keeps an eye on them and changes his plans when he realises that there's a fire."

Smith nodded.

"That's it."

"That's what?" Bridge said.

"I did this," Smith said. "That was one of the last things that Mary Lions said. If you weren't so damn ugly, I'd kiss you."

"Who said I was ugly?" Bridge said. "And I still have no idea what that brain of yours is up to."

"The fire was started to prevent the play going ahead," Smith said.

"And?"

"And," Smith said. "It was Mary who started it. her fiancé was in the play and Mary didn't want her to go on."

"Annie was supposed to be killed at the playhouse?" DC King guessed.

"She was," Smith said. "And Mary was the one who paid for the hitman."

"Are you suggesting that she had a change of heart?" Whitton said.

"I am. I think Mary saw red when she found out that Annie had been cheating on her. She organised the hit, but she changed her mind when she'd calmed down a bit. She thought that by starting a fire and thus preventing Annie from going on stage, that would be the end of it, but it only made things worse."

"There's still a few holes in that theory," Whitton said. "Why bother to follow them home and kill them both? The hit had already been paid for, so why not just walk away from the whole thing? It's not like Mary had any hope of getting her money back. She's hardly likely to press the matter, is she?"

"We're dealing with a professional," Smith said. "A man who absolutely has to finish what he's started. He will not stop until he's carried out his instructions. That's how he's wired."

"You make him sound like some kind of Terminator," Bridge said.

"That's basically what he is, isn't he?" Smith said.

"Why kill Mary?" DC King put forward. "If his instructions were to assassinate Annie, I can't understand why Mary had to die. He left Sophie Downing alive, even though she was a witness."

"I don't have an answer to that," Smith said. "Perhaps Mary's was a necessary murder. She may have put up a fight. We'll never know, but what I do know is Mary Lions took out a hit on her fiancé, she got cold feet and tried to throw a spanner in the works. But it ended badly for both her and her fiancé."

"Why are we even discussing this?" Bridge said. "It doesn't get us any closer to the people behind the murders."

"No," Smith admitted. "But it's cleared up something that was really annoying me."

"How are we going to catch this man?" Whitton said. "He's a true pro, and he operates via a network that's untraceable."

"There must be a way to trace the communication," DC King said. "He can't be getting all his instructions from somewhere in the Dark Web."

"We know that the money came from somewhere other than the bank accounts of the people who contracted the hits," Smith said. "And cybercurrency is impossible to track. The activity on the Dark Web is anonymous. That's what makes it the go to place for criminal activity. We've got Barry Stone looking into it for us, but I've got a feeling that's going to take more time than we have right now. We need to come up with something soon."

"Do you think he's going to strike again?" DC King said.

"If somebody has paid for the murder of someone in the city," Smith said. "He's going to strike again. Come on, Kerry."

"Where are we going?"

"Something is still bothering me about Mary Lions' actions," Smith said. "I want to speak to someone who knew her well once upon a time."

CHAPTER FORTY TWO

"Do you think we'll get anything from the Dark Web?" DC King asked.
She and Smith were on their way to Murton in her car.

"The whole point of it," she added. "Is absolute anonymity. How are we supposed to get anything from a place that's anonymous? How does someone even access the Dark Web?"

"If anyone can get any answers," Smith said. "It's Barry Stone. He's like one of those geeks you see in spy films. I have no idea how he does what he does and it's probably better that I don't know."

DC King parked her car outside the address they'd been given and she and Smith got out.

"I thought Mary was engaged to a woman," DC King said. "Are you sure the information you got is right?"

"Positive, Kerry," Smith said. "Mary was once married to Mark Francis."

When the door opened, Smith wondered if they had the correct address. The man looking them up and down did not look like someone who was once married to Mary Lions. Smith thought Mark Francis had to be in his mid-to-late fifties and the thick lenses on the glasses he was wearing made Smith think he was surely close to being medically blind. He introduced himself and DC King and explained the nature of their visit.

"I must admit, this has come as something of a shock," Mark Francis said.

They were sitting in his living room.

"We're very sorry, Mr Francis," DC King said.

"When was the last time you saw Mary?" Smith said.

"I haven't spoken to her for four years," Mark said. "That was shortly after the divorce."

"How long were you married?' DC King asked.

"Eighteen months," Mark said. "I should have listened to the warnings, but I suppose I was in some kind of dream world."

"How did you and Mary meet?" Smith said.

"Would you believe that she worked for me?"

"You were Mary's boss?" DC King said.

"I believe that's what it entails when someone works for you. What is it you want from me?"

"What do you do?" Smith said.

"IT," Mark said.

"And Mary worked for you?"

"She was an exceptional IT technician. And I know one when I see one. A lot of them think they know everything when they come out with their degrees, but they haven't even begun to learn."

"But Mary was different?" DC King said.

"She was. She was a natural. She had a sixth sense with computers – I always told her she was in more in tune with technology than human emotion. I haven't offered you anything to drink."

"That's fine," Smith said. "You said you haven't spoken to Mary since just after the divorce."

"It wasn't a pleasant time in my life," Mark said. "Once again I ignored the advice I was given, but you live and learn, don't you?"

"I'm not following you," Smith said.

"Eighteen months, and she walked away with half of what I'd spent years building up."

"She nailed you in the divorce?"

"You could say that. Are you sure you don't want some coffee? I'm going to make some for myself anyway."

"No thanks," Smith said.

"Are you thinking what I'm thinking?" DC King whispered when Mark had left the room.

"Mary had money," Smith said. "And she had specialist IT knowledge. But the timing with the events of Christmas Eve still don't add up."

"There was a fire at the playhouse, and they were killed shortly afterwards."

"Something about that fire is really bugging me, Kerry."

"He's coming back."

Mark Francis returned with a cup of coffee. He took a quick slurp and put the cup on the table.

"How did she die?" he said.

"We're not at liberty to talk about that," Smith said. "We were discussing the messy divorce. Do you have the details?"

"Details?" Mark said. "As in how much of my cash did she manage to squeeze out of me?"

"We can start there."

"Mary walked away with the better part of a quarter of a million," Mark said. "Not a bad score for a year and a half's work, wouldn't you say?"

"That must have made you bitter," DC King said.

"I didn't kill her, if that's what you're implying."

"It's not what we're implying at all, Mr Francis," Smith said. "We know you didn't kill her."

He was running out of questions to ask, and he was wondering if this was a waste of time.

"What was Mary like?" he said.

"Cold and calculated," Mark said without thinking. "But she also had a soft side. She blew hot and cold."

"Hot and cold?" DC King said.

"I'm sure there's a label you could attach to it these days," Mark said. "Some kind of syndrome, perhaps. One minute she would be the sweetest person in the world, and then it was as if a switch had been activated and she would be someone else. Hot and cold I call it."

"I think we've taken up enough of your time," Smith said.

"I'm sorry I couldn't be any help," Mark said. "It's been a long time since I had anything to do with Mary. I imagine she shacked up with some other poor rich bastard since."

"She was engaged to be married," DC King said.

"Poor bloke. Although he's probably just dodged a bullet, now that she's dead."

"Mary was engaged to a woman, Mr Francis," Smith said. "We'll see ourselves out."

CHAPTER FORTY THREE

Even though it was getting late, Smith managed to persuade DI Smyth to do what they should have done ages ago. They were waiting in the canteen for Callum North, Duncan Jordan and Catherine Gordon to be picked up. Smith wanted to formally interview all of them.

"You are not the only detective on this team," DI Smyth reminded him.

"I know that," Smith said. "This case is really starting to piss me off."

"All of them piss you off. It's already late, and by the time we get round to the interview stage it's going to be even later."

"I still think we should have arrested them," Smith said.

"For what?"

"Paying someone to kill someone else happens to be against the law."

"We have nothing to link any of them to the murders," DI Smyth said. "There is nothing to prove that any of them played any part in this."

"That's because they weren't the ones who carried out the actual murders," Smith said. "But they organised them."

"Without proof of that, we have nothing to justify an arrest. The only thing we can hope for is for one of them to slip up during questioning."

"Another long shot," Smith said. "Could I have your permission to go outside and smoke a cigarette?"

"Since when did you ask for my permission?"

"Since the camera was fixed over the entrance," Smith said.

DI Smyth sighed. "You have my permission."

"Thanks, boss."

It was only four in the afternoon, but the sky was pitch black. Smith lit a cigarette and inhaled deeply. He had the feeling that it was going to be a long night, and he wasn't sure what to expect from the suspects on their way to the station. Out of the three of them he couldn't really pick which one was likely to crack first. Callum, Duncan and Catherine were all cool customers, and Smith didn't think any of them would be easy to break. He was convinced of their guilt, but he was equally sure that all three of them believed that they were going to get away with it. He wondered if he could use that arrogance to his advantage in the interview room. He wasn't sure. This really was the most unusual investigation he'd ever been a part of, and he wondered if this was going to be the norm from now on. He would give anything for a good old-fashioned serial killer to get his teeth into, and he wondered if that was healthy.

The sound of his phone woke him from his thoughts about psychopaths, and when he swiped the screen, he saw it was a message from Barry Stone. The message was brief.

Think I've found your graveyard.

Smith tapped out a reply to tell Barry that he would be in touch as soon as he finished at the station, put out his cigarette and went back inside the station. The blinking light on the camera above the entrance was taunting him again, but he ignored it.

"I've been asked to let you know that Callum North and Catherine Gordon have arrived, Sarge," Baldwin told Smith as soon as he got inside.

"What about Duncan Jordan?" he asked.

"Nothing yet."

Smith still hadn't decided which one of the three he was going to tackle, but he thought that Catherine Gordon would be a safe bet. He'd sensed that she was lying when he last spoke to her, and he wanted to know what she was hiding.

"Can you do me a favour?" he asked Baldwin.

"Of course," she said.

"I need some information about the hotel that John Gordon jumped from."

"What kind of information?"

"Anything you can find," Smith said. "I don't think there was an investigation afterwards. It was ruled a suicide, nothing more and there wasn't an inquiry carried out."

"Do you think there was something more to it than a bloke jumping out of a window?"

"It's a long shot," Smith said. "But that's all we have right now."

"I'll see what I can find for you, Sarge."

"Thanks, Baldwin," Smith said.

He made his way to DI Smyth's office to let him know that he wanted to take on Catherine Gordon. The DI wasn't there. Smith went back to the front desk.

"Have you seen the boss?" he asked Baldwin.

"Not for a couple of hours."

"I was just with him in his office," Smith said. "And he's not there now."

"He didn't come past here," Baldwin said. "Perhaps he went to grab a coffee from the canteen."

DI Smyth wasn't in the canteen either. Smith got some coffee from the machine while he was there and sent DI Smyth a short message. The reply came back almost immediately. He'd been summoned to Superintendent Smyth's office. He didn't elaborate, but Smith sensed that there was a press conference on the cards. If there was one thing that Superintendent Smyth lived for it was a press conference.

He sat down at his usual table with his coffee and ran his hands through his hair. Once again, he sensed that there was something they'd overlooked. It was probably something obvious, it usually was, but it was still proving to be elusive.

Smith's thoughts turned to Barry Stone's message. He knew Barry well now, and if Barry had contacted him, it meant he had something important to report. It was intriguing and Smith decided he would head over to Barry's house as soon as the interviews had been concluded.

DI Smyth came in and Smith only had to look at him once to know that the meeting with his uncle had been unpleasant.

"When is the press conference?" he asked.

"How did you know..."

"That's why they pay me the big bucks, boss," Smith interrupted.

"Tomorrow morning," DI Smyth said. "At eleven."

"Am I invited?"

"Do you want to be invited?"

"Nope. Let me guess – the people in the offices with the views are concerned about the rumours about the hitman in the city."

"I didn't think you paid any attention to social media," DI Smyth said.

"It pays to keep abreast of the shite the people of York are lapping up," Smith said. "Shall we get these interviews over with? I want Catherine Gordon."

"Very well," DI Smyth said. "Whitton and I can interview Callum North. Duncan Jordan's lawyer is running late, but he should be here within the hour. Bridge and Harry can tackle him. Let's do this."

CHAPTER FORTY FOUR

Catherine Gordon had declined the services of a legal representative and Smith wondered why. He was convinced that she'd played a part in the staged suicide of Tom Lowe, and he'd expected her to come to the station with a lawyer. Smith didn't really care one way or the other – in his experience, interviews tended to be much simpler without the interference of legal *assistance*.

He stated the time and date for the record and outlined who was present. "Catherine," he said. "Is it OK if I call you Catherine?"

"Sure," she said. "Is this going to take long?"

"It's hard to tell," Smith said. "Is there somewhere you need to be?"

"I'm supposed to be meeting a friend for a few drinks. It's Boxing Day, in case you've forgotten."

"We'd like to talk to you about the business your husband started up with Tom Lowe," Smith said.

"What for?" Catherine asked.

"Could we get one thing straight from the start?" Smith said. "We ask the questions, and you answer them. Things go much quicker that way."

Catherine replied with a shrug of the shoulders.

"For the record," DC King. "Mrs Gordon is shrugging her shoulders."

"John and Tom created the company ten years ago," Smith said. "Is that correct?"

"More or less," Catherine said.

"Could you explain the nature of the business?"

"What has that got to do with anything?"

"Please just answer the question."

"The business model was simple," Catherine said. "LG Web Design offered high-end websites for big corporations."

"Don't businesses like that have their own people for that kind of thing?" DC King said.

"Most of the external operations are sub-contracted out these days," Catherine said. "It's something to do with tax breaks."

"And the business was doing well?" Smith said.

"Extremely well."

"LG Web Design," Smith said. "Is that Lowe-Gordon?"

"Well spotted," Catherine said. "It has more of a ring to it than GL."

"Why did John sell his share of the business?" Smith said.

"I've already told you," Catherine said. "He didn't. A buyout implies a two-way transaction, but Tom shafted him."

"OK," Smith said. "Let me rephrase that. What made John decide to get out of the business?"

"It was time," Catherine said. "Ten years of corporate life takes its toll. You can only carry on like that for so long. Let me give you an example: In 2018, John took no fewer than seventy-four flights, most of them long-haul. The body can't sustain a lifestyle like that indefinitely."

"I don't suppose it can," Smith said. "But the money was good, wasn't it?"

"Sometimes, money isn't everything."

"You won't get any arguments from me about that."

"What am I being accused of?" Catherine said.

"This is just a routine interview," Smith said.

"I don't believe that. I had nothing to do with what happened to Tom. I was nowhere near the New Tower Hotel that day."

"No," Smith said. "We've already established that. What did you think of Tom Lowe?"

"We were friends once upon a time," Catherine said. "John and Tom spent so much time together that it was inevitable that I would also see him a lot."

"Mr Lowe wasn't married, was he?" DC King said.

"Tom wasn't the marrying type."

"Tell us what happened with the buyout deal," Smith said.

"I've already explained that to you," Catherine said.

"For the record."

"It should have been relatively simple," Catherine said. "John wanted out, and Tom was the obvious person to buy him out."

"How much money are we talking about?"

"The company was assessed by an independent surveyor," Catherine said. "And a figure was agreed upon."

"You didn't answer my question."

"Tom made a generous offer," Catherine said. "And John accepted."

"I'm still waiting for you to answer the question," Smith said. "How much?"

"Four million."

"But the deal went sour," DC King said.

"It did."

"How was that even possible?" Smith said. "I'm not too clued up about buyouts, but I don't understand what could go wrong."

"John was tricked," Catherine said. "I'm not excusing what he did – it was partly his fault, but neither of us expected Tom to be so devious. He suggested a few drinks to seal the deal, but they hit the scotch before the contracts were even signed. You can guess the rest."

"I tend not to speculate," Smith said. "What happened?"

"John put his signature to documents he failed to read first," Catherine explained. "In a nutshell, he signed away everything he'd worked so hard for. He failed to read the small print, and he paid for it."

"And this was completely legal?" DC King said.

"Apparently, it was. We sought legal advice, for all the good that did."

"John lost everything," Smith said. "He was taken for a ride by a man he'd trusted. Do you believe that was why he chose to end his own life?"

"It's as good a reason as any," Catherine said.

"Did John give you any indication that he was planning on doing something so drastic?" Smith said.

"None at all, although he never did express his emotions. I suppose, in hindsight, some of the warning signs were there. But hindsight is only useful after the fact, isn't it?"

"Did you blame Tom for what John did?" Smith said.

"I did," Catherine said. "But I didn't kill him."

"No," Smith said. "You paid someone else to do that."

Catherine Gordon clearly wasn't expecting this. The expression on DC King's face told Smith that she hadn't anticipated him being so blunt either.

"I have no idea what you're talking about," Catherine said.

"Yes, you do. I know you hired someone to kill Tom Lowe. You paid using some kind of cryptocurrency and the transaction was carried out somewhere in the Dark Web. Both of which are supposed to be untraceable, but in fact, there are ways to track that kind of thing. Even activity buried deep in the cesspool that is the Dark Web can be found. And we have people who are especially adept at that kind of thing."

"You're talking utter nonsense."

"I do that a lot. Two weeks after your husband takes a leap from a hotel room, his business partner is thrown from another hotel window. We know that you arranged it."

"I presume you have some kind of proof of this," Catherine said.

"I don't need it," Smith told her. "Just knowing is enough for me."

"Am I under arrest for something?"

"Not right now," Smith said. "But that will change very soon. That's a promise."

"Then I assume that I'm free to go?" Catherine said.

"Does the graveyard mean anything to you?" Smith said.

Catherine smiled, and Smith wasn't expecting it.

"Well?" he said. "What can you tell me about the graveyard?"

"It's where dead people are buried."

"Very clever. You're not the only one who used the services of these people. One of them is going to crack, and that's all we need."

"I'm leaving now," Catherine said.

She emphasised this by getting to her feet.

"Are you an animal lover, Mrs Gordon?" Smith said.

"What?"

"Do you like animals?" Smith said. "Dogs and cats?"

"Who doesn't?" Catherine said. "I've had enough of this nonsense."

"That makes two of us," Smith said. "Interview with Catherine Gordon ended 19:33."

CHAPTER FORTY FIVE

The interviews with Callum North and Duncan Jordan were equally unproductive. DI Smyth and Whitton didn't get anything useful from Callum and Bridge and DC Moore had to sit through a one-sided conversation with Duncan. His lawyer had finally arrived, but his only purpose during the interview was to advise his client not to say anything. After two dozen, *no comments*, Bridge and DC Moore had no option but to bring things to a close.

Smith couldn't wait to get away from work for the day. He was exhausted and he still had to go and see Barry Stone. He remembered that he didn't have his car – he'd lent it to Darren to help his brother move, so he asked Whitton to drop him off at Barry's place.

"I can get a taxi back," he added.

"Why don't I just come with you?" Whitton said.

"I thought you'd want to get home to the girls."

"They'll be fine with Darren and Lucy for another hour or so," Whitton said.

"I want to see this set-up of Barry's."

"It's something else," Smith said.

They arrived at Barry's house fifteen minutes later. He invited them in, and they headed straight upstairs to his office.

"Wow," Whitton said when she went inside. "This is amazing."

"Do you know much about computers?" Barry said.

"A little bit. Those must have cost a fortune."

She pointed to the screens on the wall.

"I still don't know why he needs so many," Smith said.

"I'd explain it to you," Barry said. "But it would take all night, and you'd probably fall asleep halfway through. You're not here to discuss my hardware, are you?"

"What can you tell us about this graveyard?" Smith said.

"Take a seat," Barry said. "And I'll see if I can find it for you."

"What is it?" Whitton said.

"All in good time. I didn't keep the site open, for obvious reasons."

Whatever those reasons were, they weren't obvious to Smith. He didn't bother asking Barry about it.

They watched as Barry did what he did best. His fingers tapped keys, and the screens on the wall flashed on and off.

"It didn't take this long last time," he said.

"Is this the Dark Web?" Whitton said.

"It is."

"I expected it to be more sinister than this," Whitton said. "That page looks like any page you'd find on the Internet."

"Discount contract killers?" Smith read. "Are you being serious?"

"Apart from the content, I mean," Whitton said.

"Here we go," Barry said. "I must admit, whoever came up with this really has a creative streak."

"The Graveyard," Smith said in a voice no louder than a whisper.

The image on the screen looked like any normal graveyard. A full moon was overhead, lending the scene a sinister aspect.

"This is no ordinary graveyard," Smith read the words below the image.

"This isn't a place for the souls of the dead to be laid to rest – this is where the fate of the future dead is sealed."

"What does that even mean?" Whitton said. "The fate of the future dead?"

"Targets," Smith said.

"Got it in one," Barry confirmed.

"Let me get this straight," Whitton said. "The graveyard is allegorical?"

"What?" Smith said.

"It's not a literal place," Whitton said. "It's representative of something else."

"There's nothing to indicate that on the site," Barry said. "In fact, the instructions are suspiciously simple. I'll show you."

He clicked on one of the options on the menu, and what appeared to be a contract appeared on the screen.

"This could be a contract for buying a car," Smith said after reading a few lines.

The interested party was instructed to enter their details and there was a place for a virtual signature at the bottom. Below that were a number of terms and conditions in a much smaller font. It really did look like an innocent stock-standard contract.

"Can you enlarge it?" Smith asked. "My eyes are struggling to make out the bit at the bottom."

"The small print," Barry said.

He brought up his settings and magnified the screen until the letters in the terms and conditions were easy to read.

"According to this," Smith said. "Once the transaction has been completed the client will be contacted within two days. It's just like the site you showed me earlier. This bit is different though. The Hitmen R Us site promised to carry out the hit within two weeks, but here it's the client who decides when the murder will be carried out. That's service for you."

"There's something seriously wrong with you," Whitton said.

"You married him," Barry said.

"Don't remind me."

Smith ignored them.

"The hit isn't cheap," he said. "In Hitmen R Us you could hire a contract killer for ten thousand dollars – these people charge twice that."

"You get what you pay for," Barry said.

"There's nothing here about special instructions," Smith said. "Damn it."

"That part must be discussed when the company get in touch within two days," Whitton said.

"How do they even contact the client?" Smith said. "The only thing on here is the client's name and the name of the person they want killed. Where is the rest of the info?"

"There isn't any," Whitton said. "Are you sure this is related to the recent murders?"

"I'm starting to have my doubts," Smith said. "Hold on."

"I hate it when he says that," Whitton told Barry.

"They say you should always read the small print," Smith said. "Look at that."

He tapped his finger on the part of the contract that he was referring to.

"Oh my God," Whitton said.

"We've definitely found the right website," Smith said.

"That is seriously fucked up," Barry said. "Excuse my language."

"You're excused," Smith said.

"I wasn't actually talking to you."

"There is no cooling off period," Smith read. "Once the contract has been signed and funds received the deal is final. The reputation of the company relies on professionalism and outstanding attention to detail. Should either of the parties fail to adhere to the terms of the contract, clause 2.2 will apply. In the event of the client breaking any of the terms and conditions as set out in the contract, both the target and the client will be terminated."

"This is incredible," Whitton said. "You wouldn't want to overlook the small print in this instance."

"Mary Lions did," Smith said. "She obviously didn't read the terms and conditions and that's why she was killed. That's one mystery cleared up at least."

"This is all very well and good," Whitton said. "Not to mention extremely disturbing, but it doesn't really give us much."

"It most certainly does," Smith said.

"Such as?"

"I have a plan."

"I get worried when you say things like that," Whitton said. "What did you have in mind?"

"I'm going to persuade the boss to blow the entire budget on hiring a hitman."

CHAPTER FORTY SIX

"Are you out of your mind?"

Smith didn't think it would be easy to convince DI Smyth that the only way forward in the investigation was to fill out the contract on the Graveyard website and pay the money to arrange an assassination. He wasn't wrong. "You're seriously suggesting we spend thousands of pounds of taxpayers' money to hire a hitman?" DI Smyth added.

"I suppose it does sound bad when you phrase it like that," Smith said.

"There is no other way to phrase it. The coffers are already stretched as it is. Cutbacks have meant we have to be frugal with the budget, and there is no way this can be justified."

"It'll get us closer to these people, boss," Smith insisted.

"Are you even listening to yourself? And who are we planning on having them take out?"

"That's not going to happen," Smith said. "We'll stop them before it gets that far. This is the only way."

"The budget simply won't stretch to it."

"Then we invite someone with a bigger budget to the party," Smith said.

"Contrary to popular belief," DI Smyth said. "The specialist criminal agencies do not have unlimited budgets. We're all in the same boat."

"We need to do this, boss," Smith said. "There's no other way."

DI Smyth sighed so deeply that Smith could feel his breath across the desk. "OK," the DI said. "Let's talk this through, hypothetically. You want us to sign a contract that is tantamount to signing someone's death warrant?"

"That's about the size of it."

"Who did you have in mind?" DI Smyth said. "Target and potential client?"

"I hadn't given the target much thought," Smith said. "But I think Kerry should be the client."

"Reasons?"

"It can't be me," Smith said. "I'm too well known in the city. Whoever is behind this will smell a rat straight away if I pose as the client."

"I thought all of this was organised behind closed doors," DI Smyth said. "On the Dark Web."

"I could be wrong, but I think that's just the first step. The details of how the killing is to take place happens later."

"Do you believe this info gathering occurs face to face?"

"I really don't know, but I don't want to risk it if that's the case. My ugly mug has been widely broadcast over the years, but Kerry's hasn't."

"Let's say the second phase of the operation does happen face to face," DI Smyth said. "What then?"

"I haven't given that part much thought yet," Smith said. "But I don't get the impression that the hired gun will be a part of that. His role is strictly the killing itself, and that's where we'll catch him, hopefully before he's carried out the assassination. That last bit was a joke by the way."

"Do I look amused?"

"Sorry, boss. This is the only way."

"This is a massive undertaking," DI Smyth said. "Money aside, this kind of sting is riddled with risk and uncertainty."

"That's why I came straight to you," Smith said.

"Of course you came to me. I'm your boss."

"And you just happen to have years of experience in operations of this nature."

"I left the army a long time ago," DI Smyth said.

"But you never forget training like that."

"Let me carry out a risk assessment before we come up with a plan of action."

"Can I make a suggestion?" Smith said.

"Make it quick. I've got a press conference to get through before I can even consider this."

"While you're assessing the risks, could you disregard public opinion, the danger of a leak to the press, and it might be beneficial to forget about what top brass might think about it."

"I have to take this higher up, Smith," DI Smyth said. "This isn't something we can do without authorisation, unless we want to be jobless by the end of the year."

"I don't want the decision to be influenced by irrelevant stuff. I know it's a hell of a risk, but it's the only way."

"Leave it with me," DI Smyth said.

"We have to do this," Smith said.

"I said leave it with me. I think I've been more than generous by even having this discussion with you."

Smith knew when to quit while he was ahead.

"Good luck with the press conference," he said and left the office.

After smoking a cigarette and letting the camera over the door know what he thought of it with a subtle middle finger, he went to his office and booted up his laptop. He went to get some coffee from the canteen while the laptop was waking up for the day.

Bridge was alone at the table by the window. He was staring out, lost in his own world.

"Morning," Smith said. "Daydreaming on the job isn't recommended."

"I was miles away there," Bridge said. "Barry told me about the Graveyard site. Mary Lions died because she didn't read the small print, didn't she?"

"It looks like it. She thought she'd prevented a murder, but all she did was create another. The website gave me an idea."

He spent the next five minutes telling Bridge about his plan.

"It's risky," Bridge said. "And where are we going to get twenty thousand dollars from? What is that – about seventeen grand?"

"Something like that," Smith said.

"Who are we going to have killed?"

"We're not going to have anybody killed," Smith said. "Although I can think of a few names off the top of my head."

"You do know that top brass is not going to go for this," Bridge said. "It's not just the cash."

"Then I'll come up with another plan," Smith said. "I'll pay for it myself if I have to."

"And you've got seventeen grand lying around?"

"I've still got about half of what The Ghoul left me in his will," Smith said. "More than enough to pay for a hitman."

"There must be another way."

"There isn't," Smith decided. "The only way we're going to get anywhere near these people is if we make them believe that we're requesting their services."

CHAPTER FORTY SEVEN

Smith decided to hide inside his office for the duration of the press conference. He despised them at the best of times, and he knew that this one wouldn't be pleasant. That's why, when there was a knock on the door, he was reluctant to see who it was. It was possible that his presence was required at the press conference and that was the last thing he felt like.

It was Baldwin. Smith invited her in and told her to take a seat.

"I've done some digging into the hotel where John Gordon committed suicide," she said. "And I think I've found something."

"I was hoping you would," Smith said. "What is it?"

"You were right," Baldwin said. "There was no investigation into Mr Gordon's death. It was ruled a suicide and there wasn't an enquiry. I got hold of one of the receptionists there and I also managed to get a list of the guests staying at the hotel at the time."

"How did you manage that?"

"I have my ways."

"I won't ask what they are," Smith said. "And..."

"And," Baldwin said. "It looks like John wasn't there alone."

"I knew it. I knew there was something more to his suicide."

"Unfortunately," Baldwin said. "We're just too late with the CCTV cameras. The footage is stored on a cloud for fourteen days and automatically deleted. Anyway, one of the guests I spoke to remembered Mr Gordon. She was staying in the room next to his, and she definitely recalled seeing a woman going into the room with him."

"Do we know if anyone else was booked into the room?"

"According to the hotel records," Baldwin said. "He was there alone, but the witness is convinced there was someone else there with him."

"Did she give you a description of this mystery guest?" Smith said.

"She didn't want to talk over the phone."

"Where is this woman?" Smith said.

"Leeds."

"Grab your coat," Smith said. "We're heading over to Leeds."

Half an hour later they were a few miles south of Tadcaster on the A64. There wasn't much traffic on the roads and, according to the GPS, they would be in Leeds in twenty-five minutes.

"Do you believe John Gordon's suicide was suspicious?" Baldwin asked.

"I don't know what to think," Smith said. "His leap from the hotel room was the catalyst for what happened to Tom Lowe, but if it wasn't a simple suicide then everything gets a whole load more complicated. What else did this witness tell you?"

"Not much," Baldwin said. "She stayed in the Albert Hotel the same time as John Gordon, and she definitely remembered seeing a woman going into his room."

"Why didn't she want to talk over the phone?"

"Some people don't."

"Did you tell her you were with the police?"

"Of course," Baldwin said. "I said I was talking to everyone who stayed in the hotel on that particular night, and she told me she would prefer to talk face to face."

"That's a bit odd, don't you think?"

"Some people just don't like talking on the phone," Baldwin said. "And I always find it more productive having a conversation with a witness in person."

"I'm with you there," Smith said.

The woman from the hotel was Rachel Hill and she lived in a house in Holbeck, south of the city centre. Smith found a parking space and he and Baldwin walked up the path to the front door. Smith rang the bell, and the door opened soon afterwards. Rachel looked to be in her mid-twenties. Her blond hair was definitely not her natural colour and a couple of inches of darker hair had grown out at the roots. She had big blue eyes and Smith thought she looked tired.

"Mrs Hill?" he said.

"Miss," Rachel corrected him. "You must be from the police. Come in."

She led them to a tiny living room.

"Take a seat. Do you want something to drink?"

"No thanks," Smith said. "Thank you for agreeing to speak to us."

"I don't know how much help I'll be," Rachel said. "Your colleague told me that you were speaking to people in connection with the suicide earlier in the month. Do you think he didn't kill himself?"

"We don't think anything at the moment," Smith said. "We're just tying up a few loose ends. You stayed at The Albert Hotel on the 11th and 12th of this month, is that correct?"

"That's right."

"What were you doing there?" Smith said. "Why stay at a hotel in your hometown?"

"It was a work thing," Rachel said. "A teambuilding exercise."

"What do you do?" Baldwin asked.

"Advertising. It was actually quite painful. We were forced to partake in all these role-playing exercises. It was supposed to build team morale, but most of us were only really there for the free food and booze."

"PC Baldwin told me you remembered a woman in John Gordon's room."

"I was in the room next to his," Rachel said. "On the thirty-fourth floor. I was actually in the room when he jumped."

"That must have been terrible," Baldwin said.

"I didn't see him do it," Rachel said. "But I heard the screaming, even from that high up. I only realised what had happened afterwards. The teambuilding thing was cancelled after that."

"Can you describe this woman," Smith said.

"She was about your age. Mid-thirties."

"I'll take that as a compliment," Smith said.

In two months, he would be celebrating his fortieth birthday, and he wasn't looking forward to it.

"Her hair was short and brown, and she was about five-six. I suppose she was quite pretty in a fake kind of way."

"Fake?" Baldwin said.

"It was clear that she had money," Rachel said. "You could tell by the way she was dressed, and money can do wonders for a person's appearance, can't it? My mother used to say that there were no such things as ugly people – only poor people."

"Can you remember when you saw this woman?" Smith said.

"I saw her a few times," Rachel said. "All on Saturday."

"That was the day of the suicide," Baldwin said. "According to the report, John Gordon jumped from the window at seven in the evening of the Saturday."

"When did you last see the woman?" Smith said.

"I think it was when I returned to my room after the day's activities. It was. That will have been around half-six. She was going into the room when I walked down the hallway."

"Interesting," Smith said.

"Do you think she had something to do with the suicide?"

"We don't think anything," Smith said.

Baldwin took out her mobile phone and swiped the screen. She tapped a few times and handed the phone to Rachel.

"Is this the woman?"

Rachel didn't have to speak. The recognition was quite apparent in her face. She nodded and gave Baldwin the phone back.

"Thank you for your time," Smith said. "We won't take up any more of it."

"Will I be expected to make some kind of statement?" Rachel said.

"I don't think that will be necessary at the moment," Smith told her. "But Leeds Police will probably need to talk to you at some stage. Thank you again."

CHAPTER FORTY EIGHT

Smith's arrival back at the station coincided with the conclusion of the press conference and he thought the timing couldn't have been better. He grabbed some coffee from the canteen and took it to the small conference room. He made a beeline for the whiteboard and focused on the names scrawled on it. Certain things were much clearer today.

"Where did you disappear to?" Whitton's voice was heard behind him.

"A brief hunting expedition in Leeds," Smith said. "John Gordon wasn't alone the day he jumped from that hotel window. Baldwin tracked down a witness who saw a woman going in and out of his room, and her name just happens to be on the whiteboard there."

"Catherine Gordon?" Whitton guessed.

"Your powers of deduction are extraordinary," Smith said.

"Idiot," Whitton said. "You referred to a woman, and Catherine is the only one it could be. What do you think it means?"

"I think she either pushed her husband out of that window," Smith said. "Or she talked him into jumping, but I'm inclined to go for the former."

"I thought hotel windows didn't open far enough to allow that sort of thing to happen."

"According to the receptionist at The Albert Hotel, the mechanism that prevented the window from opening was broken. Someone forced it open."

"If Catherine was the one responsible for her husband's death," Whitton said. "It throws a bit of confusion into the mix. It means her motive for Tom Lowe's murder flies out of the window."

"It does," Smith said. "And I haven't quite figured out what that means in terms of the investigation."

The rest of the team came in together. Bridge, DC Moore and DC King seemed to be in high spirits, but DI Smyth most definitely wasn't.

"Good press conference, boss?" Smith said.

"There is no such thing as a good press conference," DI Smyth said. "But at least it's over with now."

Smith told him about the trip to Leeds. He also outlined his confusion about Catherine Gordon's motive for Tom Lowe's murder.

"That is baffling," DI Smyth said. "Are you sure this witness is reliable?"

"I saw it with my own eyes," Smith said. "As soon as she saw the photo of Catherine there was a spark of recognition. Even before she saw the photo, she described Catherine to a T. It was her in the room the evening her husband died."

"Have you shared this information with Leeds?"

"Not yet."

"Why not?"

"Because this is our party, boss," Smith said. "Leeds will be invited at some stage, but not yet. I want Catherine Gordon for the murder of Tom Lowe and things could get a bit messy if Leeds is investigating her at the same time."

"You do realise that this goes against protocol."

"What's your point?"

"I give up," DI Smyth said.

"There was no investigation into John's suicide," Smith said.

"Why would there be?" Bridge said. "According to the accounts of the people at the hotel, he was alone in the room at the time."

"Those accounts are inaccurate," Smith said. "We have a witness who confirmed that there was a woman there around the time when he jumped."

"Catherine Gordon," DI Smyth said. "Let me get this straight. Mrs Gordon denied being anywhere near Leeds on that fateful day. In her brief statement to the press, she made the same claim. What does this mean in terms of the investigation?"

"That's what we need to focus on," Smith said. "The witness is convinced that Catherine was in that room. Unfortunately, we only have her word for it – the CCTV footage from that day has been deleted. From an evidence perspective, it's flimsy."

"Witness statements always are," Bridge said. "What do we do with this information?"

"We press Catherine until she tells us the truth," Smith said.

"She's not going to admit it," DI Smyth said. "Why would she?"

"Then we find something else that links her to the murders," Smith said.

"Murders?" DC Moore said. "As in plural?"

"Have you not been paying attention, Harry?" Smith said. "Catherine Gordon played a big part in the deaths of her husband and Tom Lowe. I want her for both of them. She killed her husband, and two weeks later she paid someone to kill his business partner. We need to bite the bullet and take out a contract on the Graveyard site."

"Hold your horses," DI Smyth said. "This is not something you do on a whim. I haven't had time to consider the pros and cons, and I will do that in my own time."

"We're wasting *time*, boss," Smith said. "We need to do this now."

"Before we even think about using drastic measures," DI Smyth said. "I want to go back to the beginning. You've said yourself that there is something we've missed along the line, and I agree. There is something on there that we haven't spotted yet."

He nodded to the whiteboard at the back of the room.

Smith walked over to it again. "I'll be seeing this bastard in my sleep."

"We'll go through it chronologically," DI Smyth said.

"Janet Downing was killed first," Smith said.

The date of her murder was written on the board opposite her name.

"Thursday the 23rd," Smith said. "We believe that her murder was precipitated by the death of Brian North. Janet was driving the car that resulted in him ending up in a wheelchair. Brian died two weeks before Janet's murder."

"Harriet Jordan was next," DC King said. "She was killed later the same day."

"Harriet's murder was the result of her adultery," Smith said. "I for one believe that her punishment was a bit harsh, but who knows what goes through the head of someone who's been betrayed time and time again. Tom Lowe was thrown from the hotel window the next day. We initially thought that the catalyst for his murder was the suicide of John Gordon. John took a leap from the hotel in Leeds two weeks earlier, but we also know that he wasn't alone in the hotel room. I'm not seeing anything different here."

"Mary Lions and Annie Drew were killed later that day," Bridge carried on. "Soon after the fire that Mary started, both of them were slain at home."

"I'm convinced that Mary ordered the hit on Annie," Smith said. "She got cold feet and started the fire to prevent the murder from going ahead. She failed to read the small print in the contract and that cost her dearly."

"She organised the hit because she caught her fiancé with the stage manager two weeks ago," DC King said.

Smith turned around and smiled at her.

"Are you OK, Sarge?" she said.

"Two weeks," Smith said.

He tapped the board next to Janet Downing.

"Two weeks."

He repeated the process with Tom Lowe, Mary Lions and Annie Drew.

"Two fucking weeks. All of the hits were taken out in the space of a couple of days. The catalysts for three of the assassinations occurred two weeks ago."

"It's a feasible connection," Whitton said. "But what does it tell us, apart from the timescale involved?"

"I think this Graveyard thing is new," Smith said. "Two weeks old to be more precise. And I think we've been looking at this whole thing upside down."

"Is your brain going to do one of its weird things again, Sarge?" DC Moore wondered.

"My brain is functioning perfectly well, Harry. I'm fully lucid. We've been working on the assumption that these people sought out the Graveyard site in order to get away with the murder of someone they hate, but what if The Graveyard was created to do precisely that?"

"Could you say that once more in plain English," Bridge said.

"It's a chicken and egg thing," Smith said. "Which one came first? I think one of our suspects not only made use of the services offered by the Graveyard – I'm now convinced that one of them was the person who created it."

CHAPTER FORTY NINE

"We need to act quickly, boss," Smith said.

He'd requested a one-on-one in DI Smyth's office.

"I don't think the Graveyard site is going to be active for much longer," he added.

"There is nothing to substantiate your theory," DI Smyth said.

"I'm convinced that one of our suspects designed that website," Smith said. "It all makes sense."

"You're the only one who believes that. There is no proof that this is the case."

"I don't need proof," Smith said. "The pieces of the puzzle are beginning to fit. One of them came up with an idea so brilliant, I have to admit, I take my hat off to them. It's genius when you think about it. You create a website that offers a service that is tailor made to your own requirements. You wait for someone else to make use of these services and you put phase two of the plan into action. You eliminate your prime target, using the skills of the hired gun. The police believe it to be an anonymous, untraceable website and we don't even consider that one of the people who hired the hitman could be involved in the site itself. You don't give a shit about the other victims – you get paid your fee, and when the time is right you eliminate your primary target and get away with it. It really is genius."

"I hate to poke holes in your theory," DI Smyth said. "But if what you're suggesting is fact, there are a number of variables you've failed to consider. If this is an elaborate plot to commit the perfect murder, it relies on someone else actually making use of the services you're offering. That part is beyond the control of the website designer."

"That's a minor detail," Smith said.

"It's a massive detail," DI Smyth said. "And why not just make use of one of the other contract killer sites on the Dark Web? You said it yourself that they're anonymous and untraceable. You're clutching at straws."

"I'm not," Smith insisted. "I'm onto something here, and I know for a fact that the Graveyard site is going to be shut down soon. The primary target has been taken out, and there's no reason for it to carry on. We need to strike now."

"It's not going to happen," DI Smyth said.

"You haven't even given it any thought."

"What you're suggesting is preposterous. You want to blow thousands of pounds on something that is riddled with risks. Based on a hunch."

"Is that a no then?" Smith said.

"Do you want me to put it in black and white for you? I'll write it in block capitals on the whiteboard in the small conference room if you like."

"I'm right about this," Smith said.

"The answer is no. Let's say this theory of yours is correct – who did you have in mind? Who do you think set up The Graveyard?"

"My money is on Catherine Gordon," Smith said without thinking.

"More holes," DI Smyth said. "We were working on the assumption that Mrs Gordon arranged the murder of Tom Lowe because of John Gordon's suicide, but we now believe that she had a hand in her husband's death. That theory is contradictory."

"Fuck it," Smith said. "I know I'm right."

"Knowing and being able to prove it are very different animals."

Smith nodded. "Thanks for listening."

He stood up and headed for the door.

"Don't do anything stupid, Smith," DI Smyth said.

"Wouldn't dream of it," Smith said without turning around.

He made his way to the small conference room and stood facing the whiteboard once more. His eyes were immediately drawn to Catherine Gordon's name, and he ran through the chain of events again. Catherine's husband had died after jumping from his hotel room. It was assumed that John's money worries had led to his self-termination, but now they knew that Catherine was in Leeds with him. That was the first question that Smith needed to ask himself.

"Why would Catherine kill her husband?"

The team hadn't discussed this, and Smith knew that they should have. If Catherine really did kill John, what was her motivation?

"Money is always a good place to start."

DC King came into the room.

"Am I interrupting something?"

"I'm having an internal debate, Kerry," Smith said. "But feel free to join in. Why would Catherine Gordon want her husband dead?"

"Insurance money?" DC King said.

"We haven't checked, have we?" Smith said. "No, that's not it."

"Why not?"

"Most insurance companies don't pay out in the event of a suicide."

"That's not true, Sarge," DC King said. "There's usually a clause that stipulates a period of time after the policy is taken out, but the majority of insurance companies will pay out for a death by suicide."

"But where does Tom Lowe come into the equation?" Smith said. "Why make it look like Tom's death was a revenge killing?"

"And if this was a simple case of murder for money," DC King said. "Why transfer Tom Lowe's money to a load of animal charities?"

"That part makes no sense whatsoever," Smith agreed. "What else?"

"Catherine isn't short of cash herself," DC King said. "She got rich with the Bitcoin boom. And if Tom wasn't really the reason for John's death, why kill him like that?"

Smith tapped the whiteboard a few times and closed his eyes. "Misdirection," he said a moment later. "Good old-fashioned sleight of hand. Catherine wanted us to look the other way while she carried out her plan."

"What *was* her plan?" DC King asked. "Did she kill her husband to cover up the murder of Tom Lowe or vice versa?"

"She could have wanted them both out of the way."

"Why?"

"Money," Smith said. "I think this really has been all about money. But we have nothing linking Catherine to either death right now, and without evidence we have no chance of gaining access to Catherine's financial affairs."

"Hold on," DC King said.

"That's my line," Smith told her.

"Bona vacantia," DC King said.

"That rings a bell."

"Roughly translated," DC King said. "It means *ownerless property*. When someone dies without any dependents, the estate is passed down to the Crown."

"But John Gordon was married," Smith pointed out. "His estate will pass to Catherine."

"I'm not talking about John, Sarge," DC King said. "Tom Lowe died *bona vacantia*, and therefore the details of his estate are bound by different rules."

"How do you know so much about the law?"

"I took a few modules at university."

"What does this mean in terms of the investigation?" Smith said.

"Mr Lowe's finances will be dealt with by the Crown," DC King said. "And it's possible we'll be able to access the details without having to go through the usual channels. I could be wrong."

"I still don't know how that will help us. It's Catherine Gordon's financial situation that we're interested in – not her husband's business partner."

"You've just hit the nail on the head, Sarge," DC King said. "Tom Lowe was John's business partner. It's possible that the answers we're looking for are somewhere in the fine print of Tom's assets."

CHAPTER FIFTY

It took over an hour for Smith to get hold of someone who might be able to help him with the details of what Tom Lowe left behind when he died, but the friendly man on the other end of the phone informed him that he wouldn't be able to get an appointment until tomorrow. Smith didn't want to wait, but it couldn't be helped so he set up a meeting with a woman called Deirdre Southern. She was Tom Lowe's lawyer, and she told Smith that she could spare an hour in the morning.

Smith had no option but to wait to see what mysteries were contained in Tom Lowe's finances. In the meantime, he needed to do something to occupy his time. The rest of the team had been tasked with delving deeper into the lives of the victims. DI Smyth was convinced that there were a number of things they'd overlooked and Whitton, Bridge and the DCs King and Moore were speaking to everyone connected to the victims again.

Smith had other things on his mind. He was convinced that the murders of John Gordon and Tom Lowe were at the heart of the investigation, and he managed to find a man who might be able to shed some light on the nature of the relationship between the two men. Ian Crow was listed on the LG website as the operations manager. Smith had no idea what that meant, but Ian's name was listed directly below John's and Tom's so he reckoned he must be someone important in the company. Ian was happy to talk. He suggested they meet at a coffee shop in the city centre, and Smith didn't have a problem with that.

There were only two people in the coffee shop on Walmgate when Smith went inside. One of them was a woman so he assumed the other customer was Ian Crow, and when the man stood up as he approached the table his assumptions were proved correct.

"DS Smith."

Ian was a thin man with a friendly face. He looked to be in his mid-thirties and Smith thought he looked open and honest.

"Ian," Smith said. "Thanks for agreeing to meet."

"Sorry about this place," Ian said. "It serves my favourite coffee, and I didn't want to talk at home. I have three kids – all girls, all under five and trying to have a conversation with them around is impossible."

"I know what you mean," Smith said. "I've got three girls too."

"You really have to try the Pumpkin Spice here," Ian said. "Believe me, it sounds worse than it is."

"I'll stick with a normal coffee, thanks," Smith said. "I'm not very adventurous."

They ordered the drinks and Smith got down to business.

"You work for LG Web Design," he said.

"I'm not really sure what's going to happen now," Ian said. "We're all still in shock. First John and now Tom."

"How long have you worked for them?"

"Seven years."

"What exactly does the company do?" Smith asked. "Mrs Gordon explained it, but I'm not too clued up on technology."

"We offer world class web design to big corporations," Ian said. "It's a common belief that anyone can find a template on the Net and have a website done in an hour, but there's a lot more to it than that. LG takes it to another level. We don't just match the client to the site – we get inside the heart of the company they want to promote."

"That must be a lot of work."

"That's an understatement. Before we even begin with the design itself, we familiarise ourselves with the nature of the business. By the time we have the finished product ready to go live, the people at LG are probably qualified to work for the clients we represent. We offer twenty-four-seven after sales service, and nothing is too much to ask. I remember once, John dropped everything and booked a last-minute flight to Shanghai because a client preferred to discuss things face-to-face. There was nothing to discuss. When John arrived in China, he was presented with a case of single malt as a thank you for the incredible service."

"That must have annoyed him a bit," Smith said.

"Not at all," Ian said. "You need to understand that the clients on our books are not your average businesses. Most of them are listed companies, and the fees we charge justify a bit of inconvenience once in a while."

The drinks arrived and the conversation was paused for a while. Smith took a sip of his coffee and savoured the flavour. It really was good coffee. "What is it you do at the company?" he asked.

"I oversee the operations," Ian said. "My background is in IT, and I make sure the finished product is as polished as it's possible to get it."

"Did you work closely with John and Tom?"

"Sometimes," Ian said. "We have monthly progress meetings to discuss new possibilities and ongoing projects, but mostly I'm left to my own devices."

"Who takes care of the financial side of the business?"

"Even though LG has a turnover in the high eight figures, the personnel is relatively small. John was the CEO and Tom was the CFO. I still can't believe it. You must think me terribly cold – already I'm referring to them in the past tense."

"It's OK," Smith said.

"What really happened to them?" Ian said.

"What do you think happened?" Smith said.

"John committed suicide. And Tom was murdered. That's what the papers are saying anyway."

"You said Tom was the CFO," Smith said. "He dealt with the financial side of the business then?"

"His background was in finance," Ian said. "John was more hand's on with the web design aspect."

"Were you surprised when John announced that he wanted out?" Smith said.

"That's the first I've heard of it."

"John Gordon offered his share of the business to Tom Lowe," Smith said. "And, according to Catherine Gordon, John was ripped off in the process."

"I very much doubt that."

"It happened a few weeks ago," Smith said. "John failed to read the small print – Tom got the business and John walked away with next to nothing."

Ian took a drink of his pumpkin coffee and Smith was forced to look away. He couldn't think of anything more unpleasant than pumpkin flavoured coffee.

"What you're suggesting is impossible," Ian said.

"Go on."

"John and Tom weren't just business partners, they were friends. Tom would never rip him off."

"Catherine believes otherwise," Smith said. "She believes the deal went south and when there was nothing legally, they could do about it, John decided to end his own life."

"Have you corroborated Catherine's claim?" Ian said.

Smith realised that they hadn't, and he cursed himself. They'd taken Catherine's word for it, and in hindsight that was a really stupid thing to do.

"Why do you think John took his own life?" he asked.

"It came as a blow to all of us," Ian said.

"You didn't see it coming?"

"Not in a million years."

"And you didn't know that John was thinking of retiring?"

"He wouldn't have kept something like that to himself. Even though he was the CEO of the company, he didn't keep secrets. What transpired in the boardroom soon made its way down to the rest of the workforce. John was a good bloke."

"What about Tom Lowe?" Smith said.

"He was a bit of a rogue," Ian said. "He liked the rock 'n roll lifestyle, but he was a lovable rogue. You've got it all wrong about the dodgy deal."

Smith thought so too, and he was annoyed with himself for believing the words of the woman whom he was now convinced was at the heart of the investigation.

CHAPTER FIFTY ONE

"Catherine Gordon was telling the truth."
DC King's words weren't the words that Smith wanted to hear. After the meeting with Ian Crow, Smith had asked her to contact John Gordon's lawyer. A two-minute conversation with a rather grumpy man confirmed that John Gordon had indeed sold his share of the company to Tom Lowe. John's lawyer had refused to discuss the details, but Smith was convinced he would get more from Tom Lowe's legal representative when he met her tomorrow.

"What the hell is going on here?" Smith said. "If Catherine was telling us the truth, where does it leave us?"
"I don't have an answer to that," DC King said.
"I know she killed them both, Kerry. Or at least, she had a hand in their deaths, but why? What did she stand to gain from it?"
"Not money," DC King said. "If John sold the company for next to nothing, he had nothing to leave her."
"Did you find out about any insurance policies?"
"Harry is looking into it," DC King said. "But so far, he hasn't been able to unearth any policies. This isn't about money, is it?"
"I haven't a fucking clue about what it's about anymore. I need a smoke."

He didn't even make it to the front desk. DI Smyth caught up with him.
"You're off the hook in the professor thing."
"That was quick," Smith said.
"There wasn't much to investigate. I didn't expect it to go any further."
"I got away with it then."
"Keep your damn voice down," DI Smyth said.
"Relax, boss. Nobody can hear me."
"Take this as a sign," DI Smyth said. "You got away with it this time, but you might not be so lucky next time, so make sure there isn't a next time."

"About that..."

"I've already told you, the answer is no," DI Smyth said. "We are not going to hire a hitman. Not now, not ever."

"Fair enough. Permission to have a smoke?"

"Will you quit with this *permission to have a smoke* nonsense?"

"I'll take that as a yes then," Smith said.

He went outside and lit a cigarette. The sky overhead was grey and drops of rain were starting to fall. The weather reflected Smith's mood beautifully. They'd reached a brick wall in the investigation, and he wasn't sure how they were going to break it down. He couldn't think of a way forward and it irritated him. He knew he should be relieved about the outcome of the disciplinary hearing, but he couldn't really care less about it.

The rain stopped suddenly, and a patch of blue sky appeared. Smith took a long drag of his cigarette and exhaled a cloud of smoke.

"Fuck it," he said.

He took out his phone and brought up Barry Stone's number. The IT man answered immediately.

"Barry," Smith said. "How do I convert hard cash to that techno money?"

"Cryptocurrency," Barry corrected. "It's pretty simple."

"Your idea of simple is worlds away from mine where technology is concerned."

"I can help you. What have you got in mind?"

"Something that's probably going to cost me my job, my marriage and my liberty," Smith said.

"That doesn't sound good," Barry said.

"No," Smith said. "It sounds fucking terrible, but I'm running out of ideas."

"Pop round," Barry said. "And I'll see if I can come up with some more attractive alternatives."

"Thanks, Barry," Smith said. "I'll be there in ten minutes."

He finished the cigarette and headed for his car. He got inside and closed the door. He found the banking app on his phone and logged in. After getting a bit lost, he managed to navigate to his savings account. According to the screen of the phone the current balance in this account was just over thirty thousand pounds. The account hadn't been touched for quite some time, and Smith wondered if Whitton had forgotten all about it.

The money had come from an inheritance he hadn't expected to receive. When the old Head of Pathology, Paul *The Ghoul* Johnson had been killed by a car bomb he'd surprised everybody with the contents of his Will. Smith and a few others had inherited a substantial amount of money, and Smith hadn't spent much of his share, even though it had been in his account for more than ten years. He closed the app and sighed. This could end badly. He wasn't sure if he was about to make the worst mistake of his life, and he made up his mind to decide one way or the other during the short drive to Barry Stone's house.

He arrived at the house fifteen minutes later. He'd taken his time getting there, and by the time he'd switched off the engine his mind was made up. It was extremely risky, but it was a risk he was willing to take. He got out of the car, lit another cigarette and he realised that he'd become a chain smoker. He made a mental note to try and cut down a bit when the investigation was over. A terrible thought occurred to him. He wondered if inmates were allowed to smoke in prison. He quickly put the thought out of his mind.

His phone started to ring when he was halfway through the cigarette. The ringtone told him that it wasn't anyone at work and when he looked at the screen, he saw that it wasn't a number stored in his contacts.

"Smith," he answered it.

"DS Smith," a man said. "My name is David Platt. We spoke earlier about Tom Lowe."

"Go on," Smith said.

"You have an appointment with Mrs Southern tomorrow," David said.

"Please don't tell me that she can't make it? It's extremely important that I speak to her."

"Then you'll be glad to hear that Mrs Southern can fit you in this afternoon. Does two-thirty work for you?"

"What time is it now?" Smith asked and realised how ridiculous the question was.

"Just after one," David replied anyway.

"I'll be there," Smith said. "Where do I meet her? Are your offices even open?"

"Of course. I'll ping you the location."

"You'll do what?"

"The GPS location."

"Can you just give me the address?" Smith said. "Me and technology don't really get on."

David gave it to him. Smith thanked him and rang off. As he stood outside Barry Stone's house he wondered again if he was about to make the biggest mistake of his life.

CHAPTER FIFTY TWO

"Come on up," Barry said.

Smith followed him upstairs. There was a strange smell inside the house. Smith knew the pungent, peppery odour very well.

"Have you been smoking weed?" he asked Barry inside his office.

"Do you want some?" Barry said.

Smith laughed. "That chapter of my life is ancient history. Do I need to remind you that I'm a police officer?"

"You're not going to arrest me while you're in the process of carrying out something far more illegal than a bit of weed. The dope helps me to think. I've been trying to find your Graveyard again and it's proving to be problematic. I think the site has been taken down."

"I was worried about that," Smith said. "Although if it has, it'll probably save me a lot of heartache. Is there any way to know for certain?"

"Unfortunately, not. The active sites leave very little trace when they're shut down on a computer, and the ones that are no longer live don't even cast a shadow on the ground of the Dark Web. Although shadows are rarely seen in the dark, are they?"

"How much weed have you had?" Smith said.

"Not much," Barry said. "It's good shit though. Are you sure you don't want some? Just a little toke."

"I'm good thanks," Smith said.

"It took me a while to get in last time," Barry said. "But I really get the feeling that it's been taken down."

"How long are we talking about if it is still live?" Smith said. "To gain access, I mean?"

"How long is an Eskimo's todger?" Barry said. "It all depends, doesn't it?"

"I'm not even going to answer that. I have an appointment at half-two."

Barry glanced at the clock at the bottom of one of the screens. "That's in an hour. I don't think we'll be done by then, even if I do manage to find the website. Get to your appointment and I'll give you a call if I do manage to find your Graveyard."

"Thanks, Barry," Smith said. "And could you do me a favour?"

"Of course."

"Could you stop referring to it as my Graveyard?" Smith said. "It gives me the creeps when you do that."

* * *

Deidre Southern was a grey-haired woman in her mid-fifties. She invited Smith into her office and informed him she only had an hour to spare. Smith told her that an hour was all he needed.

"I'm here by myself," she added. "So don't be offended if I don't offer you anything to drink."

"I've not long had a cup of coffee," Smith said. "What can you tell me about Tom Lowe's estate?"

"Mr Lowe died with no dependents," Deirdre said.

"Bona vacantia," Smith said.

"You know something of the law?"

"Bits and pieces," Smith said. "I believe his estate will be handed to the Crown."

"Eventually. These things take time."

"Why's that?"

"Before an estate can be taken over by the Crown, it needs to be absolutely certain that there are no dependents lurking somewhere. Mr Lowe wasn't married, he had no brothers or sisters, but there could be some long-lost cousin somewhere who may decide to lay a claim to his assets."

"Is that likely to happen?" Smith asked.

"You can never tell."

"Did you deal with the sale of the company that Tom co-owned with John Gordon?" Smith got to the real reason he was there.

"I did," Deidre confirmed.

"Can you talk about it?"

"I don't see why not. It was rather unorthodox."

"In what way?"

"LG Web Design turned over millions," Deirdre said. "It should have been sold for considerably more than it was."

"I believe the deal was kosher," Smith said. "In accordance with the law."

"Kosher is not a term we tend to use in the legal world, but yes, everything was above board."

"How much did John Gordon get out of the deal?" Smith said.

"I'm not quite sure about the exact details."

"Could you dig out the contract for me?" Smith said. "It's really important that I see it."

Deirdre got up and left the room without explanation.

She returned a few minutes later with a file under her arm.

"I'm not at liberty to offer you a copy of this," she said. "But you're welcome to peruse it while you're here."

"Thanks," Smith said. "I really appreciate it."

"It's a standard contract," Deirdre said. "With some drastic differences. Could you excuse me? I need to make a couple of private phone calls."

"No worries," Smith said.

He opened the file and skim-read the first couple of pages. It did appear to be a stock standard contract. The wording could have been better, but Smith expected nothing else. He could never understand why these kinds of things had to be written in legalese. It was indecipherable to mere mortals, and he could understand why people like John Gordon got ripped off along the way.

He was shocked to see the asking price for a business that turned over millions. John Gordon had started the company from scratch – he'd given it ten years of service, and he walked away with four-hundred pounds. Smith wondered how Tom Lowe had managed to get away with it. Catherine Gordon had mentioned something about Tom plying John with whiskey before the contract was signed, but Smith didn't buy that. There was something really wrong with this contract, and he didn't know what to make of it.

Deirdre Southern came back inside the office.

"Can I ask you something?" Smith said.

"Please make it quick."

"Do you know who represents LG Web Design? In a legal capacity, I mean."

"You're looking at her," Deirdre said.

"You're LG's lawyer?"

"Is that a problem?"

"Doesn't that constitute a conflict of interests?" Smith said. "If you represent LG and Tom Lowe, I mean?"

"Not at all."

"But you're not John Gordon's lawyer?" Smith said. "In a personal capacity."

"No. Where are you going with this?"

"Can I ask you one more thing?" Smith said. "And I'll let you get back to work."

"I suppose so."

"Did John and Tom have some kind of business contract? Surely, they must have signed an agreement when they set up the company."

"Of course."

"Can I see it?"

"I don't know…"

"Please," Smith cut her short. "I promise I'll get out of your hair as soon as I've taken a look."

"It's rather complicated," Deirdre said. "If I recall, the business contract between Mr Lowe and John Gordon is some fifty pages long."

"I wouldn't ask if it wasn't important," Smith said.

Deirdre sighed deeply. "Give me your email address."

Smith whipped out one of his cards before she had the chance to change her mind.

"Could you send it through today please?" he said.

Deirdre nodded. "You're a persistent man, DS Smith."

"It's one of my better traits," Smith said.

"I'd hate to know what the bad ones are. I'll email the contract to you immediately."

"Thank you," Smith said. "I have to say this – you're probably the nicest lawyer I've ever met, and I've had the pleasure of dealing with a lot of them. I won't take up any more of your time."

CHAPTER FIFTY THREE

Found it.

Barry Stone's two-word message filled Smith with mixed emotions. He was relieved that the Graveyard site was still live, but he had secretly wished that the cursed website had disappeared into whatever black hole devoured the deleted sites on the Internet. He realised that he still had a choice about how to proceed, but he couldn't see any other way forward. If he took out a contract on the hitman site it could cost him everything, but it could also lead him to the people behind the recent murders.

"Are you sure about this?" Barry asked him on the doorstep.

"No," Smith admitted. "It's highly likely that things could go tit's up, but there's also a strong possibility that this could help us catch these bastards."

"You're a braver man than me, Jason Smith. Come on then."

They went upstairs and Barry woke up his laptop. The now familiar home screen of The Graveyard website stared at Smith from all seven screens on the wall. Barry tapped the keypad on one of the other laptops and the screen in the centre changed. He clicked a few times, and his fingers flew across the keyboard so quickly that Smith couldn't see what he'd typed.

"What is this?" he asked.

"Just checking that I can afford it," Barry said.

"Afford what?"

"Don't worry about that."

Smith glanced at the screen.

"I can't let you pay for this," he said when he realised what he was looking at.

"You can pay me back sometime," Barry told him.

"I've got the cash in my savings account."

"Therein lies the problem," Barry explained. "This Graveyard thing isn't child's play. Whoever designed this site knows a hell of a lot more than you think. They will know where the money is coming from – it's in their best interests to know, and they will smell a rat immediately if you make the payment. Let me do this. Consider it me performing my civic duty. I've got a good few grand in Bitcoin, and I'm not short of a few bob."

"There is something else I want you to do for me," Smith said.

"You're pushing your luck now, mate," Barry said.

"I thought about it on the drive over," Smith said. "I was planning on having one of my DCs play the part of the client, but it's too risky. The person I believe to be behind this has met DC King, and it's possible they'll be watching. We need someone unknown. Will you do it?"

"Why not?" Barry said. "I'm paying for it so I might as well get my money's worth."

"It could be dangerous," Smith warned. "I have to tell you that."

"What's the worst that can happen? I won't be alone, will I? I'll have you lot watching me the whole time."

Smith remained silent.

"Won't I?" Barry said.

"This hasn't exactly been authorised," Smith said. "But I'll make absolutely sure that you're safe. I promise."

Barry leaned over and picked a half-smoked joint out of an ashtray. He lit the end and took a long drag. The cloud of smoke he exhaled made Smith cough.

"Who do we want dead?" Barry said.

"What?"

"I'm kidding," Barry said. "But we need a target, don't we? Is there anyone you really don't like? That was also a joke, by the way. But if this is to appear genuine, we need a genuine target."

"I might have someone in mind," Smith said.

He'd also thought about this on the way to Barry's house. Something about the appointment with Tom Lowe's lawyer had sounded some warning bells. And when the email came through and Smith had stopped the car so he could read it, those warning bells had increased in volume. He'd been wrong about a lot of things during the course of the investigation, but he didn't think he was barking up the wrong tree now.

Twenty minutes later, the deal with the devil had been done. According to the instructions on the screen once the payment had been made, Barry would be contacted within two days. There was no indication of how he would be contacted, but he was assured that contact would be made, and further instructions would follow.

"They didn't even want to know how I wanted it to be carried out," Barry said.

"I think that comes later," Smith said.

"I don't think I'm going to get much sleep tonight."

"Smoke some more weed," Smith advised. "It always used to help me sleep."

"I never had you pegged as a dope fiend."

"I wasn't a dope fiend," Smith said. "I gave up drinking for a while and it was a half-decent alternative."

"Besides the illegal bit," Barry said.

"That was a bit problematic," Smith admitted. "Thanks for doing this."

"It does you good to live a little once in a while. Are you sure you won't have a wee toke on the joint? I can make up a bong if you prefer."

"Definitely not," Smith said. "Let me know as soon as these people make contact, and we'll take it from there."

"That doesn't exactly fill me with confidence. Are you going to let your bosses know about this, or are we working alone?"

"I haven't decided yet," Smith said. "I let you know when I've figured it out."

"Rupert reckons you say that too much."

"Rupert is probably right," Smith said. "I'll speak to you soon."

He made up his mind before he'd even opened the door of his car. He couldn't do this alone – he needed to involve the rest of the team, and he wasn't looking forward to giving DI Smyth the news.

CHAPTER FIFTY FOUR

The team were in the middle of a briefing when Smith made an appearance. He decided not to bring up the topic of the contract he and Barry Stone had taken out. Now wasn't the ideal time.

"Where have you been?" DI Smyth asked.

"I had an appointment with Tom Lowe's lawyer," Smith said.

At least this was the truth.

"What have I missed?" he asked.

It didn't take long for DI Smyth to tell him. The team had revisited the friends and relatives of the victims and nothing new had come to light.

"Me and Kerry paid a visit to Callum North," Whitton said. "And we had the pleasure of meeting his mother."

"And?" Smith said.

"She wasn't what I was expecting," Whitton said. "I imagined her as a frail old lady, but she's anything but."

"I thought as much."

"She didn't come across as a grieving widow," DC King said. "In fact, I think she's relieved to be rid of the burden of caring for her husband."

"It happens," Smith said. "Did they let anything slip?"

DC King frowned and remained silent, and Smith took that as a reply in the negative.

"I found out something interesting from Tom Lowe's lawyer," he said.

"You got info from a lawyer?" DC Moore said.

"She was a lovely woman, and she gave me a copy of the contract that Tom Lowe and John Gordon had drawn up when they started the company. It's a novel of a contract, but there was something in amongst the drivel of legalese that caught my eye. It was the bit that dealt with what happens in the event of one or both partners kicking the bucket."

"I like the sound of this," DI Smyth said.

"The contract stipulates that, in the event of John Gordon's death, his share of the company will go to his wife Catherine. It's standard procedure and I imagine it will be in John's private Will too. But Tom Lowe had no dependents and as such, his share of the company will automatically go to John if he dies. And this is where it gets interesting."

"What happens in the event of both of them dying?" DC Moore said.

"If you'd let me finish," Smith said. "As things stood at the time of John Gordon's death, Catherine wouldn't get anything from LG Web Design because John had recently sold it to Tom."

"For peanuts," Bridge said.

"Four hundred quid," Smith elaborated. "I got that out of the lawyer too, but that's not important. Like I said, as things stood when John fell to his death, Catherine wouldn't get a penny out of the company."

"But..." It was DC King.

Smith grinned at her. "But Tom's death changed things. The purchase offer that was drawn up for the sale of the company was time bound. To simplify it, it means the deal wouldn't actually come into effect until three weeks had passed after the signing of the contract."

"Why do that?" DC Moore said.

"I don't know, Harry," Smith said. "Perhaps it's to give the respective legal representatives time to finalise all the details."

"Catherine Gordon is going to get the company, isn't she?" Whitton said.

"She most certainly is," Smith said. "The three weeks weren't up when Tom Lowe was murdered, and as such, Tom's share of the company will be transferred to John Gordon, or in this instance, his estate. And Catherine will inherit the lot."

"This is insane," DC Moore said.

"And extremely clever," Smith said. "Catherine knew about the time clause in the sale contract, and she acted just before that clause expired."

"Money," DI Smyth said. "It's always about money. Mrs Gordon didn't care about donating Tom Lowe's millions to charity – she was due to inherit five times that in the form of the company."

"And Catherine wouldn't have been able to get her hands on Tom Lowe's personal assets anyway," Smith pointed out. "So, it was nothing to her to give it all away."

"Do you still believe she was the one behind the Graveyard website?" DI Smyth said.

"Without a shadow of a doubt," Smith said. "But we're not going to be able to find any proof of it."

"Why are you smiling then?" Whitton said.

"I'm not smiling."

"You're grinning like a moron. You've just told us that we won't find proof of Catherine's involvement in The Graveyard, and you've got a face like a kid who's just got a new bike."

"I might have found a way around this problem," Smith said.

"Let's hear it then," DI Smyth said.

"Before I start, I need you to consider this with open minds."

"Why do I already not like the sound of this?" DI Smyth said.

"You know me, boss."

"That's what concerns me."

"Just hear me out," Smith said. "As far as I can see it, the only way we're going to get anywhere near the professional killer and the host of the Graveyard website is if we make use of their services."

"Absolutely not," DI Smyth said. "This topic of conversation is closed. How do I get that through your thick skull?"

"It's too late, boss," Smith said. "I've already set things in motion. The contract has been signed, and the money has been paid."

The small conference room fell silent for quite some time.

Whitton was the first to speak.

"What money? You didn't pay for this yourself, did you?"

"Just listen," Smith said.

"Did you use the money in our savings account?"

"I didn't think you knew about that."

"Of course, I bloody know about it," Whitton said. "Please tell me you didn't do that."

"I didn't do that," Smith said. "It doesn't matter where the cash came from. This is happening."

"When is it happening?" DI Smyth asked after another moment of silence had passed.

"Soon. We'll be contacted in the next couple of days and the who, where and when will be sorted out then."

"Just exactly *who* are we talking about?" DI Smyth said.

"Catherine Gordon."

"Are you insane?" DC Moore said.

"It has crossed my mind on the odd occasion, Harry," Smith said. "Catherine Gordon is the perfect target."

"Are you forgetting that she's the one in charge of the Graveyard?" Bridge said.

"No. And that's the beauty of it. She won't be expecting it. The bloke she's hired doesn't know who she is. Everything that's happened has taken place anonymously – under the cloak of the Dark Web, and this way we get the puppet and the puppet master in the same place at the same time. We're going to use the anonymity that Catherine's relied upon to catch her."

CHAPTER FIFTY FIVE

Barry Stone received the phone the next day. It was a prepaid mobile and it was lying on the mat below the letterbox. Barry assumed that someone had posted it during the night. When he brought it to life, he realised that it wasn't password protected, and it didn't require a fingerprint to access it. The message icon was flashing and when Barry opened the message, he saw that it consisted of nothing but a pin location. Barry took out his own phone and took a photograph of the location. This was sent straight to Smith.

The prepaid phone beeped, and Barry jumped. This message contained text. The instructions were clear – he was to use the GPS on the phone to go to the location he'd been sent. He was to come alone, and he was told not to bring anything with him. No phones, tablets, not even his wallet. He would receive further instructions soon. Barry took a photo of this too and forwarded it to Smith. The reply came soon afterwards and consisted of just two words.

Stand by.

Barry had never felt so scared in his life. He'd ventured deep into the depths of the Dark Web many times but that was all done in the comfort of his home, without any danger to himself. But now he felt exposed. He was going to follow the instructions of a complete stranger, and even though he'd paid a lot of money to this stranger, he still felt extremely nervous. What if it was a trap? What if they were onto the fact that this was a set up? Smith had assured him that he wouldn't be alone. He wouldn't be aware of them, but they would be there, nonetheless.

Another message had arrived on Barry's phone. It was from Smith again, telling him that everything was in place and he was to do exactly what he was told. They would be there with him every step of the way. Barry hoped to God that Smith was true to his word.

* * *

"This is in the middle of nowhere," DC Moore tapped the screen of his tablet.

"That was the pin location Barry was given," Smith said.

"Are you sure?"

"Of course I'm sure," Smith said. "He sent me a screenshot of the pin location."

"Where is it exactly?" DI Smyth said.

"About a mile west of Holtby," DC Moore said. "There's nothing around there but fields."

"And graveyards," Smith said.

"What?" DC Moore said.

"Just thinking out loud. That's where Barry has been told to go, so that's where he has to go. We can keep an eye on him from a hidden location, close by."

"According to the map," DC Moore said. "There's no cover for miles around there. It's going to be tricky to track him without being seen."

"I don't think anyone will be watching," Smith said.

"Are you sure there won't be people keeping an eye on him?" Bridge asked.

"I don't think there will be. I get the impression that the only ones involved in all of this are Catherine Gordon and the man she hired to carry out the murders. The fewer people who know what's going on, the better. Show me that map again."

DC Moore handed him the tablet. He wasn't lying when he'd told them that there was nothing but fields for miles and Smith wondered if The Graveyard was located in one of these fields.

"I don't like this," he said.

"Now you tell us," DI Smyth said. "You were the one who decided to put a civilian at risk. If anything goes wrong, that business with the professor is going to seem like a walk in the park."

"Is there still time to call it off?" Whitton said.

Smith shook his head. "It's too late for that. You saw what happened to Mary Lions when she tried to interfere."

"What if the pin location isn't the final destination?" DC King said. "What then?"

"Then we'll have to come up with a change of plan," Smith said.

"Barry has no way of contacting us," Bridge said. "If anything happens to him, I will never forgive you."

"Nothing is going to happen to him," Smith assured him. "If he carries out his part of the plan, he'll be fine. If the pin location he's been sent is a test of sorts, there's nothing we can do about it. This is just phase one of the plot – the crucial part comes later."

"What do we do in the meantime?" DC Moore wondered.

"We wait. Barry won't let us down. He knows what he's doing."

* * *

Barry Stone had no idea what he was doing. He knew he was out of his depth, and he was starting to feel sick. The voice on the GPS informed him that his destination was seven hundred metres away, and when Barry glanced at the screen he couldn't figure out what that destination actually was. The terrain around Holtby consisted of nothing but abandoned fields. The whole area was deserted and that only served to intensify the feeling of unease.

Barry slowed down when the GPS told him his destination was coming up on the right. He stopped the car next to a narrow dirt path and switched off the engine. There was nothing here, and he wondered if he'd been lured into a trap. He'd opened the door to get out of the car when the prepaid phone beeped. It was another pin location. Barry recalled the instructions in the contract he'd signed. He was to come alone, and he was to bring nothing with him, not even his wallet.

He got out of the car and started to walk down the dirt road. The GPS told him that his destination was just under a mile away. Barry stopped and took a look around. The fields were brown and dead. Nothing would grow here for a good few months. Barry wondered if anything had ever grown there. It really was a desolate place.

The barn looked disused too. It was the only structure for miles, and it had a derelict feeling about it. Behind the barn was a field that looked like it had been ploughed. There were no vehicles anywhere, and Barry wondered what he was walking into. Once again, he sensed that something was terribly wrong.

The figured appeared from nowhere. The man was tall, and he wasn't very old.

"Follow me."

Barry didn't have much choice. The man walked over to the barn and Barry followed him inside.

He was handed a wooden box, and the man tore a piece of paper from an A4 pad.

"Answer all the questions carefully."

Barry recognised the accent. It was more obvious than Smith's, but it was unmistakably Australian.

"We can only do what you want if you fill in the form precisely. Once you've done that, go to the field behind the barn. Place the box in the hole that has been prepared. Only one hole has been dug. Do not look at the other graves in the graveyard, and make sure the box is locked. Please leave the phone on the desk."

With that, he left Barry alone inside the barn.

It took him fifteen minutes to complete the questionnaire. His hands were shaking, and it wasn't as a result of the biting cold. The words he was putting onto the page were disturbing, and it felt terribly wrong. He did as he'd been instructed and placed the paper in the box. The lock was a combination type, and Barry made sure it was definitely locked.

He went back outside and headed for the ploughed field. He wondered if this was The Graveyard, and the thought made him shiver. He spotted the hole in the dirt. There was a row of mounds next to it. Each of them was marked with an inverted cross and Barry couldn't help staring at them. There were no names on the crosses.

He placed the box in the hole and kicked some dirt on top of it. He needed to get out of there and he needed to do it quickly. He turned around, walked past the barn and rejoined the track. He'd only managed a few steps when he felt hands on his shoulders. The grip was incredible. Barry wondered if this was it. Was this where it all ended, in a barren field in the middle of nowhere?

He was spun round to face the Australian man. He realised that he'd pissed himself. The warm patch spread from his crotch and down his leg. It cooled quickly in the icy air, and Barry looked into the face of the hired killer.

"You forgot to leave the phone behind."

The man held out his hand.

"Phone please," he added when Barry didn't respond.

Barry gave it to him and headed back to his car as quickly as possible. He caught a whiff of the urine on his jeans as he walked.

CHAPTER FIFTY SIX

Smith knocked on the door of the house in Knavesmire and rubbed his hands together. A cold front had crept down from Scandinavia and the air was bitterly cold. The door opened and Catherine Gordon looked him up and down.

"What do you want?"

"Can I come in?" Smith said. "I have something important to tell you."

"I've said all I have to say," Catherine told him.

"You're going to want to hear this," Smith said. "It's in your best interests to listen to what I have to say. Come on, it's freezing out here."

"Make it quick," Catherine said. "I have a meeting with my lawyer in a couple of hours."

"This won't take long," Smith said.

Catherine opened the door wider, and Smith followed her to the living room. He sat down without being asked. There was a laptop on a desk against the wall. Attached to it were a number of devices that Smith didn't recognise.

"What is this all about?" she said. "I thought we'd already established the facts."

"Not at all," Smith said. "We haven't established anything."

"What's so important that you came all the way over here to tell me?"

"All in good time," Smith said. "I'll tell you what it is, but first you're going to tell me everything about The Graveyard."

"You really are delusional," Catherine said.

"You're going to tell me everything, and you're going to do it on tape."

He emphasised this by placing a small recording device on the coffee table.

It had been four days since the worst few hours of Barry Stone's life. The deal had been done, and the details of the contract had been buried in The

Graveyard. Barry's part in it was over, but there was still a long way to go for Smith and the team. The instructions that Barry had written on the questionnaire included the time and the place that the murder was to be carried out. It was going to take place in less than an hour.

"As I mentioned already," Smith said. "You're going to give me every little detail about The Graveyard."

"I have no idea what you're talking about," Catherine said.

"Then I'll give you a bit of help, shall I? Hold on – I almost forgot."

He switched on the tape recorder.

"Can you confirm for the record that you're aware that this conversation is being recorded?"

"This is ridiculous."

"Please," Smith said. "Just humour me."

"I am aware that we're being recorded," Catherine said.

"I've always believed that a decent story needs to have a bit of background to it," Smith said. "It gives it a certain context that way – adds a bit of meat to the bones. This particular story starts with a deal that didn't exactly go to plan. Was John in the habit of making blunders like the one he made with the contract for the sale of the company?"

"It's your story," Catherine said. "You tell me."

"I don't think he was. I think you had a hand in it. That's not important though. The deal was done, and the company was sold for no more than the average weekly wage. John lost everything, and you, by association, did too. But there's a twist in the tale already, isn't there? The time-bound clause in the contract meant you had a bit of breathing space to come up with a plan. You had three weeks to get John out of the picture, and you came up with the idea for The Graveyard."

"Is this going to take much longer?" Catherine said. "I'm running out of time."

"You certainly are," Smith said. "In more ways than one.

"Could you please get to the point," Catherine said.

"Once you helped John out of the window in Leeds," Smith said. "You created The Graveyard and contacted a pro to carry out the dirty work. And please don't deny that you were in Leeds that day – we have a reliable witness who can put you there. You set up the contract killer site and you waited. It didn't take long – pretty soon you had some interested parties. That's when you realised that you were probably going to get away with it. There was no contact between you and the killer – the cash that changed hands was untraceable and the details of the murders were given out in an isolated field that nobody would even think about digging up. You get your hands on the company, and you get a few quid for the hits into the bargain. Would you care to tell me about it on the tape?"

"You've got no proof that any of what you've just said ever happened," Catherine said.

Smith took out his phone and checked the time on the screen, "You've got twenty-six minutes."

"I have no idea what you're talking about," Catherine said.

"On Sunday, another contract was signed, wasn't it? You received the money, and you paid your hired gun his share. But and this is a huge but – you had no idea who the target was. That was all part of the plan. Absolute anonymity. But in this instance, it would probably have been better to know the details."

Catherine rolled her eyes.

"You're the target, Catherine."

Smith didn't detect any change in her face.

"It's you. In just over twenty minutes, the most exceptional professional killer I've ever seen is going to come here, and he's going to terminate you."

"You're bluffing."

"I don't really care what you think," Smith said. "This is happening, and I'd quite like to get the hell away before he does turn up. Where did you even find this man?"

Catherine didn't reply, but Smith sensed that she was mulling things over.

"I want to know everything," he said.

"And then what?" Catherine said.

"Then I'll get you out of here safely," Smith said. "This man is ruthless. He is motivated and he's driven, and he will absolutely not stop until he's carried out his instructions."

"You stole that from *The Terminator* movie."

"It's a great film," Smith said. "And if you'll allow me to use another quote from it – you need to come with me if you want to live."

"How do I know you're telling the truth?"

"You don't," Smith said. "But look at it this way. Everything I've told you is on tape. If I've been lying to you, then nothing you tell me is admissible as evidence."

This was a blatant lie, but Smith hoped that Catherine Gordon didn't know that.

"Time is running out, Catherine," he said. "Talk to me."

"I still don't believe you," she said.

"I told you that I don't care whether you believe me or not. Your man is on his way, and even though you've been paying his salary, you have no idea what he's capable of. Talk to me and make it quick."

She didn't get the chance. The sound of the doorbell seemed to freeze her in time. Her facial features stiffened, and her eyes grew wide.

"I'll get it," Smith offered. "Stay where you are."

CHAPTER FIFTY SEVEN

It was Barry Stone. Smith let him in and took him to the living room. Catherine Gordon was on her feet now, and she backed away when Barry approached.

"Relax," the IT man said. "Do I look like a trained assassin?"

"He's with me," Smith explained. "I need his expertise with the technical stuff. You've got nine minutes, Catherine."

"Boot up your laptop," Barry said.

Catherine flipped it open and switched it on.

"Nice equipment," Barry said. "Are you using GhostServe?"

Catherine nodded. "It guarantees against any web logs and DNS leaks."

"It's not infallible though. I could get past it in ten minutes."

"We don't have ten minutes," Smith told him.

"Then you're going to have to give me a bit of help," Barry told Catherine. "I want your logins and your passwords. Plus, I'm going to need the codes you use for your host access."

"Give him what he wants," Smith said.

"It wasn't supposed to go this far," Catherine said. "It was only meant to be John and Tom."

"You can fill in the gaps while you do your computer stuff," Smith said. "Did you really concoct all of this to get away with killing your husband and his business partner?"

"I'm not a bad person."

"It's not my job to judge," Smith said. "But I'm going to anyway. You are a bad person. Innocent people have been murdered, and you're responsible for that. A young girl had to witness the brutal slaying of her grandmother. Do you want to tell her that you're sorry? Do you want to apologise for the nightmares she's going to suffer because of it? That little girl is never going to get over what she saw that day."

"It was never meant to go this far. I didn't think it through carefully."

"I need the details of every transaction," Barry interrupted them.

"I can't give them to you," Catherine said.

"It's in your best interest to cooperate," Smith said.

"It's not that," Catherine said. "The encryption means there's no link to the clients on here."

"You're lying, Catherine," Barry said. "We've got a live one here, Smith. She's minutes away from death and she's still full of tricks. How do you think he'll kill her?"

"You were the one who took out the hit," Smith reminded him.

"Oh right," Barry said. "I nearly forgot."

Catherine looked at him and he wasn't expecting what happened next.

The slap was loud, and it made Smith flinch. Barry's head shot back, and he raised his hand to his face.

"Can we carry on?" Smith said. "Now you've got that out of your system."

"That fucking hurt," Barry said. "Where were we?"

"Clients," Smith reminded him.

"Right. I don't think we've got time to do it now. I can go through it later – I just need the codes."

"We've got five minutes," Smith said.

"I really didn't want it to go this far," Catherine said.

"Talk to us about that," Smith said. "The tape is still running. You were in Leeds the day your husband died, weren't you?"

Catherine nodded. "I was there. I drugged him."

"There wasn't an investigation," Smith said. "Did you have something to do with that?"

"I told the police in Leeds that John had been depressed for some time. I played the part of the distressed window, and I broke down and said I should have seen it coming. They didn't doubt me."

"You wanted the company," Smith said. "You already had half of it, in a way. You killed for the sake of the other half. I don't understand that."

"I stopped loving my husband a very long time ago. It's a long story."

"And time isn't something you have the luxury of right now. How did you come up with the idea for The Graveyard?"

"I inherited the land from my uncle," Catherine said. "Nothing ever grew there. I think there's something wrong with the soil."

"So, you turned it into a graveyard where the fate of the future dead is sealed?"

"I thought it was brilliant. A client orders a hit. I pocket the cash and alert the hitman. There are no details of the killing in the contract, and there is nothing to link me to the hired gun."

"You're wrong about that." It was Barry Stone. "You made five separate payments this month alone. Bloody hell. It's nice work if you can get it. That psycho pocketed over fifty grand for a few days work."

"How..."

Barry tapped the keypad on the laptop. "It's all a question of knowing where to look. How long have we got?"

This question was addressed to Smith.

"Not long," Smith said.

"It didn't take long to get the first client," Catherine said. "I knew nothing of the details of the killing. All I knew was the man I hired would be in touch with them and the nitty gritty would be ironed out at The Graveyard."

"Why all the drama?" Barry said. "I had to fill in some kind of questionnaire, and I had to lock it in a box and bury it in The Graveyard. What was all that about?"

"Evidence," Smith said. "Catherine wasn't privy to the identities of the targets, and she believed that she would come away from it squeaky clean because there was nothing to connect her to any of it. The hired gun doesn't ask the client to describe the target verbally. Everything is written down and buried in a graveyard in the middle of nowhere. It really was clever."

"How did you know I was behind it?" Catherine said. "How did you know that I created The Graveyard?"

"Because of the timing involved," Smith said. "There was just something wrong with the timeline. It was more guesswork than anything else. I must just be naturally lucky."

"All done." Barry looked up from the laptop.

"Will you be able to assist our tech team with that?" Smith said.

"No problem. If she makes it out of this alive, I suggest you don't let her anywhere near any phones, tablets or laptops until we're finished."

"She's probably not going to make it out alive," Smith said. "Times almost up."

"Let's get out of here then," Barry said. "I'm not in any hurry to bump into that bloke again. I had to wash my underwear and my jeans after last time."

"You pissed yourself?"

"I'm not ashamed to admit it."

"Let's go," Smith said.

Catherine shot to her feet. "What about me?"

"What about you?" Smith said.

"You said you'd protect me."

"I lied. You hired the bloke – you can fire him."

The doorbell sounded again, and Smith sighed.

"Shit, looks like we're too late."

Catherine raced out of the room and made a beeline for the back door. She was stopped in her tracks by PC Simon Miller. He'd been waiting outside the door the whole time.

"Thank God for that," Catherine said. "He's coming. You have to help me."

"You're lucky I'm wearing this uniform," PC Miller said. "I saw the result of your sick fuck mind. I hope you rot in whatever hell you're heading for."

"He's coming for me," Catherine pleaded. "You have to help me."

Smith came into the kitchen. "Nobody is coming for you, Catherine. No psychotic professional killers, anyway. Simon, do you want to do the honours and arrest her? I'm sick of the sight of her."

"With pleasure, Sarge," PC Miller said.

"What is this?" Catherine asked when she'd been read her rights. "What about the hitman?"

Smith took out his phone and swiped the screen.

"Here he is."

The photograph had been taken at the station. In it, a tall man in his twenties was looking directly at the camera. His hands were tied behind his back, and he was being restrained by two officers.

"He was never coming here," Smith said.

He didn't think that Catherine Gordon deserved any more than that, so he didn't elaborate. The truth was – Catherine was never the target. That honour went to a man that Barry Stone hadn't seen in years. In his panic at The Graveyard he'd written down the first name that had come into his head. He still couldn't understand where the blast from the past had come from.

A team was waiting for the Australian killer when he arrived at the man's house. It took six highly trained officers to disarm him and immobilise him, and he was taken away shortly afterwards. They still didn't know who he was – he had no ID on him, and he'd refused to talk since he was brought in.

"You tricked me," Catherine said. "You were bluffing all along."

"Shit happens," Smith said. "I need a smoke – the air in here has suddenly turned foul."

CHAPTER FIFTY EIGHT

"That was quite a confession," DI Smyth said.

He was standing with Smith outside the station. Smith was smoking his second cigarette in quick succession.

Catherine Gordon had admitted to everything. She'd told them everything about the murder of her husband in Leeds and the subsequent creation of The Graveyard. Her story started out slowly, but when she got into the rhythm of it, everything she'd done had come gushing out.

"She was more of an IT expert than her husband was," Smith said. "It took Barry and our team of IT boffins all night to pick apart her Graveyard site, and even then, they didn't even scratch the surface."

"The details of the clients are still eluding us," DI Smyth said.

Barry had been bluffing when he promised Catherine that they would be able to trace the clients from the website. In fact, there was no possible way to do that. It was the same story with the transactions that had taken place. When Barry had pretended to be able to find how much the hired gun had been paid for his services, that was a bluff too. He'd plucked a figure out of the air, and he'd been rather accurate.

"We seem to be on a roll with the bluff thing," Smith said. "We'll keep it going with Callum North and Duncan Jordan. We will get them to confess."

"Webber should have something from The Graveyard before the end of the day," DI Smyth said.

The field had been dug up and the boxes had been retrieved. There were five of them in total, including the one Barry Stone had buried there.

"It won't take long to connect some of those boxes to Callum and Duncan," Smith said. "We'll get a handwriting expert in if we have to, and I bet they won't have been too careful about leaving fingerprints. The concept was brilliant, but it was still no match for forensic science. We'll have them before we know it."

"I believe Barry Stone got his money back," DI Smyth said.

"I had to laugh when he told me. He demanded a full refund because he didn't get what he'd paid for, and Catherine Gordon gave it to him without any arguments."

"Even though he was partly responsible for the hit going wrong?"

"Even so. It all turned out well in the end."

"What about the Australian?" DI Smyth said.

"I'm not too stressed about him, boss."

"Is this some kind of countryman solidarity thing?"

"You know I don't give a shit about that kind of thing," Smith said. "No, the bloke was just doing a job – it wasn't personal."

"He butchered five people," DI Smyth said.

"And if it wasn't him, it would have been some other hired pro. I'm really not bothered about him."

If Smith had a crystal ball, and he was able to see into the future, he would be aware that the Australian man wasn't going to be their problem for much longer anyway. On a dreary day in the near future he would be transferred to court from his temporary place of incarceration and the officers in charge of getting him there safely would underestimate what they were dealing with. They would be overpowered, and the courteous Australian hitman would disappear, never to be seen again. Smith would be given the news, and he would react with just four words.

Tell someone who cares.

DI Smyth's phone beeped. He looked at the message and smiled.

"Webber has come up trumps with one of the boxes from The Graveyard."

"Which one?" Smith said.

"The box with the details of the murder of Harriet Jordan in it had her husband's prints all over it."

"Duncan Jordan won't be able to talk his way out of that," Smith said. "What about the one with the instructions on how Janet Downing was to be dispatched? Surely there must be some trace of Callum North on it."

"Nothing at all. We have yet to compare the handwriting on the paper to Callum's but his prints weren't there."

"Do you think he wore gloves?"

"Somebody didn't. There were scores of prints on the box. None of them were Callum's."

"We'll get him," Smith said. "What time are they getting picked up?"

"Callum and Duncan are being arrested as we speak," DI Smyth said. "I assume you'll want to be involved in their interviews?"

"No," Smith said. "This case has left me feeling a bit ill, and I'd prefer to step away from it before it contaminates my soul anymore."

"Are you feeling alright?"

"I'm feeling sick to the pit of my stomach, boss. And I'm wondering if we're ever going to have a good old-fashioned psychopath to sink our teeth into."

"You don't mean that."

"I really do. These techno investigations irritate the hell out of me. I'd give anything for a severely disturbed serial killer again."

"Be careful what you wish for."

"Right now, I'm wishing for a sick fuck who kills like a proper serial killer," Smith said. "Someone who I can relate to."

"I would advise you not to repeat that to anyone."

"It's the truth. Whatever happened to the old school psychos? They appear to be a dying breed."

"Take a break," DI Smyth said. "Go and grab a coffee. We still have a lot of loose ends to tie up, and that's not going to be a quick process."

Smith didn't wait to be asked twice. He left the office and headed for the canteen. He was deadly serious when he told DI Smyth that he longed for an old school psychopath to deal with. It had been a while, and he missed it. He didn't know then that the DI's words were going to come back to haunt him. *Be careful what you wish for.*

Soon, Smith was going to get his wish – it would be in the form of possibly the most twisted, disturbed mind he'd ever had the pleasure of, and he was going to regret ever tempting fate in this way.

He got some coffee from the machine and took it to the table by the window. Whitton was already seated.

"You OK?" she asked.

"Never better. Duncan Jordan and Callum North are on their way here. Forensics found Duncan's prints on the box in The Graveyard, so we've got him."

"What about Callum North?"

"Nothing yet," Smith said. "But it's only a matter of time before he cracks too. I'll be glad to put this one behind me."

"We all will," Whitton said.

Bridge came into the canteen.

"The DI is looking for you," he said to Whitton. "You're needed in the interview with Duncan Jordan."

"It should be a quick one," Smith said. "Who's interrogating Callum North?"

"Me and Harry," Bridge said. "How did you get out of it?"

"I reckon I've done enough," Smith said. "I want no further part of this investigation. I'm going out for a smoke."

CHAPTER FIFTY NINE

Smith lit the cigarette and walked over to his car. He was planning on smoking the cigarette and driving away. He had no idea where he was going to go – he just needed to go somewhere else. The Graveyard investigation had taken its toll on all of them, but Smith had been affected by it more than anyone else on the team. He was never going to forget Sophie Downing's revelations under hypnosis, and he wondered if the little girl was ever going to be able to put the events of her grandmother's murder out of her mind. Smith hoped she would.

It still sickened him to think that one woman's greed had contributed to so much heartache, and he hoped that Catherine Gordon would suffer in the worst possible way for her crimes. It was the least she deserved. Six people were dead because of her hunger for money, and it only made Smith despise money even more.

There was a silver lining of sorts on the dark cloud that was the investigation. The animal charities and dog shelters were probably going to be able to keep the money that was transferred from Tom Lowe's accounts. Once the news had been broadcast, a public appeal had been launched. It had grown in momentum until the people who made the decisions had no option but to listen. Social media appeals had sprung up, and the general consensus was the dogs and cats of the city deserved the money. The outcome had a feelgood aspect to it and in the end public opinion won by a landslide. Tom Lowe hadn't lost his life and five of his fingers for nothing.

Smith finished his cigarette and threw the butt into the distance.

"You look like a man with the weight of the world on his shoulders."

The woman had approached without him realising.

"You could say that," Smith said.

He guessed her age to be somewhere in the mid-forties, early-fifties. She was slim and she was dressed like a woman two decades younger in a pair of jeans and a denim jacket.

"Penny for them?"

Smith looked into her eyes. "Excuse me?"

"Penny for your thoughts," she said. "It sometimes helps to share."

"You really don't want to hear my thoughts right now," Smith said. "Do I know you?"

"The name's Rachel. We've never met, but I know who you are."

"Quite a few people do," Smith said. "I'd love to stay and chat, but I have somewhere I need to be."

"Everything will work out in the end," Rachel said. "It usually does."

"I wish I shared your optimism."

"Take me for example. I feel free for the first time in years."

"That's good to hear," Smith said.

"Thirty-six years," Rachel said.

Smith was wide awake.

"What did you say your name was again?"

"Rachel," she said. "Rachel North. You've met my boy, Callum."

"You're Callum's mother?"

Rachel nodded.

"Is he here?"

Another nod. "He asked me to come for moral support. He claims that he's innocent, but you'll soon see that he isn't."

"I shouldn't be talking to you," Smith said.

"Then listen instead. For thirty-six years I ran around after that boy and his father, and now it's over. Do you know what that feels like? Can you imagine how liberating it is?"

"I really need to be going," Smith said.

"He'll deny it, you know," Rachel said. "And he'll be very convincing."

"You're talking to the wrong person, Mrs North."

Smith opened the door of his car.

"Call me Rachel. Mrs North no longer exists."

"Goodbye Rachel," Smith said.

"You'll find Callum's fingerprints on a Bic pen in the desk inside the barn next to the graveyard. You really have no idea what freedom feels like until times like these. Good luck, Detective Smith – I hope you find your peace."

Smith watched her walk away.

"What the fuck just happened?" he asked himself.

He got into the car and closed the door. He took out his phone and typed a short message to Grant Webber. The blue ticks told him that the Head of Forensics read it almost immediately.

A reply arrived just as quickly but Smith didn't bother to read it. He turned the key in the ignition, engaged first gear and drove away from the station. Rachel North's words didn't leave much room for interpretation, but Smith still wasn't interested. It was quite clear what Callum's mother had implied, and Smith knew that he ought to share the conversation with the rest of the team, but he wasn't going to. He turned onto the main road and increased his speed. He wanted to put as much distance between himself and The Graveyard investigation as possible. As far as he was concerned, it was all over.

THE END

Printed in Dunstable, United Kingdom